"I cannot blam̲̲̲̲̲**y.
It is not irratio**̲**
if you try. You** **
your shoulder."**

"No, but I won't always have you to protect me."
She spoke quietly, with feeling.

His finger was still beneath her chin, her eyes
large and luminous as they held his.

"You will soon be under your godmother's
protection, but until then, you have me."

"Yes," she breathed, moving closer to him, turning
her face up to his, her lips moist and partly open.

Unable to resist doing so, Christopher's mouth
settled on hers. Her lips opened like a flower
beneath his own, her warm, sweet breath entering
his mouth. He kissed her tenderly, but then his
senses started to flee and his breathing quickened
and he deepened the kiss. Dear Lord, what was he
doing? Kissing her and loving it. It had to stop.

Author Note

Here we are with another Regency romance—
a romance between two people destined for
each other.

Lucy Walsh, born and raised in Louisiana and
heiress to a vast plantation, is fresh out of school
when her stepmother arrives in London to arrange
her marriage to Mr. Barrington, a stranger to Lucy.
Unbeknownst to Lucy, her father is dead, and her
stepmother and Mr. Barrington have concocted a
scheme for Mr. Barrington to marry Lucy in order
to get their hands on her inheritance. Unable to
believe her father would want her to do this, Lucy
stands against them and is befriended by Captain
Christopher Wilding.

Also born and raised in America, and having learned
at an early age that the only way to survive was to
fight back or die trying and use his own initiative,
Christopher became a reckless adventurer and
privateer. He is also the estranged grandson of the
Duke of Rockley and has recently come to England
to face his responsibilities.

Christopher and Lucy's romance is played out in
London society as she struggles to break free of
her stepmother and Mr. Barrington.

Enjoy!

HELEN
DICKSON

—

A Viscount to Save
Her Reputation

If you purchased this book without a cover you should be aware
that this book is stolen property. It was reported as "unsold and
destroyed" to the publisher, and neither the author nor the
publisher has received any payment for this "stripped book."

H HARLEQUIN®
HISTORICAL™

Recycling programs
for this product may
not exist in your area.

ISBN-13: 978-1-335-50621-4

A Viscount to Save Her Reputation

Copyright © 2021 by Helen Dickson

All rights reserved. No part of this book may be used or reproduced in
any manner whatsoever without written permission except in the case of
brief quotations embodied in critical articles and reviews.

This is a work of fiction. Names, characters, places and incidents
are either the product of the author's imagination or are used fictitiously.
Any resemblance to actual persons, living or dead, businesses,
companies, events or locales is entirely coincidental.

This edition published by arrangement with Harlequin Books S.A.

For questions and comments about the quality of this book,
please contact us at CustomerService@Harlequin.com.

Harlequin Enterprises ULC
22 Adelaide St. West, 40th Floor
Toronto, Ontario M5H 4E3, Canada
www.Harlequin.com

Printed in U.S.A.

Helen Dickson was born and still lives in South Yorkshire, UK, with her retired farm manager husband. Having moved out of the busy farmhouse where she raised their two sons, she now has more time to indulge in her favorite pastimes. She enjoys being outdoors, traveling, reading and music. An incurable romantic, she writes for pleasure. It was a love of history that drove her to writing historical fiction.

Books by Helen Dickson

Harlequin Historical

When Marrying a Duke...
The Devil Claims a Wife
The Master of Stonegrave Hall
Mishap Marriage
A Traitor's Touch
Caught in Scandal's Storm
Lucy Lane and the Lieutenant
Lord Lansbury's Christmas Wedding
Royalist on the Run
The Foundling Bride
Carrying the Gentleman's Secret
A Vow for an Heiress
The Governess's Scandalous Marriage
Reunited at the King's Court
Wedded for His Secret Child
Resisting Her Enemy Lord
A Viscount to Save Her Reputation

Castonbury Park

The Housemaid's Scandalous Secret

Visit the Author Profile page
at Harlequin.com for more titles.

Chapter One

1816

Lucy had been summoned to Miss Brody's study at the Academy for Young Ladies, at a loss to guess at the reason. Of medium height and as slender as a wand, she hurried along the corridor. The Spanish blood from her mother was evident in her dark eyes and dark curling hair and passionate nature. She had attempted to scrape her hair back into a ribbon at the nape without much success. The effect was softened by several escaping stray curls brushing her cheeks.

She had been born and raised at Aspendale, her father's ranch in Louisiana, but when her mother had died when she was nine years old, her father, a man of unimaginable wealth, had sent her to England to receive her education and to learn to be a lady. Lucy adored her tall, golden-haired father and had wept copious tears on the ship that had brought her to England. He had made Lady Caroline Sutton, who had been her mother's closest friend and Lucy's god-mother, her official guardian for the time she was in England. Lucy would stay with her at her house on Curzon Street when not at the academy.

Miss Brody, the proprietress of the academy for the past twenty years, was a tall, stately woman. Her grey-ing hair crowned a lined, intelligent face and shrewd grey eyes. Her graceful movements, calm features and soft voice disguised a formidable efficiency and en-ergy. She put all her great emphasis on learning and devoted all her time to crusading for the education of women. She ran her academy efficiently and employed only the best teachers. She was seated at her desk, her head bent over a letter. Looking up when Lucy en-tered, she smiled, but Lucy noted the concern on her face and the frown that furrowed her brow.

'Come and sit down, Lucy. I have received a letter from your father and wanted to make you aware of its contents straight away.'

Lucy sank on to a hard wooden chair in front of the desk, sitting stiff and straight-backed on the edge. The summer sun shining through the window fell on Lucy's face, illuminating her fine skin to a soft shade of golden honey and lighting the brown eyes with a luminous quality. She had a natural poise and unaf-fected warmth, and at that moment an air of serious-ness as she waited for Miss Brody to proceed. 'He is aware that your time at the academy is almost over—indeed, you have taken advantage of all the academy has to offer and excelled admirably in all your studies.

Your father is extremely proud of you and has made arrangements for your future.'

Lucy's heart leapt with sudden hope that he had arranged for her to go home. 'Am I to return to Louisiana?'

'No—at least not immediately. He—he has arranged for you to be married, Lucy.'

'Married!' Lucy gasped, so taken aback that her façade of dignity dropped and for a split second she felt like a bewildered child. 'But I don't want to get married—not to anyone.'

She wanted to scream at Miss Brody that she was too young, that when she did marry it would be to a man of her choosing. But she had learned some self-control, taught her by this very woman, so she folded her hands in front of her. She looked the perfect image of piety and humility as she looked guilelessly into Miss Brody's narrowed, watching eyes, but Miss Brody knew better and would not be misled by her show of meekness that for the present concealed her recalcitrant nature.

'I'm sorry, Miss Brody.'

'You should be. You must learn to guard that tongue of yours.'

'Yes—but I have no desire to be married.' Reckless, in spite of Miss Brody's reproachful look, she cried out, 'I will not be forced into this. I will write to my father and explain how I feel. He will not make me do this—to—to marry a complete stranger. Why? There has to be more to this.'

Miss Brody had always been extremely sympathetic to the trials and tribulations of all her pupils and in particular this young lady who was so far from her home in America. But on this matter, on a direct instruction from her father, then she must support that. 'I realise that the letter from your father has come as something of a shock, Lucy, and you will need time to adjust, but he is acting within his rights. Since Lady Sutton is on an extensive stay in France and not expected back for at least another month at least, your stepmother, Mrs Walsh, will be here shortly. She is looking forward to meeting you. She will be taking a house in London. You are to go to her there. As your father's wife she will undertake your chaperonage and take full charge of the marriage proceedings.'

'But—she is not a blood relative of mine. I have never met her.' In spite of all her efforts, she found that she could not check her wild, resentful thoughts. They flew around in her mind like bird wings beating against the bars of a cage. She felt a trap closing around her and she endured a nauseating turmoil of distress. 'And—and this man he wants me to marry— does he have a name?'

'Your father writes that he is Mark Barrington— a friend of his and your stepmother and also a ranch owner in Louisiana.'

'I see. Then—what is he doing in England?'

'He is coming to London on affairs of business. I dare say he will return to Louisiana when they have been settled and you are married.'

'But—my godmother, Aunt Caroline, has arranged for me to remain here at the academy until she returns or sends someone to escort me to Paris where she will be expecting me.'

'Then I will write to her and explain everything.'

As Miss Brody returned to her work Lucy made her way to the garden, which was quiet at this time of day when classes were in full sway. She would have returned to her lesson, but her knees were shaking so violently that she had to sit herself down on a bench. She was so angry that she could hardly think straight. The letter from her father filled her mind, obliterating everything else. Tension vibrated in her highly strung body and her hands, instead of being clasped demurely in front of her, were now clenched by her sides in a passion of anger. Her large, brown eyes, flecked with gold, were stormy. No matter how hard her teachers had tried to instil discipline in her, they had failed to cleanse her mind of rebellious thoughts. There was no sign of resignation, obedience and humility in her now.

She had hoped for so much on leaving the academy. She and her godmother had talked of her debut and of the balls she would attend, the travelling they would do together—France, Italy and Spain—but all she felt was betrayed and led down by her own father, and she had not even left the academy.

As an only child she had been her father's pride and joy and he had given her anything she wished for, so why was he doing this to her? Without being consulted or offered the choice, she was to marry a man she had never even heard of. Because of circumstances was she any less her own person because she was a woman under her father's domination and because she had a mind of her own and a will to go with it? She was eighteen years old with her whole life in front of her, a future of excitement and new experiences. And now, without warning, the exciting future she had hoped for was being snatched away from her.

She found herself wondering what kind of woman her stepmother was. From her father's letters she knew her name was Sofia and that he had met her on a visit to New Orleans. They had married after a short courtship. There must be something endearing about her to have captivated her ageing father. But Lucy felt nervous about meeting her. How would they react to each other when they met?

Broughton Fair was a tremendous social event, when the close-knit families of the surrounding countryside came together to enjoy and revel in the two days of festivities. It was also of economic importance, for livestock and farm produce were brought in from nearby farms and villages to be sold, and wandering gypsies came in gaily painted caravans, positioning them in fields adjacent to the fairground. Fairgoers would go and have their palms read and buy good luck charms. There was music and dancing and games to play with the riotous children. It was a colourful, exciting affair and everyone could forget their troubles for a while and enjoy what was on offer.

It was mid-afternoon when some of the girls from the academy were allowed out to attend the fair. Miss Hope, one of the teachers at the academy who was in her middle years and sadly overweight, was in charge of them, which she found tiresome at the best of times. Having found herself a comfortable bench in the shade of a leafy elm, she had soon dozed off, unaware of the mischief her young charges got up to.

Lucy was with her friend Emma. Missing her Louisiana home, Emma had been her salvation when she had arrived at the academy. She had entered Lucy's life like a shining light. They often quarrelled, but this did not spoil their friendship. They talked with the easy camaraderie of kindred spirits and would be eternally united by girlhood memories. Emma charmed all her companions and could not be found wanting in those accomplishments that characterise a young lady. She was so very different to Lucy. Emma was petite with a profusion of golden curls, cornflower-blue eyes and was sweet tempered, whereas Lucy was slightly taller and exotic with her darker hair and creamy complexion.

Dressed in identical blue skirts and white blouses, which marked them as pupils at the academy, lying on the grass on the edge of the crowd beneath a warm July sun, with the appetising aroma of cooked food filling the air, they were discussing the letter Lucy's father had sent to Miss Brody. Emma was a dreadful romantic at heart, and was of the opinion that Lucy was lucky to find herself in a situation where she was to marry and had immediately launched into a torrent of questions.

'You might not be so displeased when you see him. Your father might have made a good choice. And he's to come to England. Perhaps he's impatient to take a look at his bride.'

Emma's words weren't meant to provoke Lucy, but they did just that. 'Really, Emma! Are you saying that I should be grateful to my father for choosing my husband? I am eighteen years old and not ready to be married off. When I leave the academy I want to have some fun and enjoy myself. I don't care how rich he is or how handsome, I don't want to meet him. I have every intention of foiling their arrangements. I absolutely will not marry yet. There are more important things in life.'

Emma sighed, sitting up and picking a bonbon out of a box she had purchased from one of the stalls. 'I don't know what. I hope my papa soon finds me a husband—a handsome one, of course. I wouldn't want to marry an ugly man,' she said, popping the bonbon in her mouth and proceeding to lick her sticky fingers.

'I'm sure he will, Emma. Men find you attractive and the way you flirt with them is quite shameless. You'll soon have yourself a husband—although,' she said, as she watched Emma's soft pink lips close around the sugary sweet, 'if you carry on eating those bonbons like that you'll become so fat you'll put them off.'

'No, I won't. I don't intend to get fat. But what will you do when you meet with your stepmother and this gentleman your father wants you to marry? You can't very well ignore him. He's not going to go away after travelling all the way from Louisiana.'

'I know.' Lucy frowned. She would have to give it

careful thought. 'I don't know what I'm going to do. I'll think about what to do when I reach London.' Sitting up, she brushed the stray pieces of grass from her skirt. 'I wish you were coming with me, Emma. I'm going to miss you when we leave here.'

'We'll keep in touch. You must come and stay with me and we'll write often.'

'Yes. I promise.'

Emma declared the she was thirsty and wandered off to the stall selling lemonade. There was a dark-haired young man in front of her and the two soon got into conversation. Purchasing their drinks, the two wandered off towards the archery range. In the company of such an attractive young man and suspecting Emma wouldn't be in too much of a hurry to return—unless Miss Hope woke up and went looking for her—Lucy got to her feet and mingled with the crowd.

Groups of people jostled each other and the clamour of voices was all around her. She sauntered past acrobats and a man with a performing bear. Across the field horses brought by the gypsies were being auctioned off. This piqued her interest and she strolled towards them, failing to see the man with his shoulder propped against a tree, his arms folded across his broad chest, a leather satchel slung over his shoulder. One horse was particularly beautiful, a grey stallion, which appeared to have attracted a great deal of attention. It tossed its head and flowing white mane, the hint of restrained power in every movement of its muscular body. It would prove a challenge to even the most accomplished rider.

Unobserved to Lucy, a youth carrying a wriggling young goat walked by, the goat determined to be free. The youth stumbled and dropped the goat, whereupon it leaped to its feet and zigzagged across the grass. The stallion sidestepped and the man holding the leading rope let go when it reared up. Finding itself free, it then began to prance with its hooves flailing, scattering all those around it and raising shouts from the crowd.

Somebody shouted a warning to Lucy to get back, to get out of the way, but she stood, not out of bravado, but as one mesmerised by the fabulous animal as it reared up and shook its head. But then suddenly, all her senses alert to danger, never of a nervous disposition, she felt the chilling hand of fear clutch at her. That was when a swift, agile figure appeared from nowhere and a powerful pair of hands reached out and grabbed her, lifting her off her feet and she was borne backwards into the safety of the trees. Then she was held quite still. She was unable to struggle, unable to utter even the smallest sound as she watched as the horse was caught and brought under control. She knew at once that her saviour was a man, a tall individual with immensely strong arms and fingers that gripped her arms like bands of steel.

'You silly little fool,' he said. 'You court danger.'

The voice was rich and hypnotically deep and pleasant. It lacked the roughness that would have marked him as a common countryman. He sounded cultured. He continued to hold her, his long-limbed body pressed close to hers. His hot breath touched her skin as the voice sounded close to her ear. She could feel his steady heartbeat and she could smell his male-ness. The contact was electric. It flashed like a power-ful current, charging the air between them. Her skin tingled and grew warm with pleasure.

To Lucy it seemed as if the moment was suddenly suspended, along with the noise of the fair and even the movements of the crowd. Only after a lengthy pause did she become aware that the powerful grip was being eased by degrees until her hands were free. For all its intensity the moment from when the horse had bolted until now was brief, but Lucy felt a shift-ing deep inside her and experienced an unmistakable sense of longing.

Slowly she turned to face her rescuer. He was wear-ing fawn riding breeches that were tucked into high-topped brown leather riding boots. He wore a white shirt, left open at the front to expose his tanned chest, the sleeves rolled back over powerful brown forearms. Tilting her head, she shielded her eyes in the sunlight, squinting into a face that made her breath catch in her throat when she found herself looking into eyes like shards of splintered glass, piercing her. There was a tiny scar on his cheek and a slight cleft in his chin, and those small imperfections only marked him as more handsome, more dangerously desirable than any man she had ever seen. His thick, softly curling black hair glistened in the sun.

She was used to handsome men—had met sev-eral when she had stayed with her society-loving godmother, but this man was in a different class al-together. There was something so forceful, so compelling in the confrontation that gooseflesh raised itself on her forearms and an icy tingle raced down her spine.

The incident had made them the focal point of the crowd's attention, but when the runaway horse was caught and brought under control, people turned away. Lucy's rescuer drew her aside, casting a glance at his horse which had wandered off when he'd let go of its bridle to pull Lucy out of the way of the runaway horse. It was nibbling contentedly at the grass, unaware of the furore.

Mesmerised, Lucy gazed up into his recklessly handsome face. She knew she should do something, say something, if only to express her gratitude. His eyes seemed to bore right through her and she felt her secret thoughts were revealed to him, her petty vanities and jealousies, her less than admirable nature. 'Thank you, sir. Why did you risk your life for me?'

'I didn't,' he answered, his voice faintly amused. 'I know how to avoid a runaway horse—which is what you should have done instead of waiting for it to trample you.'

The authority in his calm tone brought Lucy up short. Feeling like a child who had been caught misbehaving, she sighed. 'I suppose I should, but I couldn't move. It's such a beautiful creature. But it could have killed you.'

'You were in dire need of rescuing—and I'm not that easy to dispose of.'

'No,' she said quietly. 'I don't believe you are.'

'It's not difficult to survive if you see from where the danger is coming.'

'You are fearless, sir.'

'I like to think so.'

'But—that cannot be. Everyone has something to fear.'

'That is not always the case.'

'There isn't a man alive who doesn't fear something.'

'Had I not pulled you back the horse would have trampled you to death.'

'Then I owe you my life. My name is Lucy Walsh.'

'And are you enjoying yourself, Miss Walsh?'

'Oh, yes, very much. I would offer you a reward if I had something to give.'

A fleeting grin flashed white against his tanned face and a roguish glint that must surely be what would charm any female he came into contact with made his eyes dance with silver lights. 'As pretty as you are, you can give me all the reward you want. It is a pleasure to meet such a beautiful young lady.'

His eyes gleamed as he looked at her and she was aware of an acute pleasure because, having reached eighteen, she was becoming rather susceptible to admiration from the opposite sex and experienced a warm feeling towards those who expressed it. Cheeks burning, she offered him her most brilliant smile. 'There can be no doubt that you saved my life. Should I offer money?'

'Good Lord, no!' he exclaimed, then lowered his voice and smiled into her eyes. 'I am fiercely proud,

Lucy Walsh. To offer money would offend me deeply and I could never expect payment from a lady for services rendered. Although,' he murmured, a glint entering his narrowed eyes, 'were you older, a kiss would be reward enough.'

Lucy laughed. She could tell from the teasing note in his voice that he was jesting. 'That would be highly improper, I'm afraid. Old or young, I don't go around kissing people because they saved my life. There must be something else.' Tilting her head to one side, she gave him a frowning look. 'What makes you think I want to kiss you?'

'I can see it in her eyes when a woman wants me.'

'You can? You are arrogant, sir.'

He grinned. 'It's in my nature. Tell me, Miss Walsh, do you live in Broughton?'

No. I'm at the academy for young ladies here—it's just outside the village.'

'A schoolgirl.'

Lucy bristled with indignation. 'I'm not so young. I'm eighteen.'

'Not so young, then. A veritable ancient, in fact.' He laughed lightly when her cheeks flushed pink with embarrassment.

Lucy detected a glint of silver in his penetrating eyes—it was a dangerous light, which warned anyone rash enough to challenge him that he would be a formidable adversary. But not today. Not with her. 'I'm leaving shortly.'

'And where is home?'

'I live with my godmother in London when I'm on

holiday from the academy—although at present she is in Paris. I hope to join her shortly.'

'You have been before?'

'No. I have that to look forward to.'

'I might be going myself in the next week or so—relating to business.' He looked annoyed when a group of rowdy young males who had imbibed too much of the ale on sale came too close, a couple of them looking at Lucy with undisguised interest. 'Shall we move away from here and see what the fair has to offer—if you have the time?'

Thinking he was the most handsome and exciting man she had met in a long time, if ever, she was reluctant to be parted from him just yet. However, aware of the impropriety of going off with a strange gentleman, she hesitated. She could almost feel the force of Miss Hope's cold stare and was relieved when, on glancing in her direction, she saw she was still dozing.

Lucy had no doubt that should Miss Hope be made aware of her impropriety she would have to listen to her telling her how a perfect lady should behave, quoting as an example Lydia Brownlow. Lydia was prim and proper, refined and easily shaped, whereas Lucy was quite the opposite. She had tried to be like Lydia and adopt her demure mannerisms, but it was no use. She could not be like Lydia no matter how hard she tried.

'Well?' he said, waiting for her answer, seeing her hesitation. 'I promise I shall behave like the perfect gentleman at all times. No one is going to bother you with me at your side.'

When he looked at her and smiled the way he was doing now her spirits soared. Suddenly all the condemnations Miss Hope would heap on her, telling her that she was without a grain of sense or propriety and taking a morbid delight in listing all her transgressions should she find out, would be worthwhile. Besides, since she was to leave the academy and be forced into marriage with the man her father had chosen for her, then this would be the last time to have some fun before entering the world of adults.

'Oh, yes,' she said in answer to the gentleman's suggestion. 'I'm in no hurry to return to the academy.'

They strolled, looking at the various stalls selling all manner of goods, pausing to look at a puppet theatre that had attracted a large number of children, booing and cheering their enthusiasm. Eventually they sat under the trees in the shade on the edge of the fair to eat warm gingerbread, neither of them in any hurry to end the camaraderie between them. He told her he was a sea captain, owning his own vessel.

Tucking her legs beneath her skirts, Lucy sat facing him. 'You don't look like a sea captain.'

'I trust you will not hold that against me.'

'No, of course not. Why should I?'

'Because you might think a sailor to be out of place at an event such as this.'

Lucy fancied he was laughing at her so she smiled. 'Not in the least.'

'I like to go where the will and the spirit takes me. I'm used to being at sea beneath the wide open sky and with a never-ending expanse of water before me.

There's something about the sea that makes one conscious of life's blessings and to enjoy it to the full. I like to feel the hot sun by day and watch the moon and stars by night.'

'And the wind and the storms?'

'We weather them—as sailors do.'

She laughed. 'How poetic you sound.'

'I am many things, but a poet is not one of them. And yet here I am today—a sailor partaking of what the fair has to offer and in the company of a beautiful young lady.'

'There is nothing strange in that.'

'Ah, but if I were a gentleman I would not have taken the opportunity, just bowed in a deferential manner and declared myself unworthy of the honour of passing a moment or two in conversation with a young lady of note.'

Lucy smile broadly. 'Deferential? Oh, sir! I doubt you have a deferential bone in your body and consider yourself worthy to sit down with the King himself.' He looked at her steadily and she felt herself flushing.

'And what would a young lady like you know what is in a sailor's heart?'

'I don't, of course.'

'But you are a clever young lady, Miss Walsh, with a great life ahead of you because you are bold and will take what you want with both hands. It will be a lucky man who wins your heart and shares that life with you.'

As he spoke he was looking at her very steadily. Lucy felt her cheeks heat with warmth. Suddenly everything about the day was beautiful, everything bathed in a soft glow—and the glow came from within herself. Never had she felt like this—so secure, so happy. As she gazed at her handsome companion it was as though a vital part of her had been missing until now. The feeling had come over her all of a sudden, it seemed, and she was slightly bewildered, but she revelled in it. Glancing to where Miss Hope still dozed in perfect ignorance of what her charges were up to, Lucy knew she should have left him then and walked away, but she did not. Knowing what her future had in store for her, she wanted to hold on to what could be her last taste of freedom.

'Miss Hope, who is supposed to be chaperoning us, is asleep. She would have a seizure if she knew I was talking to you like this.'

'Then we shall keep it to ourselves. I find it is the things we are not supposed to do that we enjoy doing the most.'

Lucy listened to him intently lest she missed a word or an expression on his face as he described the countries he had visited, east and west, and the cargoes he had carried, not even looking at her which, if she had more experience of men, would have told her of his consuming interest in what he had chosen to do. He talked about crossing vast oceans as if it were a mere sailing up the Thames. She hung on to his every word, the glow inside her spreading, coursing through her veins like a glorious elixir, filling her with new emotions and instincts.

'You were born in London?' he asked, getting to his feet and holding out his hand to assist her.

Lucy took it, grasping it firmly. 'No. I was born in Louisiana.'

He looked surprised. They began heading in the direction of where they had met. 'You are an American?'

'Yes. Have you been there?'

'Yes—quite recently, in fact. Like you, I too am an American. I was born and brought up there—Charleston, South Carolina. My father came from Surrey, but before he died he considered himself an American. He helped fight the Revolutionary War back in the early eighties. When the fighting was finished and America won the war, things changed. He started a shipping company in Charleston. How did you come to leave Louisiana?'

'When my mother died my father sent me to England to be educated and to be taught to be a lady. He sets great store by such things.'

'He is English—or was he born out there?'

'He was born there. My grandfather went to America when he was a young man. The lure of America was too great for him to resist—he was bitten by the bug that bit everyone else in those days. He toured about—travelling west for a while—hungry to see it all for himself.'

'He wasn't the only man lured by the Promised Land. It was a dream shared by many—thousands of men all seeking a better life, a different life, to raise their families, all the time pushing further west in a valiant attempt to tame the land and carve themselves a niche. What made your grandfather settle in Louisiana?'

'He got tired of wandering and eventually settled near Baton Rouge—which was where my father was born and later met and married my mother. She was Spanish.'

'I see. You have a colourful and interesting background. You must have missed it when you left.'

'I did—very much. I was homesick for a long time.' Lucy would never forget the day when she'd had to leave Louisiana. She'd been so happy there that she hadn't wanted to leave. Oppressed by a terrible feeling of isolation, when she had first come to England she'd felt out of place. With her exotic upbringing and the freedom and vibrant colour of Louisiana coursing through her veins, it had been difficult that first year, try as she did, for her to conform to an English young lady's way of life.

'Will you return to Louisiana to be worshipped by the handsome sons of wealthy planters?' he said teasingly.

'No—at least not yet. I would like to see my father, but I like England very well. Besides, Louisiana might not be the idyllic paradise I remember—and yet, even though I have settled down here, there are times when I still feel like a stranger in a strange land. Do you trade with England and do business with the people your father fought?'

He grinned. 'I don't hold grudges when it comes to business. My father liked trading with the English— like your own father—for a profit.'

'And will you carry on your father's business?'

'No. Things change—things have changed for me. My parents are both dead. I sold the business.'

'I'm sorry.' Despite his self-assurance, she sensed a deep sadness in him, something frozen and withdrawn. 'You have no siblings who can take it on?'

'Sadly, no. I have a younger sister, but no brothers.'

His eyes had clouded over and, sensing he didn't want to talk about it, she didn't question him further about his family. 'You said things have changed for you. If you are not going to run a shipping company, will you remain at sea?'

'No. I'm in the process of selling my ship. I have a buyer. Hopefully the sale will go through.'

The breeze blew her hair across her face and she reached up and absently drew it back, combing her fingers through it and sweeping it behind her ears, unconscious of how seductive the gesture was to her companion. Her eyes moved over him in the bright sunlight, memorising the gleam of his dark hair, the firm lines of his jaw, his mouth, the lean, hard strength of his body.

He met and held her gaze, his lips curving in a smile. 'You seem to be greatly preoccupied with my looks. Do you like what you see?'

'Why—I...' She bit her lip, suddenly realising the imprudence of letting her tongue run away with her. This man was a stranger to her and there was no reason to share the intimate details of her life with him.

Appearing to enjoy the confusion his question caused her, chuckling softly, he brought a finger up to her face and followed the arc of her cheek, ever so gently, then brushed back a stray curl and tucked it behind her ear. Lucy shivered at his touch, but she did not draw away. She recognised the obvious admiration she read in his eyes and suddenly became aware of the boldness of his body, his maleness and the impropriety of being alone in his company.

Her heart beat hard in her chest and pounded in her ears and he moved closer, but then stopped. His mouth curled in one corner. He looked at her for a long time, his eyes studying her darkening, and she thought she knew what he was thinking. It alarmed her just a little, but she didn't lower her eyes.

'If you were not so young and innocent, Lucy Walsh, I would most definitely be tempted to kiss you to see if those lips are as soft and sweet as I imagine them to be—just something to remember in the coming days.'

'Why, do you mean you would claim a kiss from me as pay back after all?' she murmured cheekily.

'My dear Miss Walsh,' he said, looking at her face directly with a frank leer of approval that raked down over her body, 'I am a seaman and if you were on my ship, and older and with more experience of the world at large, believe me when I tell you that you would pay me back, only I don't think you would like the price.'

Shocked, Lucy drew herself up, a hot flush mantling her cheeks, but strangely she was not offended. 'Sir, you are no gentleman.'

He grinned. 'So you've finally figured that out. But worry not. I mean you no harm. Keep your innocence, Lucy Walsh. Hold on to it as long as you can. Your virtue is the most precious thing you have. Never forget that.'

Lucy stared at him, thinking it was a strange thing for him to say and wondered what had prompted it. Then he smiled, a slow, sensual, brilliant smile that made her feel as if she'd stared at the sun too long. 'You are going far?'

'I've been visiting a relative here in Surrey. I'm with a friend, Jacob Higgins, and we're on our way back to London. Jacob couldn't resist dropping in to see what the fair was all about and to partake of refreshment—the liquid kind. Speaking of which, I should go and look for him. Then I really should be going. I want to make it back before dark. Captain Christopher Wilding at your service.' With a smile he inclined his head in the briefest of bows. 'I bid you good day, Lucy Walsh. It's been a pleasure talking to you.' He turned from her and walked away.

Lucy's eyes followed him as he strode across the grass with a casual grace, took hold of the bridle of a splendid chestnut stallion and swung himself on to its back with all the ease of a trained athlete. She noted how he rode his horse as if he were part of the animal. She still felt the undercurrents created by his presence and, as he disappeared into the trees, she was touched by an incredible sense of loss.

She had no idea what had possessed her to go off with him like she had, for she had been unable to stop herself. It was as if the innocent part of her had undergone an extraordinary transformation beneath the intense silver gaze and she had become a shameless wanton. When she thought of it and their conversation and he had said that, had she been older, a kiss would be the reward for saving her from a runaway horse, an acute embarrassment washed over her, along with an odd, breathless excitement that she was certain could not be anything but wicked.

She was sure he had been attracted to her in a special sort of way and there was no doubt he'd had an effect on her. He had made her feel she was no longer a child. She felt frustrated that he had gone before she could understand the meaning of this attraction between them.

Hearing someone call her name, she looked round to see Emma, who came to stand beside her.

'Who was that man you were talking to?' Emma asked, looking in the direction in which he had disappeared.

'Christopher Wilding, apparently,' she murmured a little dreamily, completely unaware that there was a sparkle in her eyes and a delicate pink flush on her cheeks that hadn't been there before her meeting with the handsome sea captain. From the moment she had set eyes on him she had felt a strong sense of attraction to him, right from the moment she had looked into his silver-grey eyes when he had saved her from being trampled to death by the horse. 'He came to my rescue when a horse threatened to run me down. He's a sea captain.'

'Then he must have been with the person I was talking to. He told me he was a sailor. He said his friend was a sea captain, a privateer—the owner of a vessel called *Sea Nymph*, which is docked in London—and quite famous for escaping at the most crucial moment from impossible situations.'

Lucy gave her an indulgent smile. 'I think he might have been trying to impress you, Emma, with his story of derring-do.'

'Perhaps you're right, but he was nice—and see,' Emma said, running towards a leather satchel on the ground, 'your captain must have dropped this.' She handed it to Lucy. 'Do you think we should look in-side?'

'No. If he did indeed drop it—or it might have fallen from his horse—then we should try to find him.' She looked around, hoping to catch sight of him, but he was nowhere to be seen. 'He must have left with his friend.'

'Perhaps there's an address inside where he can be reached. Have a look, Lucy. There will be no harm done.'

Nervously Lucy unwrapped the package, but there was nothing inside to identify the stranger, just papers with an address in Hanover Square which she imme-diately put back without reading them.'

'We'll take them back with us. He knows I am at the academy so when he misses them, if they are im-portant, he might very well go to there.'

Chapter Two

Riding away from the fair with Jacob, Christopher found his thoughts turning to his pleasurable meeting with Lucy Walsh, unable to believe he had felt such delight spending time with a young woman fresh out of school eating warm gingerbread under a tree. She had roused his interest and he had been immediately drawn to her, attracted by her physical beauty. He had been at sea until two days ago when he had put in at the port in London.

It had been a while since he had seen such fresh beauty. When she had turned her face up to the sun, the light had caught her eyes, which were brown and flecked with pure gold, deep and transparent like sunshine on water, and surrounded by incredibly long lashes. If he had looked into them too long he knew he would have become lost. Her skin was soft and golden, and she had a mouth that enjoyed laughter.

For the short time they had been together he had revelled in her presence and fought down the insane impulse to bend his head and slowly kiss the laughter from her soft, inviting lips. Give her another year or so and she would be a natural temptress, alluring and provocative. But for now she was an innocent, young and with the face of an angel and an unspoiled charm that made him smile. She was also in possession of a strength of character that would mature as she became older—though she had been sadly in need of grooming.

Her rich cloud of dark hair was highlighted with streaks of gold and boasted dried leaves and bits of grass. The plain white blouse and blue skirt that she wore accentuated her tiny waist and the body beneath, outlining the curve of her young breasts. Her face was enchanting. The primal rush of attraction he had felt for her had surprised him. He was an experienced man of the world, but he was also an honourable man and sincerely hoped she would not be chastised for spending time with him.

The strength of his desire was unexpected. How, in a matter of moments, had he gone from contemplating an evening's wanton revelry in London with his friends to finding himself attracted to an eighteen-year-old girl he would very much like to see again? All the time they had been together she had watched him with the wide-eyed, fascinated attention of an innocent, untouched girl for a man older and presumably experienced. It was probably the first time in her young life that she had been in the presence of a mature male with a colourful existence and therefore delightfully dangerous—it would not have occurred to her she could be out of her depth.

Most of his adult life had been spent on board his ship so he had to take advantage of carnal relationships when he put into port—be it the Caribbean, America or England. He was single by choice and, because long absences would be certain to strain a relationship, he wanted no emotional intimacy or entanglements that having a wife or keeping a mistress would have entailed.

Born and raised in America, he was a man who liked to make his own fortune—or die trying. Having learned at an early age that the only way to survive was to fight back and use his own initiative, he had become a reckless adventurer and privateer. As the estranged grandson of the Duke of Rockwood he was also heir to a dukedom and the estate of Rockwood Park in Surrey. It was an inheritance shunned by his own father, who had become estranged from his father when, thirty-five years ago, he had married an American woman of lowly birth and chosen to live in America. His grandfather had disowned him for marrying a woman he considered to be so far beneath him that he could not accept her at the time.

As the years went by it was a decision he had come to regret and sought absolution from his son, but where his son was concerned there was no forgiveness. When Christopher had come to England for his education and spent time at Rockwood Park, his grandfather had been prepared to go to any lengths in order to win his respect. If he could not have his forgiveness, then he would take comfort from the times he spent at Rockwood Park.

When he had been a boy the estrangement and the nature of it had caused Christopher considerable heartache and bitterness at his grandfather's rejection of his mother—a gentle woman who had not deserved such harsh treatment and would have given her life to repair the damage her marriage to Christopher's father had caused. His father had died in America six months earlier, his mother several months before him.

Christopher had notified his grandfather of the death of his father. Whether it was regret or his effort to make amends for what had happened between them so long ago now, the Duke had taken to writing to Christopher on a regular basis, asking him to give serious thought to his position and not to turn his back on his inheritance, that it was up to him to cherish and safeguard what generations of Wildings had built and would pass on to his descendants. Christopher was the rightful heir to Rockwood Park, the Wildings' ancestral home, and the Duke genuinely wanted him to take on the responsibility.

Christopher had known the time would come when he would have to give serious thought to accepting his inheritance and settling down. Having developed an understanding of his grandfather, out of which had come respect and a closeness having grown out of the times they had spent together at Rockwood Park, with his ship docked in London and up for sale, and a dearly loved sister—who had attempted to take her own life following an unhappy love affair—at Rockwood Park recovering, he knew this was the time.

Having arrived back at the academy, the handsome sea captain was temporarily forgotten when, after tidying herself up in the room she shared with Emma, Lucy was summoned to Miss Brody's study. As soon as she saw the woman seated stiffly on the gold and green sofa, she knew this was her stepmother. She rose when Lucy entered, her hazel eyes focusing steadily and unnervingly on her.

'Why, you must be Lucy.' Her voice was low and husky—like honey, Lucy thought. Catlike, she crossed towards her and gave her a peck on the cheek. Standing back, she smiled, the smile remaining fixed on her lips without reaching her eyes, giving a lie to any words of welcome and instant fondness for her stepdaughter. 'I'm so pleased to meet you at last. I've heard so much about you from your dear father that I feel that I know you already.'

Totally unprepared for this attractive, perfectly formed woman, within seconds of their meeting Lucy felt gauche and terribly unfeminine. Sofia's long dark brown hair coiled beneath an elegant hat that matched her saffron-coloured dress, and tall slender body, gave her a regal effect. Her mouth was full and red and there were a few lines of age on her face and her cheeks owed some of their glow to the rouge pot, but there was no denying that Sofia Walsh was still a handsome woman and also much younger than her ageing and ailing father.

'You have arrived earlier than I expected,' Lucy said. 'I wasn't expecting you for several weeks.'

'I know, my dear, but I was impatient to see my stepdaughter. I arrived in London several days ago and couldn't see the point of waiting any longer. I know we will get on well together and soon come to understand each other. Miss Brody has been giving me an account of your time and achievements at the academy. You have done well. I had no idea I had such a clever stepdaughter.'

'Lucy,' Miss Brody said, getting to her feet and coming to her. 'You are to leave with Mrs Walsh today. I know you have already packed some of your things, which we will send on later, so I think you should go and pack what you would like to take with you today. I've ordered refreshment to be brought for Mrs Walsh while you say goodbye to your friends and collect your things.'

'Yes—of course. Please excuse me.'

She went out, closing the door softly behind her, And returned to her room, taken completely by surprise by her stepmother's unexpected arrival. There were so many conflicting and confusing thoughts going round in her head that she couldn't think straight. The undercurrents she had sensed from the moment she had set eyes on the sleekly beautiful woman gave her a feeling of unease. She began to pack the things she would take with her, while Emma sat on her bed, unable to believe they were to part and not knowing when they would see each other again.

'But—it's absolutely ghastly,' Emma retorted. 'Why would she want to whisk you away without notice?'

'I have no idea, Emma,' she said, thrusting anything she could lay her hands on willy-nilly into her large bag, 'but from what I have seen of Sofia, she is a woman who knows exactly what she wants and is not a woman to cross.'

'Oh, dear! You don't like her, do you? Although I recall when your father wrote telling you of his marriage that you were not prepared to like her.'

'No, I wasn't. But goodness! How shall I endure it—being thrust into the company of a woman I don't know and who will probably look on me as something of a freak. Oh, why did my godmother decide to go to France at this time? It would have been reassuring to have her in London.'

'And the gentleman you are to marry? Did your stepmother mention him?'

'No—and I'm not going to marry him, Emma,' she said adamantly, absently shoving the sea captain's leather satchel into her bag. 'No doubt she'll lose no time in telling me all about him.'

By the time Lucy had packed and had her bags carried down to the elegant carriage standing in the drive, Sofia was ready and impatient to return to London. Lucy said hurried goodbyes to Miss Brody and all those who came to see her off. The hardest thing of all was leaving Emma. Both girls were tearful and Lucy wondered how on earth she was going to survive without her dear friend.

* * *

'You will be able to write to your friends when you are settled, Lucy,' Sofia said as Lucy dabbed away her tears.

'Yes, I will, although I am going to miss Emma. We started at the academy together.'

'And your godmother? She is in France, I understand.'

'Yes—on an extended visit. She—hoped I would join her when I finished at the academy.'

'Your father has placed me in the role of chaperon, Lucy. You must write to your godmother and tell her what has transpired, what it is your father has arranged for you.'

'You mean my betrothal to Mr Barrington.'

Sofia looked at her coldly. 'Exactly.'

'Even though I am against it.'

'Yes, even so.'

'Aunt Caroline will not like it at all.'

'There is not a thing Lady Sutton can do about it. I have a letter from your father to give to her explaining everything. Your father has your best interest at heart, Lucy. He sent you to England to take advantage of all the country has to offer a young lady of means. But he never forgot that you are the daughter of a person who has earned his fortune through business and trade— the type of person the *ton* look down their aristocratic noses at. There are many vicious tongues who will not fail to remind you of that connection. Your father, who is astute in matters of business and knows the way of the world, sees this and is of the opinion that you will be better off marrying into your own kind.'

'I remember that my father told me to remember who I am and to be proud.'

'Which is good advice. Mark Barrington is also a ranch owner, looking for a wife.'

'And I happen to fit the bill,' Lucy said stiffly. There was stubborn pride in the set of her small chin.

Sofia gave her a sharp look or reproach. 'Exactly. There, I knew you would see sense. Make the most of the opportunity that has been offered. Your father is determined to secure a suitable match for you in Louisiana.'

'Even though I am against it?'

Sofia's eyes narrowed with annoyance. 'Don't be tiresome, Lucy. You must be obedient to my wishes. I do not wish to have to tell your father that you are disobedient. I am sure that would grieve him. The matter is settled. You have a duty and a responsibility to your father,' she reminded her coldly.

'I do not want to marry a man who is a complete stranger to me. I will not.'

Sofia looked at her as she would a recalcitrant child. 'He will not always be a stranger to you.'

Lucy fought back the anger Sofia's words stirred, but she was determined to speak her mind. Certainly she owed it to her father to treat Sofia with polite deference, but filial duty only went so far. 'Getting to know him holds little interest to me—now or in the future. I will never love him and I will not marry him.'

'Really, Lucy, what foolishness is this—what nonsense?'

'Not to me. Do you mind telling me Mr Barrington's age? Is he young, old—what?'

'He is a sophisticated man—almost forty. He might not be the essence of a young woman's romantic dreams, but he is caring and will make you a good husband. He is also possessed of a cool, steady temperament and is ready to marry you whenever it might be.'

'Without even seeing me? Goodness, for all he knows I might be fat, ugly and stupid.'

'Your father has assured him that you are none of those things. You are still very young, but you will learn that few people marry for love when there is business to transact.'

'So, I am a business transaction. Well, at least now I know where I stand. When am I to meet Mr Barrington?'

'Later today, when he comes for dinner. He's taken rooms at Pulteney's Hotel in Piccadilly for the time he is in London. You will get to know him before you wed—and I hope for a little fun myself. I haven't come all this way, to the most famous capital in the world, not to enjoy the pleasure the city has to offer.'

'Why did my father not accompany you to England?'

'He—he had important matters to take care of— but he is looking forward to seeing you when we return to Louisiana.'

'Has he not sent a letter to me, explaining why he is doing this?'

'I'm afraid not.'

'It is most unusual. How was he when you left?'

'I have no wish to worry you, but of late he's not been himself—indeed, when the doctor told him he must take things easy, he became concerned about you, about your future. If anything should happen to him he wants to be entirely sure that you'll be taken care of, which is why he arranged for you to marry Mark Barrington, so that you would be left in capable hands.'

'Then we must leave for America at once. I would like to see him,' Lucy said, deeply concerned about her father's failing health.

'Unfortunately, that's not possible. Mark has some business to take care of. These things cannot be done in a hurry—but rest assured we will leave before the month is out.'

Arriving at the house in Belgravia Sofia was renting for the time she was in London, a fashionable and tastefully furnished house, Lucy asked to be excused so that she could go to her room and freshen up. She was relieved to be by herself at last, away from Sofia's oppressive presence. Kicking off her shoes, she lay on the bed and tried to sort out her thoughts. It had been an eventful day and she had much to think about. One thing she was certain about was that she did not like her stepmother. Lucy sensed a scheming nature behind her smiles. Knowing there was little she could do to change things just then, but feeling she must do something, she immediately wrote a letter to her godmother, begging her to help her.

Christopher had been halfway to London when he missed the satchel. The papers it contained were pertaining to the sale of his ship. He had a buyer in Paris who was interested in purchasing it so it was imperative that he retrieved the satchel. Cursing his carelessness, he had told Jacob to go on ahead while he rode back to Broughton to look for it, although he didn't hold out much hope of finding it. He was right. After doing a thorough search and making enquiries it could not be located. It was as he was about to leave that he thought of Lucy Walsh.

He recalled having it on his shoulder when he rushed to her aid. That was the moment it had dropped off his shoulder on to the grass. It was a long shot, but it could be possible that she had found it and handed it in to someone.

Having asked for directions to the academy, he was soon there. The proprietress, Miss Brody, was pleased to help. Knowing that Lucy had been at the fair with Emma, she immediately sent for her. Emma told him that, yes, they had found the satchel and that in the mayhem that followed her stepmother's arrival, Lucy had taken it with her to her stepmother's house in Belgravia. In fact, Captain Wilding must have passed the carriage on the way.

Thanking them, Christopher left for London, happy

that the retrieval of his satchel gave him the opportunity to see Miss Walsh once more.

Lucy didn't want to meet Mr Barrington, yet pride and vanity made her take care of her toilette and choose a suitable gown. She had few fashionable clothes for social occasions, which her godmother had told her would be remedied once she had finished her education and she could take her out in society before leaving for America.

With a smooth and practised grace, Sofia presented Lucy to Mr Barrington. He was tall, dressed in a dark blue frock suit, and handsome enough, with sultry features and dangerously hooded eyes. There was a certain swagger about him and he exuded all the confidence of a conceited charmer. But he didn't charm Lucy. His expression was one of hauteur and he stared at her with masculine speculation. She sensed the scrutiny of his gaze, and some instinct told her that this was a man she should be very careful with. When Sofia introduced them there was a light in his eyes and a wrongness about him Lucy could not explain. Whatever it was it made the contents of her stomach curdle.

'Miss Walsh, it is a pleasure to meet you at last. I have heard a great deal about you from your father.'

His voice was as smooth as silk. While his eyes noted her perfunctory curtsy, he studied her closely, his eyes absorbing every detail of her face and figure with its tiny waist, the watered silk of her gown with the gentle swelling of her bosom. Concealing the rush of dislike and repugnancy that washed over her, Lucy struggled to maintain her composure.

'Sofia tells me you are a planter, Mr Barrington, in Louisiana.' He nodded. 'Do you know my father well?'

'I do. We have known each other for many years and I hold him in the highest esteem.'

'Mark is a frequent visitor to Aspendale, Lucy. My dear husband always welcomes his company.'

'Yes,' Lucy remarked. 'Father is a sociable person. I remember the house always being full of guests— more so when my mother was alive.'

Lucy hadn't missed the grimace on Sofia's face at the mention of her husband's first wife. She had realised that when Sofia's mind was made up about anything she would not take kindly to being taken to task and would lose no opportunity to undermine her confidence and belittle her, so she wasn't surprised when during the main course she immediately brought up the subject she had been dreading.

'Tomorrow we will visit the shops, Lucy. I think we should put our mind to having you fitted for some new gowns now you are no longer at the academy and about to move in society. We will also give some thought to your wedding gown—something creamy white, I think.'

Lucy stopped eating and stared at her. 'A wedding gown? I have told you, Sofia, I have no wish to get married—not to Mr Barrington or anyone else for that matter. I do not know Mr Barrington and I certainly don't recall him doing me the courtesy of asking me to be his wife.'

'Lucy, kindly guard your tongue,' Sofia chided.

'I'll thank you to stay out of this, Sofia,' Mr Barrington said sharply.

He continued to converse, respectful and polite and solicitous to Lucy's comfort. His manner was rather stiff at first, but he relaxed over the meal and several glasses of wine. He paid Lucy a good deal of attention. She wasn't flattered by it, but unnerved. They talked of trivialities—she talked of life at the academy, he talked of places like New Orleans and Natchez. For her part Sofia spoke very little as she watched the by-play between these two, her eyes sharp and assessing. Lucy couldn't wait for the meal to end so she could escape to her room.

Then Mr Barrington's eyes narrowed and his mouth pulled itself into a smile so contrived that it was little more than a sneer. 'So, Lucy, you imply that you are not enthusiastic about marrying me.'

Lucy did not shrink from his sarcasm. 'Indeed, that is so, sir.'

'I can understand that perfectly. You are young. You have just finished your education. Every young lady wants to experience her first soirée, her first ball. I will make sure you do not lack for entertainment for the short time we are in London.'

'You are all kindness, Mr Barrington.'

His eyes narrowed at the irony in her tone of voice. 'However, I see no reason why we cannot become affianced in the meantime.'

'I will do nothing until I have heard from my father. Might I remind you that I have not agreed to a marriage between us and, since there is no pressure of circumstance, I see no reason to rush into a marriage with anyone.'

'Forgive my bluntness, but the matter is far more complex than you could possibly understand.'

Lucy felt her hackles rise, but forced herself to remain calm. 'Really? You underestimate my intelligence, Mr Barrington.'

'Not at all, my dear. I simply recognise that young ladies like yourself have no head for these things. Your father has agreed to the marriage—indeed, he is anxious for the wedding to take place before we leave for Louisiana.'

'And I have told you that I will do nothing until I have confirmation from my father that this is what he wants.'

'You must allow yourself to be guided by those who understand these things.'

'And my dowry?' she asked bluntly. He talked as if as a woman, her life, had neither worth nor meaning in the real world of men. 'Has he been generous with that?'

'We have come to an agreement—but I sought to spare you the trivial details. However, if you insist on a full explanation…'

'I insist on it,' she said, very much to his surprise.

'Very well—but it is not a subject for the dinner table.'

'No. I agree,' she said, with a tight smile.

There was a hint of presumptuousness in his manner and there were times when he could not veil the look of calculation in his eyes. Mark Barrington looked like an elegant predatory animal who had discovered his prey and was biding his time before pouncing. The thought sent a shudder down her spine. She did not like him. He was determined and grasping, but he would not find her as easy to manipulate as he imagined.

But she must not underestimate him. This was definitely a man she should be careful of. Her cloak of cynicism and the feeling that all was not as it should be stayed with her long after Mr Barrington had left. She had always sailed through life, happy and carefree. Now she felt there was something malevolent in it.

Having no desire to remain in Sofia's company a moment longer, Lucy excused herself.

Sofia allowed herself a little smile. 'Well, Lucy, what do you think of Mark? He's charming, don't you agree?'

'No, Sofia. Mr Barrington did not make a favourable impression on me and, now I have met him I am more determined not to marry him than I was before.'

Sofia's smile faded abruptly as she rose to her feet. 'You wretched girl. You will marry him. If it's the last thing I do I will see you wed.' In a swirl of silver and blue chenille and a cloud of expensive perfume, she marched from the room, apparently not caring that the door shook as she slammed it forcefully behind her.

When she had gone, Lucy finally allowed her defences to crumble—her shoulders slumped and she buried her face in her hands. By heaven, she would not stay here and be forced to marry Mr Barrington, no matter how much her father wanted it or how advantageous the match. Despite his intentions where she was concerned, Lucy was determined to rid herself of him as soon as Aunt Caroline returned. She couldn't go through with becoming his wife. Anything, even returning to the academy and becoming a tutor herself, would be preferable to marrying Mr Barrington. There had to be some way out of her predicament.

She did have money of her own, enough to pay her passage to America if need be or to go to Paris to see her godmother, but she was aware of the dangers of a young woman travelling alone so she made up her mind to wait before taking such drastic action. But in the meantime she must be wary.

Was there no one to protect her? The two people she loved most in the world—her father and her godmother—were too far away to be of help, but an image of Captain Wilding suddenly rose in her mind. He was a sea captain, a man who had to be intelligent, with practical common sense, a man capable of forming an independent assessment in any given situation. He had to be fair but hard, dependable, a man his crew could respect and have absolute confidence in.

She recalled that he had mentioned he was to go to Paris. Was it possible that he could be persuaded to take her with him? It was presumptuous of her, she knew that, and it was highly likely he would refuse, but it was a lifeline she had to cling to, hoping it would get her out of this intolerable situation.

* * *

The next morning when Lucy left the house, attired in a cloak over a lavender gown and carrying Captain Wilding's satchel, she did so quietly so as not to disturb Sofia. Hiring a hackney, she instructed the driver to take her to Hanover Square. There was no sign that she had spent a sleepless night trying to come to a decision about her future course of action or that she was still trying to bolster the courage to carry out the wild plan she had conceived. But her delicate jaw was set with determination. Sofia had provoked more than her own anger—the woman had aroused in Lucy an instinct for self-preservation. But she was also struck with the fear that, as she had no one else to turn to, only this stranger, if he would not help her then she was doomed.

London was gilded with sunlight and bustling with activity. In the elite environs of Mayfair, dwellings were elegant, smart cabriolets driven by prideful drivers passed up and down the thoroughfares, along with carriages pulled by well-matched, fine-blooded teams. When the cab halted outside the address she had given him, handing the driver his fee, with her heart pounding in her chest, she climbed the steps to the house.

It was the same as all the others in the square—large and elegant with Doric columns flanking the black-painted door. Gathering all her courage, she squared her shoulders and made perhaps the most dangerous and important decision of her life. Raising the brass knocker with a determined lift of her arm, she hit the door to announce her arrival.

A man she assumed to be the butler opened the
door and, yes, he said, Captain Wilding was at home.
Forcing herself to ignore the fluttering in her stomach, she stepped inside. The hall was bathed in sunlight, revealing the fine plastering and elegant marble
stairs rising to a gallery. Decorated in soothing shades
of cream and green, it possessed a simple elegance.
Tasteful paintings and shimmering gilt mirrors hung
on the walls. She was shown into a large room and told
to wait. He would ask Captain Wilding if he would
see her.

Gingerly perching on a sofa, she looked around
her. Fresh flowers in a porcelain vase were arranged
on the marble mantelpiece. She admired the elegant
silk damask furniture and the Persian carpet, which
shimmered with vivid colours. Tall French windows
overlooked a terraced garden. It was not the kind of
house in which she imagined a seaman would have
lodgings. Did Captain Wilding own this house? she
wondered. If so, he must be very rich.

Minutes passed. She sat there, clutching the satchel,
feeling the tension mounting inside her. Then she heard
footsteps and, fixing her eyes on the door, watched
him enter. He was as tall as she remembered, slender
and as handsome as a god with those perfectly chiselled features. She could see he was surprised to see
her. Clearly he had not been expecting callers at this
hour of the morning. His linen shirt was open at the
throat and thin enough to reveal the sculpted muscles
beneath, and his snug black breeches were moulded to
his legs. Standing up, she threw back the hood of her

cloak, unaware that even without ornamentation she appeared as young and fresh as a spring breeze. She waited for him to cross towards her, watching him, admiring him, suddenly shy of him. She was physically attracted to him—no woman could be immune to that potent magnetism. He inspired emotions she had never felt before, marvellous, conflicting emotions.

'You—you remember me? We met at the fair.' He smiled at her, a heated, knowing smile, which gave her hope that he would help her.

'This is my lucky day. I remember, for once having made your acquaintance that would not be something I would forget. This is a pleasant surprise. Indeed it is. Ah, I see you have my satchel. Thank God you found it. You have also saved me a journey. I was going to call on you later.'

'You were? How did you know I had it?'

'When I realised I had mislaid it I went back to the fair and made enquiries. I went to your academy on the off chance that you might have found it. Your friend Emma told me that you had and that you had it with you.'

'I see. I hope you don't mind, but I looked inside and saw this address on one of the papers.'

'No, I don't mind. I'm glad you did. Thank you. Are you alone?'

'Yes—I—I...' Lowering her eyes, she chewed on her lip, at a loss as to how to continue. How could she ask someone she didn't know to help her? But whoever he was, her excellent instincts told her that she could trust this man.

He looked down at her, frowning, his eyes delving into hers. 'You appear troubled. Is something wrong?'

'Yes,' she replied quickly, meeting his gaze. Summoning up her nerve, she said, 'I—I'm sure you will think me presumptuous, and I cannot blame you, but I would like to ask you a favour.'

'A favour?' His eyes narrowed in sudden wariness. 'What sort of favour, exactly?'

Her confidence wavered a little, but with her heart in her throat she lifted her chin and squared her shoulders. 'I—I was wondering—I recall you telling me that you were going to Paris shortly.'

He stiffened, his eyes glittering with the wary gaze of a seasoned warrior. Putting his hands on his lean hips, he regarded her with a frown. 'You do have a way of knocking a man between the eyes, don't you, Miss Walsh? I did say that, although I'm surprised you remember. Why?'

'Will you take me with you—to France?' Too naive to know how to hide her feelings, the words came out in a rush and she waited, holding her breath, for him to reply. She lifted her eyes to his and her longing for him to agree to her wish was there in their soft depths.

'Good Lord!' The words were exhaled slowly, but otherwise, he simply stared at her.

Somewhat heartened that she hadn't been refused outright, Lucy went on. 'Before you give me your answer, perhaps I should mention that I am quite desperate to leave London.'

'So why are you running away?'

She stared at him, looking wary and perplexed. 'How do you know that?'

'I don't, but you've just confirmed my suspicion.' He paused, studying her. 'Has someone hurt you— been cruel to you? Frightened you?'

'No, nothing like that. If you must know, my father has arranged my marriage to a man he deems suitable. I think he's a family friend.'

'And you don't want to marry him.'

'No, absolutely not.'

'Is there someone else you would rather marry?'

'Good heavens, no. I don't want to get married— not to anyone—at least not yet. I've only just finished my education. I'm not ready to get married. But this is so unlike my father. I can't help feeling that there is something wrong.'

'I recall you telling me your godmother is in Paris. Have you written to her?'

'Yes, but it will be ages before she replies.'

'Is there no one you can stay with until you hear from your godmother?'

'No—only Emma, but she is still at the academy. If it were possible, I would take ship for America and demand to know what my father is playing at.'

'When did you last hear from him?'

'About two months ago. He writes on a regular basis.'

'And he gave no hint of what he had in mind?'

'No, nothing.'

'Did you by any chance read the letter he wrote to the academy?'

'Why—I—no, I did not. It was addressed to Miss Brody. Why do you ask?'

He shook his head. 'No reason. Have you met this man he has chosen for you?'

'Yes, last night, and I don't like him.'

'Why? What's wrong with him? Is he old, ugly, fat?'

'No—at least at nearly forty he's old to me—old enough to be my father.'

'Your father is still in Louisiana, I take it.'

'Yes. He sent my stepmother to take care of the proceedings. Being taken early out of the academy has ruined what should be a happy time for me. I find I have been thrown into the middle of an unpleasant situation.'

'Do you think you are worrying too much about all this? You might be wrong. There might be a logical answer to all these things.'

'I don't know. It's just this feeling I have that things are not quite right. I have to be prepared in case I am right.'

'So you think running away is the solution. And you want to go to Paris. That's a bit extreme, if you don't mind me saying so.'

'No, not at all, and I imagine you think with the impetuosity of youth and all that I am quite mad, but I'm not. My godmother was expecting me to go to her when I finished at the academy. She loves Paris and was simply dying to show it to me. She was unaware that my stepmother was coming to London—as I was.'

'Has it not occurred to you that a scandal might ensue should you run away from your stepmother?'

'Scandal! Why, no. Why should it? No one knows me or my stepmother—although I think she will make her presence known and will soon be invited to every soirée and ball on offer. I cannot imagine it will matter to you if I am gossiped about.'

'It happens to matter a great deal to me. For reasons of my own the last thing I want at this time is to have scandal attached to my name. Have you explained to your stepmother your aversion to marrying the man your father has chosen for you?'

'Yes, but my objections fell on deaf ears. She is determined that we will be married before she turns round and heads back to Louisiana. Why, Sofia has even suggested shopping for my wedding gown.'

Christopher was quiet for a moment, studying her, then he said, 'So you are asking me to aid and abet you in your escape.'

'If you put it like that then, yes, I am.' Her eyes looked beseechingly into his. 'The fact is that there is no one else I can ask. *Please* take me with you.'

'How do you know I'm not a madman or a seducer?'

He spoke quietly, raising an eyebrow in question. She glanced at him. He was standing perfectly still, watching her. A muscle moved spasmodically in his throat as he waited for her answer. Something in his expression made her catch her breath, for the effect of that warmly intimate look in his eyes was vibrantly, alarmingly alive, and the full impact of the risk she was taking by being here and asking him to take her to France made her realise the recklessness of her actions. She did not know this man at all—she'd only met him briefly the day before, yet her instinct told her she could trust him implicitly.

'I might be young and inexperienced in the ways of the world at large, but I do trust my judgement and believe you would not do me harm. You might be no prize, sir, but you are certainly preferable to the man who poses as my betrothed. I will sell my soul to the devil before I marry him. Will you take me to Paris?' She waited through a long moment of awful suspense.

Christopher looked at her in taut silence. Finally he spoke and his voice was rough with emotion, as if the words were being gouged out of him. 'Absolutely not.'

'But—why?'

'Because it's a mad idea, that's why.'

'No, it isn't. You told me you had to go there.'

'Not any more. The person I was going to see is here in London.'

'Oh, I see.' Disappointment swamped her.

'I'm sorry, Miss Walsh, but I'm afraid I'm not free to take you to Paris. I have a duty I am obliged to fulfil here in England.'

His tone suggested such finality that Lucy turned away, tears welling in her eyes. But while her heart began to beat in helpless misery she was determined not to let them to break free, for if she allowed them to do so she would be utterly demolished. She felt crushed by the full weight of her stupidity, her gullibility, and all that those two traits had brought down on her. She was afraid her knees were going to give way. Thankfully they didn't.

She was still under the influence of his sensual magnetism and felt her heart begin to break. His refusal shouldn't hurt so much, but she had done her best to persuade him. She couldn't force him to take her to France. What she was going to do now she didn't know and that alarmed her. There remained only for her to extricate herself from this awkward situation as gracefully as possible.

'Of course you do,' she murmured, stepping away from him. 'I understand perfectly.' Her voice seemed to belong to someone else, a flat, hollow, defeated voice that came from a great distance.

'My advice is that you return to your stepmother and try to reason with her. Perhaps you are making too much of it when she might very well have your best interests at heart. Maybe she will be willing to delay your nuptials until you are back in Louisiana.'

Lucy stared at him, offended that he had not believed a word she had said. His sweeping, masculine assumption made her eyes sparkle dangerously and she was unable to bite back the retort that sprang to her lips. 'Please do not belittle me. What I told you was the truth and I have good reason to be concerned about the plans being put in place for my future without consideration for my feelings.'

'Miss Walsh—I beg your pardon. I did not mean to belittle you.'

'Yes, you did, Captain Wilding. You intended to do just that, to make me see that I am no more than a green girl and that I am making a mountain out of a molehill. It was the sort of remark I would expect from a typical arrogant male who thinks women would be better off doing what they are told by their male superior who think they are brainless and helpless. I am neither of those things, sir.'

Taking a deep breath, she clenched her trembling hands in the folds of her skirt, her chin tilted as a thin, determined smile curved those tempting lips. 'I'm sorry. I should not have bothered you with my troubles. I must go. Thank you for your time.'

She walked away, devastated by her sense of loss and amazed by his obvious indifference. Before she could reach the door, Christopher closed the distance between them and grasped her arm. When she turned to look at him, Lucy could see the silver lights in his grey eyes and the crinkled web of laugh lines at the corners. Yet he wasn't anywhere near to laughing now. He searched her face for a long moment, then reached up to gently touch her trembling chin with a long forefinger.

'Lucy, if I were free… I really would be tempted to take you to your godmother in Paris. But I cannot.'

She forced a smile at his gallantry and had to struggle to answer. She was grateful when he released her arm and escorted her into the hall.

'I must go.'

'No—wait.'

'No, really. It was most kind of you to listen to me, but…' She mouthed the polite words which she had been taught from the nursery upwards and Captain

Wilding continued to look at her without expression. There was about him a certain air of boredom and no doubt he was impatient for her to be gone. She should not have come. She should have given his wretched satchel to one of the servants to deliver for her, for his attitude seemed to tell her that she was no more than a silly young girl and her usual exuberant confidence drained from her.

'How did you travel here?'

'In a hackney cab.'

'You really should not have come alone. A young woman taking a hackney in London, no matter how brave, has much to fear.'

'I am sure you're right, but I had to see you and I didn't want my stepmother to see me leave. She would have stopped me.'

'I'll arrange to have the carriage brought round.'

'No,' she was quick to say. 'Thank you for your offer, but I would rather go back the way I came.'

She turned abruptly and headed for the door, bewildered at the strength of her own feelings and not at all sure what she was going to do about them, only aware at this precise moment that she needed quite desperately to get away from the overwhelming hurt that had attacked her.

On her return journey anger took over, anger at her own gullibility, her innocence and inexperience in this new world into which she had been thrust. Did she not have enough spirit to refuse a suitor she despised and did not love—could never love?

Chapter Three

When the hackney had disappeared, Christopher raked his fingers through his hair in consternation, thinking of the reasons he wasn't free: his grandfather, his inheritance and a sister, injured in mind and body who needed him at this time. He shook his head in frustration. He couldn't take Lucy Walsh to Paris if he wanted to. Besides, he had received notice that the man who was interested in purchasing his vessel was in London so there was no need for him go to Paris.

Christopher couldn't deny that he was fascinated by Lucy Walsh. When he had walked into the room and seen her sitting there, waiting for him, looking so heartbreakingly young and lovely, he had welcomed the sight of her. When she had left, he felt that he had let her down and knew there would be no peace from the throbbing emptiness that was gnawing away at him that was to increase unbearably as the days passed. He felt a sudden longing, a bittersweet mixture of desire and regret for sending her away. It was a sensation so unexpected and so unwanted that the force of it astonished him.

Instead of meekly doing her father's bidding, she had, instead, set upon a course to save herself from an unwanted marriage and appealed to him for help. He recalled how she had looked at him with her soft brown eyes. She needed him. It was the kind of look that was imploring and proud, the kind of look that could stir a man's conscience. He couldn't do what she asked, it was impossible, and on that thought he had put up his defence.

But it had been damned hard, he thought with a defeated sigh, to refuse her, but he must retain his self-control or he would be lost. She was a distraction he did not need. He was here to sort out his future, not to become entangled with the delectable Miss Walsh in a fascinating web of intrigue. It was a hare-brained scheme she had concocted anyway. If he were to do as she asked, when her father found out he had abetted her in her wild escapade, he would be well within his rights to call him out. He was determined not to let her impossible request interfere with what he had to do.

He did ask himself why the inheritance should matter to him, but it did matter. Very much, in fact. The Wildings were an old and respected family and he would not have the name sullied by scandal. He could not allow himself to be distracted once he had decided on a course of action.

Suddenly irritated with her for needing his help and angry with himself for feeling guilty about refusing to give it, he snatched up the satchel and took it into the office, undid the straps and took out the papers.

'Oh, hell,' he muttered, wondering how Lucy Walsh had managed to get under his skin and make him feel like such a cad for refusing her, but he realised there must be more to her need to escape London than a mere feminine whim. He thought of her facing her troubles alone, without anyone there to protect her, and he knew that if her godmother didn't return soon the pressure would only increase.

Perhaps it was her eventful meeting with Captain Wilding earlier that day that made Lucy unable to sleep that night, for when she retired to her room, sleep evaded her. An inexplicable heaviness weighed on her heart. It didn't help that her thoughts kept returning to that devastating meeting with Captain Wilding. She couldn't stop thinking about it. When she had been with him at the fair his rugged strength and the attention he had given her had made her feel so very feminine, his earthy sensuousness so very desirable. If his treatment of her earlier had been anything to go by, then he probably hadn't been as affected by their meeting as she had been. No doubt he was the kind of seafaring adventurer with *a woman in every port*. After their acrimonious parting earlier, he would have forgotten about her entirely.

Yet she could not forget. She kept remembering the intensity of her feelings when he had snatched her out of the path of the rampaging horse, his tall strong body and his arms crushing her against him, and she remembered the sensations that had exploded inside her like tiny petals unfurling. She remembered the musky scent of his flesh and a warm, potent and unmistakable sense of longing deep inside her. She wondered what it would have felt like to be kissed by him. Abruptly she shook her head. Such fantasies were not acceptable for an unmarried young woman. She sighed. She couldn't imagine why she was thinking this way. She would do far better to try to sleep.

Drawing a robe over her white nightdress, she slipped downstairs to warm herself some milk, hoping it would help settle her. A full moon shone brightly through the windows, lighting her way as she went back up the stairs. The house was large with several bedrooms on the first floor. Reaching the landing, she was about to turn to go to her bedroom when she heard muffled voices coming from further down the landing, dragging her from her melancholy thoughts. Puzzled, she went to investigate, her bare feet making no sound on the thickly carpeted floor.

On reaching Sofia's door she paused to listen, hearing Sofia's muffled laughter and a man's voice within. He seemed to be urging her in subdued tones to be silent. Recognising the voice as belonging to Mr Barrington, for a moment she was transfixed with horror, for finding the two of them together in Sofia's bedroom could mean only one thing. Moving closer to the door, she strained her ears better to hear what was being said, shocked by what she heard next.

'I hope this is worth it, Mark,' she heard Sofia say,

'marrying a chaste little virgin. She won't give you what I can.'

Mr Barrington chuckled low in his throat. 'Of course she won't, but I have to go through the motions. Not only is she more annoyingly intelligent than I gave her credit for, she is perceptive as well—and suspicious. She is quite prepared to speak her mind.'

'Is it your intention to take her out in society?'

'To alleviate suspicion and secure our betrothal, yes—but we will keep it limited. When does her godmother return to London?'

'I really don't know. Hopefully not for some time—and not until our business is concluded.'

Lucy's mind reeled as she sought some explanation that might excuse their conduct, telling herself that things weren't always as they appeared, but there wasn't one. Feeling physically sick, she backed away from the door. How could they? How could they do this? How could Mr Barrington, with his insufferable arrogance, behave so disgustingly? As she experienced the full impact of their treachery, anger leaped in her.

She returned to her room as silently as she had come. Leaning on the closed door, she waited a moment for her limbs to stop shaking and her rage to lessen. She never wanted to look upon either of their faces again. It made her realise how little she knew of them. Mr Barrington was a bad individual and her stepmother a hard-hearted, selfish and greedy woman.

'I think I hate them both,' she whispered.

Getting into bed, she lay back on the pillows and

closed her eyes. Only gradually did she come to accept that bringing the incident out into the open would resolve nothing. Having listened to their conversation, now she had managed to get over the impact of what she had heard, she realised that her fears were not unfounded after all. Her whole life was in the hands of these two people. But what did they intend for her? What did it mean? That was when she began to fear for her father. What were they up to? Was she a pawn in some game they were playing? That was the moment she cursed her own ineptitude and her inability to control her own life.

Gradually she calmed down, but she was left feeling drained and utterly exhausted. For the time being she must swallow her own feelings of outrage and keep what she had seen and heard to herself, but she could not pretend it had never happened—nor could she forget and she would never forgive. Her natural pride and honesty urged her to a confrontation and a final settling of accounts with them, but she couldn't. Not yet. She must bide her time until she heard from her godmother—or her father.

Much to Lucy's relief there was no sign of Mr Barrington the next morning. Over the days that followed she minimised the time she spent with him and Sofia. She remained constantly alert and focused, bearing in mind everything that was happening. As a result she began to notice their small, silent exchanges.

Sofia seemed determined to create an easy atmosphere. She was always bright and encouraged Lucy to look favourably on her marriage to Mr Barrington. She took Lucy on shopping expeditions, where she was fitted for a number of gowns that Sofia insisted were necessary for the future Mrs Barrington. There were morning gowns in muslin, silks, satins and tulle, all trimmed with delicate lace. There were walking gowns with matching spencers, hats and bonnets, boots for walking and slippers for soirées in fashionable drawing rooms and, Sofia told her, no wardrobe could be complete without a ball gown. Never had Lucy seen, let alone possessed, such a fine selection of clothes. Sofia soon inveigled her way into society and was invited to soirées and even a ball at Lord and Lady Skeffington's house in Mayfair.

After attending a couple of soirées with Sofia and Mr Barrington, which left her feeling unimpressed and even more reticent towards her would-be betrothed, the day of the ball arrived. Mr Barrington intended to use the occasion to present her as his betrothed, no matter how often she reminded him that she would not marry him. He always looked at her with disdain and told her it was what her father wanted.

The Skeffington ball was to be a glittering, grand occasion, and in spite of herself Lucy was nervous about attending. She had to bathe and dress extra carefully, but her heart wasn't in it. She tried to remain patient while her maid fussed around, lacing up her stays, coiffing her hair, a white gardenia caught up in the ribbons among the crown of glossy black ringlets piled high on her head and artful tendrils caressing her cheeks. A simple gown of ivory silk, its skirt frosted with intricate silver lace, was slipped over her petticoats. The bodice was cut far lower than she considered decent, with full, puffed sleeves set well off her shoulders. By the time she was ready she was weary of the preparations.

Her hands were clad in long white gloves. The silk gown rustled softly as she made a slow progress down the stairs, where Mr Barrington draped an ermine-lined cloak over her shoulders, his hands brushing her bare flesh and lingering longer than was necessary. Attired in purple satin knee breeches and matching jacket and white silk stockings, with a frilled shirt it was Lucy's opinion that he looked overdressed, an opinion that she kept to herself.

'You look quite charming, Lucy,' Sofia said, resplendently dressed in saffron spangled gauze, her hair arranged in high and elaborate curls. 'But come along now. We must hurry. We're late as it is.'

They arrived at Skeffington House to find an unending line of carriages stretched all the way down the street. When Lucy stepped down from the carriage, never had she looked so fine and never had she felt so wretched. She looked like a lovely gilded statue and no man watching her could fail to admire her, but there was something at once remote and detached in the dazzling young woman herself. How they would laugh, she thought bitterly, if they could but know how miserable she was and how heavy her heart, which lay in her breast as silent and dead as a lump of rock.

They arrived late, hoping to avoid the early influx

of guests, but there was still a crush of an elegantly dressed assembly in the hall. The smell was a unique mixture of powder, perfume and sweat that always heralded a society event. After being received by their hosts—Mr Barrington making a point of introducing Lucy as his betrothed—they moved on, mingling with other guests. How she would have liked to tell them all that he was a liar, that he was nothing to her, but thrust into the midst of this glittering event stuffed with English elite, the last thing she wanted was to cause a scene and make herself the centre of attention.

Some of the guests Sofia knew already and lost no time in introducing Mr Barrington and Lucy to them. Lucy hated it, hated the way in which they manipulated her every move. She felt their control all around her. Mr Barrington moved to stand beside her.

'Come, my dear. Let us proceed to the ballroom.'

Giving Sofia a nod which implied she must follow, he held out his arm, leaving Lucy no recourse but to take it. Their progress up the stairs was slow since there were so many people all heading for the ballroom. Music and flowers filled the house. She noticed how the eyes of the ladies lingered on her tall, impressive escort. Then suddenly, as if a barrier had come down between them, they stopped. The man who stood before them was none other than Christopher Wilding. His gaze abruptly snapped to her face, registering not only her presence for the first time, but her worried eyes and wan smile as well. A brief impersonal smile touched the corner of his mouth before he glanced at her escort.

Lucy's attention was riveted suddenly on this man whose head rose above those of the crowd of guests. For a moment she thought she must be seeing things, suffering from a delusion brought about by some wish of her own to see him. But those handsome features—that fine-boned face and bronzed skin, those deep-set silver-grey eyes, that crooked smile at once impudent and gay—could not belong to any other man that she knew. Her heart gave a joyful leap and she almost said his name out loud, but, remembering the embarrassment of their last encounter, she lowered her eyes. As she moved past him, her eyes were drawn of their own volition to his figure in a plain but perfectly cut black coat, the darkness alleviated by the pristine whiteness of his cravat and silver waistcoat that matched his eyes.

Then, without a word, Barrington swerved away, just as if the incident had never happened. But Lucy had sensed a change in her escort. She had felt the muscles of his arm tense under her hand. Clearly aggravated by the encounter with Captain Wilding, he cursed softly, but his voice remained quite normal when he said, 'They are playing a waltz. Let's dance.'

'Are you acquainted with that particular gentleman, Lucy?' Sofia enquired, having closely observed her stepdaughter's reaction to the encounter.

'Yes, I am. We met at Broughton Fair, on the day you arrived at the academy.'

'What do you know about him?'

'Very little, only that he is a sea captain with his own vessel.'

'Well—at least he isn't a common sailor—though why any man would want to spend his life at sea when he could be on dry land is beyond me.'

'I imagine he likes the sea best or he would not do what he does,' Lucy replied coolly.

Sofia shot her a frosty stare. 'Be that is it may, if he should ask you to dance you must refuse him.'

Unbeknown to Lucy, tonight Christopher had taken his first privileged step into the realms of nobility as Viscount Rockley, attending the ball to represent his grandfather. His grandfather no longer attended society affairs so Christopher's presence tonight was bound to stir excitement in the curious.

He was unable to ignore the tide of black anger that consumed him on encountering Mark Barrington, or the contempt in which he was held. It would have been far preferable if the meeting appeared as nothing more than a chance encounter. But who would have thought Barrington, the man who had ruined his sister, had hurt her so much that she had tried taking her own life, would turn up here in London?

Mark Barrington was the son of a gambler and—like father like son—cared for nothing beyond the gaming tables. He had managed to make his money in the West Indies and New Orleans, only to lose it again. He was a social climbing individual who was well beneath the notice of London society. He was also a detestable character, but he was clever. If he had come all this way with the intention of wedding

Miss Walsh, then there had to be something sinister behind it.

He had no illusions with regard to the character of the man he hated above all others. He was dangerous. They had a past. Christopher wouldn't put it past Barrington to put a bullet or a blade in his back.

He now believed Miss Walsh to be in grave danger. Had he known that Barrington was her intended when she came to call on him, he would not have made light of the issue and considered how best to protect her. Mark Barrington would not willingly allow her to slip from his grasp. Men like him were used to taking what they wanted and would use force if necessary. He could not allow her to reside in that house for much longer.

Barrington was capable of forcing her into marriage by ruining her. What did he intend for her afterwards? There had to be more to this. What was in it for him—and what part did Miss Walsh's own father play in this? He recalled her telling him that Barrington was a ranch owner himself. Christopher knew this to be a blatant lie.

Standing on the sidelines, he continued to watch her. He regarded the elegant older woman who hovered protectively at her side, ready to steer her young charge through the set of rules of society with smooth efficiency. He assumed the woman to be Miss Walsh's stepmother. Miss Walsh had a delicate loveliness, a bright, strong spirit, which he felt would never be cast down. Just why he was drawn to her was something that eluded him.

He told himself that it was because he didn't want Barrington panting after her, but it was more than that. Her smile warmed his heart and her most innocent look sent desire raging through his veins. There was a provocative sensuality about her, a natural, unaffected sophistication that drew him to her. Even surrounded by London's most famous beauties, she managed to shine with an innocent kind of splendour that would draw the attention of any gentleman.

Feeling compelled and at liberty to look his fill, he felt his heart contract, not having grasped the full reality of her beauty until that moment. Her dark hair set off by the white gardenia gleamed in the light of the chandeliers, her face so elegantly carved that it appeared to be a magnificent work of art, yet it was pale and there was a strained look about her. He recalled their first meeting at the fair, the deep glow of admiration in her warm eyes as she had listened to him relate tales of his travels and derring-do with such rapt attention.

Lucy did her duty and danced two dances with Mr Barrington, and in between acknowledged the good wishes of those who came to congratulate them on their betrothal. Lucy would have liked to shout from the rafters that she had no intention of marrying him, but considered it prudent to keep quiet for the time being. He was not the best of dancers and she welcomed the dances she had with some of the younger set. She had her first taste of champagne, which she liked well enough, but she would drink it sparingly.

Miss Brody was of the opinion that it weakened one's inhibitions and she wanted to remain in full control of her wits. The ladies, some who flirted outrageously, fascinated her. She observed the ones who used fans and eyelashes to their advantage.

From a distance she noticed how Captain Wilding moved with ease among the crowd. There was a restless energy about him. He seemed to shine with a potent, relentless force that demanded unwavering attention. He wore his magnetism with casual disdain, taking it for granted that any woman he encountered would succumb at the snap of his fingers. She imagined that most of them did. She wanted to believe it was surprise that was causing her heart to leap and her body to tingle with excitement, but that would not explain why her gaze lingered on his tall figure that was shown to advantage by the black and white clothes he wore, or why she was wishing he would seek her out and ask her to dance.

Mr Barrington watched her constantly through heavy lidded eyes—until the draw of the card room proved too tempting for his addictive nature to resist, leaving Lucy to sip her champagne with no one but Sofia for company. It was when Sofia took to the dance floor with an elderly gentleman that Captain Wilding suddenly appeared, as if he had been awaiting the moment when she would be alone. She had surreptitiously glanced in his direction, caught up in her private impressions of his elegance and noting that he danced with no one. Now he bowed his head while holding her gaze, his expression both sombre and tender, a smile curving his lips.

'Miss Walsh! I had hoped to have the pleasure of seeing you again, but I did not think to find you here.'

'No, I don't suppose you did. For myself, your presence has also taken me by surprise.'

'You are so beautiful tonight,' he said with a husky undertone. 'Your cheeks are pink. Your eyes are gleaming. You look radiant. I am happy to see you are still smiling at me.'

'How could I not? You have done nothing wrong. The fact that you could not help me—I understand perfectly and do not hold it against you. It was wrong of me to approach you. It was extremely stupid of me. I certainly should not have asked you to take me to France. It was presumptuous of me.'

'No, it wasn't. I deeply regret I could not be of help and I am sorry,' he said, his voice edged with harsh remorse. 'I'm relieved to get you alone at last. You are a popular young lady among the young set. You have no shortage of partners.'

'Will you not ask me to dance?' she said as the lilting notes of the waltz floated around her. 'And quickly before my stepmother comes back.'

'I would be honoured.'

Completely disregarding what Sofia had said to her earlier that she was not to dance with Captain Wilding and taking immense satisfaction in disobeying her, she smiled and allowed him to lead her on to the dancefloor. She walked into his arms and felt his arm slide around her waist, bringing her close against the solid strength of his body. His free hand closed around her fingers and suddenly she was being whirled gently around the floor.

For a man who had spent most of his adult life at sea he was a superb dancer with an amazing sense of timing. His step was light. He took charge of the dance and she went where she was led. It was like dancing on air. For several moments they did not speak. Lucy enjoyed the wonderful sensation of being twirled around as though they both had wings, their bodies moving with perfect rhythm. Beneath her gloved hand she felt the strength of his shoulder and the arm encircling her waist like a band of steel was holding her much closer than was proper. She should have felt overpowered, but she felt safe and protected instead. The dance seemed to free her from the weight of her body. If only her mind could be freed of its burdens as easily.

'You dance divinely,' Captain Wilding breathed softly, a slow, admiring smile sweeping across his features.

'I love the waltz,' she said, feeling a little giddy and reckless and wonderful, wishing the dance would never end. 'Although Miss Brody is of the opinion that it is not proper for young ladies to dance the waltz.'

'They do in France. All the time.'

'Sadly, this is not France. How I wish it were, then I could find my godmother—Aunt Caroline.'

'Is she really your aunt?'

'No. She is my godmother and was my mother's closest friend. She insisted I addressed her as Aunt Caroline when I was very young.'

He twirled her round once more before capturing her eyes, a lazy smile sweeping across his face. 'Are you pleased to see me?'

'I hadn't expected to.'

'Surprises are pleasant, don't you agree?'

'Sometimes.'

'I am sure your escort would not be pleased to see you dancing with me. He should know better than to leave you to the mercy of all these unattended young men.'

'I am of the opinion that we are not as fragile as some would try to pretend.'

'Do you believe that?'

'Yes,' she replied, tilting her head to his, laughter in her soft brown eyes. 'It's a masculine idea—meant to show the superiority of the male sex.'

'And do you believe that also?'

'Believe what?'

'In the superiority of the man.'

'Absolutely not.'

'So you are saying men are inferior, then.'

'I didn't say that.'

'No, but that is what you meant.'

'Not at all.'

'That is gracious of you.'

'Not really. It's common sense. I believe the sexes should be equal, that men and women should complement each other.'

He grinned. 'That's some school you went to. I'm sure it is written somewhere that there are occasions where a woman's role is subservient.'

'Probably written by arrogant males who find females a temptation they can't resist,' she quipped. He
held her so close she could feel the warmth of his body
and smell the spicy scent of his cologne. She was suddenly conscious of his close proximity. His eyes, with
their lowered lids, had never left her face. She had
never realised before how seductive those eyes were
making her feel—so female and fragile.

Her cheeks flushed and she seemed to be having
trouble breathing. Her breasts strained against their
silken prison and her nipples were strangely taut, feeling the gaze of his lazy, indolent eyes like a subtle
caress.

'So, they transfer the blame for that on the women
rather than their own weakness.'

Looking up at him as he twirled her round again,
Lucy saw the indolence in his eyes had been replaced
by a mischievous twinkle and laughed. 'Stop teasing
me and enjoy the dance before you have to return me
to my stepmother.'

After a moment, on a more serious note, he said,
'You are betrothed to Mark Barrington. Why didn't
you tell me?'

Her face fell, the carefree feelings of a moment before melting away. 'First, I am not betrothed to anyone—especially not to Mr Barrington, however much
he likes to think so—and second, I saw no reason to
tell you his name. It didn't seem to be important and
it never occurred to me that you would know him.'

'He is still intent on marrying you. Indeed, he has

introduced you as his betrothed to anyone who will listen.'

'I know. There is nothing I can do about that without causing a scene. But be assured, I have no intention of marrying him. I would rather kill myself.'

Captain Wilding averted his gaze, but not before Lucy had seen the sudden pain that entered his eyes. It was as if her words had resurrected a time and an image he did not want to be reminded of.

'The more I resist,' Lucy went on, 'Sofia is very quick to remind me of my duty and obligation to my father. But the more I have come to know them, the more certain I am that my father doesn't want this. But what am I to do? I am quite alone and at their mercy. I am fearful of the future, which is as yet uncertain.'

'Had I known I would have whisked you away to a place of safety to avoid his clutches.'

'You know him, don't you? You recognised him. I suspected as much when he reacted to your encounter when we arrived.'

The sound he made, half-laugh, half-curse, made him turn from her. 'Dear God in heaven! Do I know him? I wish I'd never set eyes on the blackguard. Yes, I know him. We know each other from way back. He is a man of questionable suitability for the young and innocent. Are you quite certain that your father consented to your marriage to Barrington?'

'No—no, I'm not. I have reason to have strong doubts about it now. This is all very difficult for me. Sofia is beautiful and clever enough to have captured my ageing and lonely father—and young enough to find herself a lover. That is what Mr Barrington and Sofia are—lovers.'

'Are you certain about that?'

'Oh, yes. Had I not heard them together…' she paused and blushed before continuing determinedly '…in her bedroom, I would not have believed it. But what can I do about it? I was so angry that I considered facing them with it, but I considered it prudent for the time being to keep what I witnessed to myself, to bide my time until Aunt Caroline comes back from France.'

'You have heard nothing from her?'

'No. She's probably travelling. She did mention that she might go to Milan.'

He was silent as he whirled her round in the dance. Seeing an opening in the tall French windows, he deftly waltzed her through them on to a terrace that dropped down into a lantern-lit garden. Lucy stood beside a stone balustrade, breathing heavily from her exertions and appreciating the feel of the cool air on her face. Budding jasmine and honeysuckle climbing the walls around the garden gave off a heady and intoxicating scent. Warning bells began ringing inside her head, telling her of the impropriety of being on the terrace alone with this man, but she felt safe for the first time since she'd left the academy, and far too happy just being with him to listen to them.

Her companion was so utterly relaxed, so confident. Most women would have felt a thrill of anticipation were he to gaze at them as he gazed at her now. 'I don't know what you hope to achieve by waltzing me out here in the middle of a dance—unless it is to catch your breath.' With his hands clasped behind his back, he stood looking down at her. Despite her firm resolve to remain calm and unmoved by him, Lucy felt her heart give a sudden leap on being alone with him.

'Oh, I can think of plenty of things that would interest me, Miss Walsh, and catching my breath is certainly not one of them.' He boldly stared his appreciation until Lucy had the distinct feeling that his imagination went further than the material of her gown. A treacherous warmth was slowly beginning to seep up her arms and down her legs and she fought the weakness with all her might.

She stood quite still when he reached out and traced her cheek and along her jaw with his finger. 'But I did want to speak to you privately,' he said on a more serious note. 'It's Mr Barrington and your stepmother that concerns me right now. They are up to no good. You have to get away from them.'

'I know, but I am quite helpless. I won't be bargained off like a piece of merchandise. I hate him. I hate them both.' The words burst from her and she did not try to stop them. She looked at his face and something in its hard expression made her draw in her breath sharply. His eyes darkened and his expression tightened in a way that left her in no doubt of the anger he himself felt towards Mr Barrington. 'What has he done to cause such ill feeling between the two of you?'

'It's a long and terribly sad tale, but I knew that one day, when I got my hands on him, I would make him wish he had never been born.'

There was a note in his voice that Lucy had not

heard before and it sent a cold shiver down her spine. 'Why, what is he guilty of?'

Staring straight ahead, he thought for a moment and then shook his head. 'I'd rather not say—at least not now.' Sighing deeply he turned to her. 'I'd much rather talk of something else. I'd much rather talk about you,' he said quietly.

Lucy asked herself why she suddenly felt nervous standing alone with Captain Wilding and, to her consternation, found the answer. It was because he encroached too closely upon her and because she was afraid he would come even closer.

'You are flushed,' he said softly. 'Are you all right? Not too warm?'

She stared up at him and shook her head. She wasn't sure she could speak without betraying the emotions that filled her with a sweet, unfamiliar torment. She wanted nothing more than to melt against him and assuage the feelings consuming her. She was unable to believe her reaction to this man. With always something to say for herself, she was now as awkward and inarticulate as the adolescent girl she was.

They stood in silence for a moment and she knew he was as aware as she was of the combustible nature of their relationship. It was disturbing, an awareness that was uncomfortable. He was standing perfectly still, watching her. Those hooded, seductive eyes glowed darkly and told her things she had only ever been able to dream of. Something in his expression made her catch her breath and the spell was broken, but the effect of that warmly intimate look in his eyes was vibrantly, alarmingly alive, and the full import of the risk she was taking by being alone with him made her begin to quake inside. This was only the third time they had met and already Captain Wilding had established himself in her mind and she was troubled by her own susceptibility.

'What are you thinking?' he asked after a moment.

'I was thinking how lovely both the night and the scent coming from the flowers in the garden are,' she answered truthfully.

'And you are enjoying the ball—which, I assume, is your first.'

'Yes, it is and I am enjoying the experience.'

'You will enjoy many more balls in the future.' He paused, looking at her appraisingly as she gazed into the garden. 'Have you any idea how lovely you look tonight?' he murmured.

There was a soft, caressing note in his voice which should have caused Lucy to take flight, but instead she merely looked at him enquiringly and smiled. 'If I do, then it is more to do with the expertise of my maid than anything else. Believe me, I am exactly the same person you met at the fair.'

He laughed, his strong white teeth flashing in the dim light, and Lucy realised that when he did that he seemed much younger than his twenty-eight or thirty years.

'Of course you are and you were just as lovely then—and I remember how it felt when I saved you from that stampeding horse and held you in my arms.'

A warm flush crept over Lucy's cheeks and through

her veins when she remembered how he had held her close, his warm breath on her neck. 'I think you recall too much,' she chided gently, smiling up at him obliquely.

'Where you are concerned, Miss Walsh, I cannot help it.' A lazy smile swept over his handsome face and the force of that white smile did treacherous things to Lucy's heart rate. 'Come, admit it. You like being out here with me.'

'I do?' He nodded. Lucy looked at him, despite her desire not to, not for the first time finding herself at a loss to understand him.

'Admit it, Miss Walsh. Admit that you are here with me because you want to be. Because you find yourself irresistibly drawn to me—as I am to you.'

With slightly raised eyebrows he glanced down at her, his gaze and his crooked smile drenching her in its sexuality and bringing an attractive flush to her cheeks. 'I don't know what it is or how you do it, but you make me feel uneasy when you speak to me like this and look at me the way you are doing now. There is nothing between us.'

'There isn't?'

'No—and I have given you no reason to suppose there is.' She looked at him helplessly. 'I don't understand you. I don't understand what it is you want.'

Lucy was too innocent and naive not to let her emotions show on her face. For a long moment Captain Wilding's gaze held hers with penetrating intensity, not having missed the emotions flitting over her expressive features. The clear silver-grey of his eyes were as enigmatic as they were silently challenging and unexpectedly Lucy felt an answering thrill of excitement. The darkening in Captain Wilding's eyes warned her he was aware of that brief response.

'I think you do, Lucy,' he said softly.

The music, the scent of the flowers, quickened her heartbeat as a thick, ready awareness heated the air between them. For a moment Lucy was thrown into such a panic she could not think coherently. He was standing so very close that she suddenly wanted to escape, to return to the dancing. Yet, at the same time, she could not move and allowed Captain Wilding to draw her against his chest, her eyes wide open as he bent his head and placed his mouth over her own, plucking the breath from between her parted lips, his mouth warm and searching. She sighed against him, sweet splendour blossoming inside.

They both felt the sudden excitement of physical contact. Lucy had never been kissed in her life and she could not have imagined how pleasurable it could be. Too innocent and naive to know how to hide her feelings, she followed his lead and instinctively yielded her mouth to his. The moment Captain Wilding felt her response his arms tightened around her, circling and possessive, desire, primitive and potent, pouring through his veins.

His lips left her mouth and trailed a path across her cheek to her ear, bushing back and forth, then his tongue touched the lobe and began delicately tracing each curve, slowly probing each crevice, until Lucy shivered with the waves of tension shooting through her.

'Don't be afraid,' he murmured, his lips against hers. 'I'll stop whenever you tell me to.'

Imprisoned by his protective embrace and reassured by his words, Lucy allowed him to take her lips once more. The sweet offering drew a half-groan from him and his lips seized hers in a kiss of melting hunger that deepened to scorching demand. Lucy felt a glorious ache inside her that slowly spread and she found herself sliding into a dark abyss of desire. He pressed his hips to hers and she could feel the hardness of his body. She trembled against him as waves of pleasure shot through her. Raising his hand, he caressed the nape of her neck, his lips leaving hers and tracing a line down the column of her throat, his hands warm on her flesh, before finding her lips once more and tasting their champagne-flavoured softness.

To Lucy, absolutely seduced by his kiss, what he was doing to her was like being wrapped in a cocoon of dangerous, pleasurable sensuality, where she had no control over anything. When Captain Wilding at last removed his mouth from hers he drew a long, shuddering breath, meeting her gaze and seeing that her eyes were naked and defenceless. His tanned features were hard with desire, and, aware that someone could appear at any moment, he knew he must keep their passion under control.

Lucy trembled in the aftermath of his kiss, unable to believe what had happened or that she desperately wanted him to repeat the kiss that had stunned her senses with its wild sweetness. Captain Wilding was still holding her gaze and she looked with longing at his lips.

'Don't look at me like that unless you want me to kiss you again, Lucy,' he murmured huskily, his eyes dark with passion.

With her heart beating hard against her ribs, slowly she raised her eyes to his and, leaning towards him, again boldly touched his mouth with her own. Unable to resist what she was so generously offering, he clamped his mouth on to hers once more, causing the blood to pound in her head and her senses to reel as her mind retreated down an unknown, forbidden path, plunging her into an oblivion that was dark and exquisitely sensual. The kiss went on longer than the first.

Out of sheer self-preservation, an eternity later Captain Wilding lifted his head.

'Don't, Lucy,' he said when she swayed against him. 'We have to stop now. Someone might come on to the terrace and then where would we be?'

Bemused, Lucy looked up at him, her eyes large and luminous. As reality began to return and she became aware of her surroundings, with the sound of the music and laughter in her ears, she was shocked by the explosion of passion between them, shocked by what she had done. She stepped back, her knees weak.

'This—this is madness. We should not be doing this. We—we must go back inside.'

Captain Wilding stopped her, putting his hand on her arm as she was about to pass him, seeing her lovely eyes were apprehensive and deceptively innocent. 'Wait,' he said gently. 'Take a moment to calm down. Don't let anyone see you like this.'

'Why? What do I look like?'

'Your eyes are aglow with passion and your cheeks flushed.' He smiled down at her and touched her cheek.

'Everyone will think I've been dancing.'

'If dancing makes you look like this, then you should dance more often.'

'Then it is your fault. You should not have kissed me. Do you enjoy inducing feelings in me that make me so confused that I can't think straight, feelings that can come to nothing?' Glancing around, she saw that other couples had ventured out on to the terrace and were curiously glancing in their direction. Feeling terribly self-conscious, she stepped away from her companion. 'See, we have drawn attention. Now I must insist on returning to the dancing. Sofia will be looking for me.'

They returned to the ballroom as the dance was about to end, but their appearance from the terrace had not gone unobserved. Unaware of the attention, Christopher took Lucy in his arms and danced her to the edge of the floor where he stopped and looked down at her. When he spoke, his voice was serious once more.

'No matter what happens, I will help you get away. I know Barrington. He's a dangerous individual—and I believe you to be in grave danger. Do you still wish to leave?'

Hope shone in her eyes. 'More than ever. You will take me to France?'

'No—not to France. But I will take you to a place where you will be safe until your godmother returns to London. Can you get away?'

'I—I don't know,' she said, seeing Sofia bearing down on them, her face like thunder. 'They tend to watch me all the time. I suppose I could tell them I would like to visit Emma—but she lives in Kent. She should be home now and it would not be an unreasonable request.'

'If you leave London, send a note to me at my address if it's possible. If not, I'll find a way of contacting you.' Taking a step back when Sofia reached them, he bowed and smiled, showing a flash of white teeth.

'You are enjoying the dancing, Lucy?' she said, her eyes snapping to her partner. Her fan shut with a click and her fingers tightened on it so viciously that the fragile ivory sticks were in danger of snapping.

'Yes, thank you, Sofia. This is Captain Wilding— Captain Wilding, my stepmother, Sofia Walsh.'

'I am charmed to meet you, Mrs Walsh, but I must correct you, Miss Walsh,' he said, addressing Lucy. 'I am here tonight under my official title, that of Viscount Rockley of Rockwood Park in Surrey.'

Lucy stared at him in astonishment. 'Oh—I—I had no idea…'

He grinned down at her. 'Of course you hadn't. Now please excuse me,' he said, inclining his head to them both. 'Mrs Walsh, Miss Walsh.'

Sofia drew her aside. 'Where have you been? When

I didn't see you I thought you'd gone to the ladies' rest room, then I see you coming in from the terrace with Captain Wilding—or perhaps I should say Viscount Rockley.'

Lucy was totally confused by Captain Wilding's disclosure that he was a peer of the realm. 'He—he asked me to dance—so I did. It was very warm so we stepped outside. We cannot have been gone longer that a few minutes.'

'Nevertheless, you should not have done that. People see these things—they talk. A young lady's reputation can be ruined by such thoughtlessness. Now come along. We'll get some refreshment from the buffet and then we'll go and find Mark.'

As the night wore on and there was no sign of Mr Barrington, after eating a light meal from the buffet with an agitated Sofia, they went in search of him. Sofia seemed to know exactly where he would be. The rooms set aside for those who favoured a game of cards or dice were well attended. Lucy tried not to appear shocked at finding herself among gamblers. But while the moralist in her disapproved of this kind of behaviour, her rebellious Bohemian instinct was inquisitive.

The room was hot, crowded and noisy. Ignoring the admiring glances of some of the gentlemen, she followed Sofia further into the room and into another where the noise was curiously muted so as not to detract the more hardened players. Green baize tables for dice, whist, French Hazard and other games that

took the guests' fancy had been set up. Lucy's eyes
scanned the groups of people clustered around them,
where several games were in progress. The players
were obscured from view.

Sofia went to speak to a gentleman Lucy had seen
Mr Barrington with earlier. The two had seemed to
know each other well.

'Where is he?' Sofia asked. 'Where is Mark? I
know he's in here.'

The gentleman, Sir Simon Bucklow, turned and
looked at her. 'He will not be pleased to see you here.
You know what he's like when he's in the thick of a
game.'

'All too well. I will speak to him. He will listen
to me.'

'He is determined. He will not listen to you.' Sir
Simon placed a restraining hand on her arm. 'Leave
him. It might surprise you to know that he is winning.
He will not thank you for interfering.'

Sofia worked her fan vigorously. 'Very well, but if
he wins the game then he must leave the table.'

'He won't do that and you know it, Sofia. We've
both seen him in this mood before when he thinks everything is going his way—and I have to tell you that
the liquor he's consumed has increased his habitual
readiness to take risks to a point of madness.'

Through a gap around the card table where Sir Simon's attention was focused, Lucy pushed her way
through to see Mr Barrington engaged in a serious
game. His full face was flushed and his cravat droop-
ing. Anger flared in his eyes when he saw Lucy and

his lips curled with disapproval, but he did not allow himself to become sidetracked from the game in hand. He looked disappointed when his partner got up from the table, having lost the game and reluctant to play on. Another man came and sat opposite, shuffling and cutting one of the two packs of cards on the green cloth with slender, flexible fingers as they prepared to begin a game of piquet. It was a game for two people which offered excellent scope for both intelligence and judgement, something Mr Barrington would have risen to had his brain not been fogged with the fumes of alcohol.

Suddenly Mr Barrington looked across at his opponent and his gaze was arrested. Lucy saw a tightening to his features as his eyes narrowed and swept Christopher Wilding, a man who had suddenly taken on a whole new persona for Lucy. The look that passed between them crackled with hidden fire and, for just a moment, she saw something savage and raw stir in the depths of Viscount Rockley's eyes, before they became icy with contempt.

'You know why I'm here, Barrington,' said Viscount Rockley in a cold voice, seeing Barrington's shoulders stiffen.

Lucy could almost feel the effort Mr Barrington was exerting to keep his rage under control and he smiled thinly, looking at his opponent with cool mockery.

'I applaud your detective work, Rockley.'

Viscount Rockley's face was like granite. 'It wasn't difficult. Your habits are well known,' he said with biting scorn. 'After what you have done, I have every reason in the world to kill you. However, I will reserve that ultimate pleasure until I have ruined you.'

Mr Barrington snorted with contempt. 'That's extremely generous of you, Rockley. Play on.'

Chapter Four

Lucy was puzzled by the incident, curious as to what had induced this unconcealed animosity between the two of them.

The game began in earnest. It followed the classic pattern with Mr Barrington winning a little, then losing more and more, until he ceased to win anything at all as his partner, who, unlike Mr Barrington, was completely unaffected by alcohol, raised the stakes higher and higher. With a mixture of languor and self-assurance, his eyes on the cards did not stir.

'His partner is Christopher Wilding—Viscount Rockley,' Sofia said quietly to Sir Simon Bucklow, distraught that the game was not going Mark's way. 'The man looks set to ruin him.'

'It's more than likely that he will,' Sir Simon murmured. 'Rockley is extremely proficient at the game— all that time he spends at sea, I suppose. A man has to have something to help him pass the time.'

Fascinated by the scene being played out before her

eyes, Lucy looked at the man now known to her as Viscount Rockley. He looked so different to the man she knew. There was a strong, arrogant set to his jaw and his face was as hard and forbidding as a granite sculpture, his fingers, long and slender, handling the cards with expert ease. He was the kind of man who was capable of silencing a room full of people just by appearing in the doorway.

She didn't realise she was staring at him until his instinct made him look up, as if sensing her gaze, and Lucy felt her breath catch in her throat when his eyes locked on to hers, compelling and piercing. His dark brows lifted a fraction and a slight smile twitched his lips at the corners.

For the next half-hour she watched every move of the game. The air was heavy with tension. It became clear early on that Viscount Rockley's mastery of the game surpassed Mr Barrington's—he had the amazing ability to reject the right cards from the original hand and an equal ability to enter into all the complicated moves which influenced the game. There was also a feeling that something else was going on between these two men, something that no one present was party to.

Beside her, the tension was becoming unbearable for Sofia as Mr Barrington lost more and more of his winnings to his partner, who presided over the game like a predatory hawk. The light from the chandeliers played on his chiselled features as he watched his opponent closely, quietly confident, and inside the room the air was charged with expectant excitement.

He was experienced and the more Mr Barrington lost, the more Viscount Rockley incited him to go on playing, to bid higher and higher. He must have been able to see Mr Barrington was inebriated and not in possession of his right senses. He would have had to be blind not to, but he lounged indifferently across from him, his expression bland as he coolly regarded his opponent, whose flushed face and shaking hands clearly betrayed his emotions. The wagers were high and Mr Barrington seemed oblivious to the muted murmurs of the spectators as he watched Viscount Rockley's flexible fingers shuffle again and again, flicking over card after card, producing from his hand an ace, another ace, a king, a queen.

When Mr Barrington had lost his former winnings, pushing a pile of banknotes into the centre of the table, Viscount Rockley raised the stake yet again to three thousand guineas.

No longer able to stand by and watch his friend lose what he suspected was every penny to his name, Sir Simon Bucklow stepped forward.

'Don't be a fool, Mark,' he told him. 'You cannot cover the bet if you lose. After losing what you have won tonight, you no longer have three thousand guineas to your name.

Impatient at being interrupted, Mr Barrington shot him a look which told him not to interfere as he put his signature to a chit and placed it with his opponent's money in the centre of the table. 'There you are mistaken. I can afford it. I will take the bet and I aim to win it back on the next hand.

The game had attracted attention. People came in from the ballroom to watch. There was a ripple of excitement from the spectators as Mr Barrington, in an agitated state and perspiration gathering on his brow, accepted the bet as Viscount Rockley piled on the agony. A pulse beat at the side of his face, his play becoming erratic and desperate as the play went on and he was reduced to signing one IOU after another.

One hour later the game was over. Lucy didn't realise she had been holding her breath, until she released it in a long sigh. Viscount Rockley rose from his chair, pocketed the IOUs and looked down at his defeated opponent coldly. A thin smile curled his lips, his eyes showing contempt for his victim, utterly unconcerned for the pain he must be feeling and knowing that in situations such as this it was not uncommon for a man who had staked his entire fortune on a game of cards to go out and shoot himself.

'Rotten luck, Barrington,' he said calmly, 'but that's how it goes. It was a fair contest. If you wish to try to recoup your losses and exact your revenge, I will be happy to give you the opportunity of doing so.'

'Oh, I will, Rockley, you can count on it. This is not the end.'

Leaning forward so his next words were heard by no one but Barrington, Rockley said, 'You robbed me of something that was priceless to me—my family. I swore then that when I found you, you would answer to me. This is just the beginning.'

With everyone talking about Mr Barrington's rotten luck, Lucy was shocked to the very core of her being by what she had just witnessed. Retreating to the back of the room, away from the players who continued to hold everyone's attention, she left the room and moved towards the top of the stairs where it was quiet, gripping the balustrade with trembling hands.

While the two men had been playing she had not really had the chance to take in the significance of what was happening. Now she thought of Viscount Rockley and wondered what Mr Barrington had done to make him hate him so much. She was at a loss to know what to say or how to deal with the situation. Suddenly Viscount Rockley came striding out of the room. Seeing her standing there, he fixed his gaze on her and walked towards her.

'Miss Walsh. I'm sorry you had to witness that. I doubt Barrington will be able to settle the IOUs.'

'What will you do? Have him thrown into a debtors' prison if he can't pay? You know what my feelings are where he is concerned, but I would take no pleasure in seeing him brought so low. He has a ranch to sell, but would you really do that to a man?'

'Your defence of Barrington is touching, but he does not own a ranch.'

'He doesn't?'

'No. I know him—have done for years. He is a gambler like his father before him.' With a slight lift to his sleek eyebrows and drenching her in his most charming smile, he studied her for a moment, his silver-grey eyes levelled on hers, penetrating and disturbing. Taking her hand, he turned it over and kissed her palm, then closed her fingers over it. 'I am all too aware of the danger Barrington poses. I will come for you soon. Be sure of it.' Inclining his head in a bow, he descended the stairs—unaware as he did so of the savage fury that lanced through Mark Barrington who had stepped out of the card room in time to witness the intimacy of their parting.

Accompanied by Sofia and Sir Simon Bucklow, as Viscount Rockley disappeared through the door into the street Mr Barrington strode to Lucy, furious with her. 'You,' he hissed. 'You know him?'

She nodded, unable to speak.

He rounded on Sofia, whose expression was blank, but in her eyes Lucy saw fear. 'Did you know of this?'

'No—I swear it, Mark.'

Lucy had to admire Sofia's composure under attack, although she saw her swallow before she replied.

Mr Barrington turned again to Lucy. 'Have you nothing to say?'

'No, because I have done nothing wrong.'

'Nothing wrong. Look around you and tell me that,' he said, sweeping his arm wide to indicate the crowd of curious onlookers gathering around the doorway to the cardroom. 'Everyone here tonight knows you are betrothed to me. It has just been brought to my attention by Sir Simon—who bore witness to the incident himself—that you accompanied Rockley on to the terrace earlier where you were seen in an intimate embrace—hardly the actions of a lady of virtue,' he hissed. 'Rockley has just made an excellent job of compromising you.'

Lucy didn't deign to reply. Never had she felt so embarrassed or so humiliated in the whole of her life. All she wanted at that moment was to escape all those watching, accusing eyes. Mr Barrington was beyond reasonable argument. Bright colour suffused his face. His pride as well as his pocket was severely dented. Seeing the expressions on the faces of those who stood around, ranging from mockery to contempt, he realised he had become a creature of ridicule. When he spoke there was a world of condemnation in it.

'That man has made me a laughing stock, an object of ridicule. But if he thinks to get the better of me he's mistaken. And you!' He glowered at Lucy. 'What in God's name do you think you're playing at? How dare you humiliate me in this manner? How dare you do this to me? I did not expect you to be in league with Rockley. It's plain that the blackguard has an eye for you himself. You should not have been in the card room—nor you, Sofia.'

Aware that they were attracting a great deal of interest and whispering among those gathered, Lucy had no intention of airing their grievances any further in public. Although she was not deaf—already she heard those gathered questioning her morals and her loyalties were roundly denounced: after all, what else could be expected from an American girl—savages all of them.

Turning to Sofia, she said, 'I would like to leave

now, Sofia. I have no stomach for dancing.' What was there left to enjoy?

Mr Barrington gave her an angry, censorious look that she'd had the temerity to witness his downfall, his humiliation. He tensed as if he would strike her or shout at her perhaps, but in the end he visibly slumped within himself, his anger spent for the present.

Feeling physically ill, Lucy accompanied Sofia down the stairs. Knowing there was no help for it but to brazen it out, in a defiant gesture she thrust out her chin and squared her shoulders.

Mr Barrington left Skeffington House embittered. In a murderous rage, he gave vent to his fury on the way back to the house. Throughout, Lucy remained impeccably calm. To retaliate would only increase his anger. Not even the scorn of those who had witnessed the whole sorry episode in the card room raised a re-action. She had learned at the academy that to keep control could win its own battles—her control over her temper sometimes astonished her.

'This isn't over by any means,' he said with an acid drawl, the cords of his neck above his cravat standing out, quivering and tense.

'I cannot imagine what you mean,' Lucy said.

His eyes became narrow and cold. 'Lord Rock-ley cut the ground from beneath my feet once before and I do not forget the wrong he did me. I intend to make him suffer for it. I'm a patient man and also a determined one. I hate and I wait for the opportunity to strike back.'

'Try not to upset yourself, Mark,' Sofia said quietly. 'Perhaps we should not have gone to the ball.'

'And how dare you announce we are to be married,' Lucy retorted. 'I refuse to be manipulated and pushed around by you.'

'Carry on with your defiance and you will regret it.'

Lucy made no reply, but it increased her curiosity about what could have happened between the two men to have made them such deadly enemies.

It was not until they reached the house that Sofia turned on her, her steely reprimands echoing those of Mr Barrington, while he poured himself a generous glass of brandy from the decanter.

'How could you do it, Lucy? How could you be so careless as to flaunt yourself with Lord Rockley? You father would be ashamed that you have learned so little at the academy.'

Lucy was regretful in that moment. There would be disappointment and hurt in her father's heart and she hated being the cause since, despite their separation, his love for her had been vast and all encompassing.

'Forgive me if I upset you, Sofia, but I will repeat what I said to Mr Barrington. I have done nothing wrong. Perhaps he would not have played so irrationally had he abstained from drinking so much before embarking on such a vital game of cards with a man who is clearly his opponent in life as well as at the gaming tables.'

'I have no idea what you are talking about, Lucy, or what has prompted that remark. What I will say is that Mark is far more amenable than you give him credit for.'

'Then it's a shame you can't marry him yourself, Sofia,' Lucy remarked sharply. 'Does my father know of your adulterous relationship with the man he has chosen for me to wed?'

Silence and the truth fell between them like a dead weight and if looks really could kill, then Lucy had no doubt she would be dead that instant. Saying nothing, her chest heaving with fury, Sofia turned and left the room.

Mr Barrington had been humiliated, ruined, and Lucy would like to know what transgression he was guilty of to warrant such vicious disgrace and humiliation from Lord Rockley. Tonight, Mr Barrington had presented her as his intended bride with the intention of sealing the deal and marrying her very soon—even though she continued to resist. He had told everyone—boasted of it, in fact. Instead she and Viscount Rockley had dragged him into a hotbed of scandal and predictable innuendo. No doubt it would entertain society for days to come, but she feared that she would be the one to suffer for it.

Never had it been as clear as this that her future hung in the balance. There was a hard, cold, tight feeling inside her and for the first time she cursed Lord Rockley for tonight's catastrophe. Why could he not have left well alone? He had apologised for the intimacies they had shared earlier, then he had left her, unaware as he did so of the catastrophe that was about to unfold around her. As she climbed the stairs to her room she seemed to be made of steel and ice, sheathed in an unnatural calm that belied the emotions seething inside her.

What was she going to do? It was time she began to think for herself and not rely on others to help her. She did consider going to her godmother's house, but when she was away she always closed the house, leaving a caretaker to keep an eye on things while the servants went to their respective homes until it was time for her to return. She had money in the bank from her father's allowance. There should be enough to see her to France—and maybe even enough to pay her passage to Louisiana. It would be difficult persuading Sofia and Mr Barrington to agree, but she must insist that her wishes be taken into account.

Whatever she decided, she must achieve it with dignity. She would not compromise herself further than she had at the Skeffington ball. But when she allowed herself to dwell on Lord Rockley's kiss, which had inspired emotions and feelings she had never felt before, she could not escape the fact that she had embarked upon a hazardous obstacle course of emotions that left her breathless and intoxicated. She had left the secure world of her learning to the more dangerous ground on to which Viscount Rockley sought to entice her. As she splashed the cold water on her face prior to going to bed, it chilled her flesh while leaving the secret fires within her uncooled.

There were so many unanswered questions that kept her awake until almost dawn, when finally she fell into an exhausted sleep.

* * *

Home alone with a raw ache inside him, the vexing tide of anger which had consumed Christopher since setting eyes on Mark Barrington began to subside. So concerned was he about Miss Walsh that his mind was locked in furious combat with the desire to go after her and snatch her from the clutches of Barrington and her stepmother, but he couldn't, at least not yet.

He was seized with a passionate longing to protect the lovely young woman who had crept into his heart. What was it that drew him to her? he asked himself. Her sincerity? Her gentleness and purity of both body and mind? Was it her smile, her touch, that set the blood pounding in his veins? Everything about her threw him off balance. Why had he kissed her? What madness had made him do that? Why had he allowed himself to get carried away?

At the time he'd been besieged by a confusion of emotions that all battled for supremacy. He was astounded by the passion that had erupted between them, astounded that this young woman had the ability to almost make him lose his mind. His conscience pricked him, reminding him of the unforgivable sin that he had been kissing a girl fresh out of the schoolroom. She had kissed so innocently, yet even though she had wanted the kiss surely she did not realise what she was doing.

He was instantly thrust back just over three years, when he had returned from the West Indies and seen his sister about to take her own life in the lake close to his Charleston home. The relief that he had been in time and anger he had felt afterwards, knowing Barrington was the cause of her misery, had almost consumed him. Even now Christopher felt the wrenching loss of first his mother and then his father—the proud man who had turned his back on his noble heritage and married the daughter of a poor clergyman.

He had been powerless when his sister had fallen into Barrington's hands, but not this time. Now he would willingly walk through hell fire before he would allow Lucy to become Barrington's next victim.

Lucy continued to listen to Mr Barrington's constant outburst of anger the following day. Unfortunately, the lurid versions of what had happened at the Skeffington ball had spread like wildfire throughout the *ton*. The story of the episode was circulated along with the added slander that while betrothed to Mr Barrington, she had been carrying on Lord Rockley. Any other man would have called off the wedding on being so humiliated, but Mr Barrington wouldn't hear of it.

Lucy was too humiliated to leave the house that day. In the eyes of everyone she was a shameless wanton and unfit company for unsullied young ladies. She had broken all the rules that governed polite society— there were many who said that it was only what could be expected from an American girl.

Sensitive to Mr Barrington's mood, Sofia went around as if she were treading on eggshells. She watched Lucy threateningly, as though daring her to make one false move or to protest in any way. Genuinely afraid for her safety, Lucy was all the more determined to visit the bank the following day to extract funds to take her to Paris.

The night following the Skeffington ball, it was gone midnight when the door to Lucy's room was pushed open. Shoving herself up in the bed and wiping the sleep from her eyes, she peered into the dimly lit room. A tall figure loomed in the doorway, swaying slightly. It was Mr Barrington and he had a robe covering his night attire.

She stared at him, stunned, feeling the weight of the trap he had sprung on her. When he started to close the door she flung herself out of bed and shot across the room, hoping to push him out before the door closed completely. But he was having none of it. She was horrified when he grasped her arm and pulled her back, yanking her arm in her shoulder. She cried, stumbling to the floor, the pain from her injured shoulder jarring through her. Ignoring it as best she could, she began to crawl towards the door where she would shout for help, but he caught hold or her before she could slip past him and pulled her back, his face harsh and distorted in the shadows of the room.

'Stop it,' he snarled. 'You're going nowhere. I'm sick of you evading me whenever I come to the house. You will be my wife if I have to shame you into it. No more hiding and dodging my attentions. I knew when I set eyes on you that I had to have you—and you so trusting it was easy to persuade you to go along with us. So you see, my dear, I plan to have you—one way or another. I intend to have what is rightfully mine.'

'Never,' she cried, kicking and fighting. 'Get out of my room! Let go of me!'

'Be still, you little hell cat,' he barked, throwing her on to the bed and putting her beneath him, his hands pawing roughly at her body.

Lucy glared at him, her hatred so virulent he almost recoiled, then he laughed.

'Stop this nonsense. I'm in no mood to play coy games—although I am not averse to some resistance from the women I make love to.'

Knowing what he would do to her, Lucy began struggling, her anger spurring her on. He tried to kiss her, but she turned her face away, unable to bear having him touch her. By some miracle she managed to wriggle from beneath him on to the floor. She made a rush for the door, but he was ahead of her, blocking her escape. Backed up to the bed, she could go no further. Seeing that loathsome face coming closer, Lucy was possessed with the sudden courage to go on fighting him no matter what. In one quick movement she dodged to the side of him but he reached out, catching her nightdress in his hand. There was a tearing sound as it ripped.

He was more agile than she had given him credit for. Again he caught her arm and jerked her back to him with frightening strength. His eyes went to the exposed flesh above the torn nightdress and his tongue passed salaciously over his lips. His desire for her was plainly visible in his eyes as they travelled over her, surveying those soft curves, impatiently anticipating the taste of that sweet young flesh. A sick feeling of nausea rose within her.

'Do you know how you tempt me, Lucy? Day after day I have to watch you I am tormented. Your skin is so soft. We will be married as soon as it can be arranged.'

'Never,' she hissed. 'I will never marry you. I would rather marry a snake. Is my stepmother not enough for you that you must have me as well?'

'Not when you are younger and prettier,' he hissed, reaching for her once more.

She pushed hard, turning her head away in disgust. Why didn't Sofia or the servants come to her aid? she thought frantically. They must know that he was in her room and what he was doing. The struggle between them went on. Lucy was exhausted and knew she couldn't fight him for much longer. At one point she fell down on to the bed and rolled away to the other side. Reaching out to the table beside the bed, her fingers closed round a heavy candlestick, the candle still in the holder unlit. Still looking down at her, he must have thought she couldn't take any more. She anticipated his move when he dropped down on to the bed and reached for her. To protect herself, in desperation she raised her arm and brought the candlestick down hard on his head. With a grunt his body went limp.

Quickly Lucy scrambled off the bed and stared at his limp form sprawled across the covers, a red stain on the sheet where his head had come to rest, the stain increasing the longer she looked. Horrified at the thought that she might have killed him, panic set in. Confusion shook her every fibre and fear raged within her body. Closing her eyes, she tried to still her fast-beating heart. Quivering, she sank to her knees. From some inner source, strength surfaced. She forced herself to look at him again before going to the washstand. Taking a towel, she lifted his head and placed it beneath. Gingerly she laid a hand against his chest, but she could detect no movement. Holding her breath, she stepped away, hearing the beat of her own heart pounding in her ears. She could not believe this was happening to her and was too shocked, too bewildered, to think clearly.

She had to get away. No one here would help her—no one here would believe she hadn't killed him on purpose. Sofia and the servants had probably been told not to interfere. There was nothing for it. She would have to help herself. Pulling herself together, with calm deliberation she dragged on some clothes and crept from the room, aching and bruised and feeling as though she were sinking into a black hole, but she had to keep going. She tried not to look at Mr Barrington sprawled across her bed, his life blood flowing out of him.

The house was quiet as she slipped as silent and swift as a shadow down the stairs and out of the house. With her heart in her mouth she was thankful that the streets were quiet, any sounds muffled by the fog that rolled over her, thick and clammy. She began to run as fast as her legs would carry her, without looking back. She would go to Lord Rockley—there was nowhere else she could go, no one she knew who would shelter her.

It was a long way from Belgravia to Hanover Square on foot. Exhausted and terrified that she had committed murder, she leaned on the door of the house where Lord Rockley lived, her legs ready to give way. Following a few sharp raps, eventually it was opened by a servant who had obviously been roused from his bed.

Archie, the Duke of Rockwood's butler, fell back when the young lady tumbled into the hall. Rendered immobile, he looked towards the study as the door opened and His Lordship came out, having just returned from his club in St James's and having a late brandy before retiring to bed.

'What is happening, Archie...?' His eyes took in the young woman lying crumpled on the floor, recognising her at once. 'Good God!' he exclaimed, alarmed, wondering what could have happened to bring Lucy to such wretchedness. Hurrying towards her, he dropped to his knees. His face lost all colour and he was heard to moan softly in his throat. Sweeping the hair back from her face, he stared down at her.

'The young lady, sir. She seems to have had some kind of accident.'

Christopher's eyes took in the crumpled form. 'This was no accident, Archie. Lucy!' Suddenly her eyes snapped open and became fixed on his face. Fear was in their depths. 'It's all right. You're safe now. Lucy, what has happened? Who has done this to you?'

'*He* did.'

The words were barely discernible, but Christopher didn't have to ask again. 'I'll take her upstairs, Archie. Wake Mrs Ward and send her to my room.' Sweeping Lucy up into his arms, he carried her upstairs and laid her on the bed in his own room. 'Lucy, are you hurt? Can you answer me?'

She nodded, opening her eyes once more, looking at him for a long moment, every nerve vibrating. His voice slowly penetrated the inner sanctum of her mind. 'Christopher. Oh, Christopher.' Quite suddenly her features crumpled. She closed her eyes and shuddered violently, clasping her arms tight around her chest. 'He—he came to my room,' she whispered, clearly traumatised by everything that Mark Barrington had done to her. 'I—I think I killed him.' A sob caught in her throat and tears formed in her eyes and began to run unheeded down her face.

'Lucy—don't. Hush. It's all right now. I've got you. I won't let any more harm come to you, I swear it.'

The painful, unfamiliar constriction in Christopher's chest made his hand tremble slightly as he reached out for the distressed young woman and gathered her to him and held her while she wept. As he held her to him, old pain rose fast and bitter. He wondered briefly if Barrington was taunting him, but dismissed it. It was agony for him to watch and listen to her anguish, raised from the vast reservoir of despair threatening to drown her. With her face pressed into the curve of his shoulder she seemed so small, so utterly female, warm, fragile and vulnerable. His heart ached with the fear of what had been done to her.

Murmuring soothing words of comfort, he held her tightly, tenderly, as she wept, soaking his shirt front with her warm tears. They remained like that until her sobbing turned to quiet whimpering and finally she grew silent and still. As if she felt the strength of his arms and the warmth of his body, she sighed but made no effort to free herself from that tight circle of arms—and as he sensed the change in her, Christopher had no intention of letting her go while she was content to remain there.

It seemed a lifetime had passed when at last she whispered, 'I didn't mean to do it—but he—he…'

Holding her away from him, he wiped away her tears with the sheet, not wanting to ask the question, but knowing he must. 'Look at me, Lucy. I have to ask. Did he…?'

Lucy knew what he was trying to ask her and she shook her head. 'No, but he tried to. That's why I had to hit him.'

'Thank God! That was brave of you.'

'I managed to get away. I didn't know where to go—Aunt Caroline's house is all shut up. I know no one else in London—only you.'

'Thank God you came.' Christopher reached out and pulled her to him once more. There was a note of bitterness in his voice before it softened somewhat. 'Tell me what happened. I'll try not to interrupt and I'll try to restrain my temper. What did you do? Tell me.'

In between sobs she told him how he had tried to

rape her, how hard she had fought him and to save herself how she had hit him over the head with a candlestick. There was a changing play of expressions on Christopher's face. They ranged from apprehension to grim-lipped rage to concern back to rage again. Several times he wanted to interrupt her, but, true to his word, he merely tightened his lips and desisted.

'There was blood everywhere. He was unconscious—I thought he was, but I couldn't rouse him. I—I'm sure I killed him. I…'

Christopher's arms tightened around her. 'Don't think of that now. We'll get you cleaned up and into bed.' He didn't release his hold on her when Mrs Ward entered. Having had no time to dress, she was wrapped in a warm dressing gown, grey hair showing beneath the white cotton of her cap. Her eyes went immediately to the young woman he was holding in his arms, clearly having no idea what to make of it. 'Ah, Mrs Ward. This is Miss Walsh—a friend of mine. I'm afraid she's had a traumatic experience and is upset. She'll be staying the night.'

Mrs Ward tutted as she inspected Miss Walsh closely. The small, thin woman had a loving heart that seemed to shine out from her pale blue eyes. She was now in her mid-fifties and had been with the Rockwood family as housekeeper for thirty years. Unlike the other servants, whose moods would fluctuate according to the duties required of them, Mrs Ward was one of those rare women blessed with a temperament that was constant and reliable.

'Poor dear looks as if she's been in the wars all

right. Dear me, such goings on. I'll go and get some warm water and we'll get her cleaned up.'

Christopher made a move to get off the bed, but Lucy clung on to him. 'Don't leave me. Stay with me.'

'I'm not going anywhere, Lucy.'

She really was an innocent, which made Barrington's assault even worse. She was a well-brought-up young woman who had been taught that any intimacy should be conducted only between a husband and wife, and he knew how shocked and horrified she would be feeling after what had occurred.

Christopher stood back while Mrs Ward ministered to Lucy, pulling a screen between them to preserve her modesty. Lucy stood up while her cloak was removed and then the gown, which she had thrown on hastily and was carelessly buttoned. When it slipped from her shoulders, Christopher was alerted when Mrs Ward let out a gasp. Immediately he tore the screen away.

'What's wrong?'

'The lady, sir—the bruising—the person who did this…'

Witnessing what had been done to her, Christopher was horrified on seeing the bruising marring the tender flesh of her shoulder from Barrington's rough handling.'

'Please, Christopher—don't look that way,' Lucy whispered. 'The bruising is nothing. It will heal.'

'You call this nothing?' His voice was oddly quiet as his hand reached out to touch her shoulder gently. 'The man's a devil,' he rasped, like the sound a splintered bone might make. 'He will be sorry for this. It will not be forgotten.'

'Shall I have a bed made up for her?'

'Yes, that would be as well, Mrs Ward. Do you have some laudanum?'

'Yes—I have some left over from when my back was playing up.'

'I don't think it will go amiss if you were to give Miss Walsh some. She needs to sleep.'

He did not leave the house until Lucy was ensconced in another room and the laudanum he had asked Mrs Ward to give her had taken effect and Lucy was curled up asleep.

Chapter Five

Christopher arrived at the house in Belgravia just as dawn was breaking. Hammering on the door, he waited, sensing that after what had occurred here at just after midnight would have the whole house in turmoil. Years of experience had taught him to keep his most violent emotions in check, but his current emotions were most certainly violent. When the door was finally opened by a bleary-eyed female servant, red faced and her cap askew, he pushed his way inside, demanding to see Mrs Walsh. When asked who she should say was calling, he made use of his title, Viscount Rockley, both to impress and intimidate. Tall and impressive, his appearance immaculate, he did not look like a man who had been up all night.

When Sofia Walsh finally appeared, her manner was frosty, but she received him with polite hospitality. It was clear to Christopher that she had assessed this new situation and, warned that she was under threat, chosen her strategy on the instant.

'Forgive me if I seem surprised to see you, Viscount Rockley. I don't usually receive guests at this early hour. What is it all about?'

'You know why I am here, Mrs Walsh, so let's dispense with the preliminaries.'

'As you wish. What brings you here? My stepdaughter? Have you found her?'

'She found me—thank God.'

'Then I would be obliged if you would return her to me—although why she would seek you out of all people begs the question as to why.'

'It would appear there is no one else in London she can trust. You may be assured, Mrs Walsh, that she will not be returning to this house.'

'Why—how dare you,' Sofia hissed, struggling to maintain her composure. 'How dare you come here and threaten me.'

'You are about to discover that there is precious little I do not dare. What occurred to her in this house in the early hours of this morning beggars belief. I am in full possession of the facts, so don't try to take me for a fool. Had you any idea she had run off to escape the brutal attack Barrington forced on her?'

'No, not until I was alerted by one of the servants who had seen her leaving the house.'

'And no one thought to go after her—a young woman alone on the streets of London is dangerous at the best of times, but between midnight and dawn it is doubly so?'

'As I said, I did not find out until it was too late and

I had no idea where she might have fled to. I believed she would return when she saw sense.'

'So where is Barrington? Miss Walsh believes she killed him.'

'She didn't. He—he suffered a head wound and was out of it for a while. He left about an hour ago.'

'Does that mean he has decided to bolt like the coward he is, or is he lying low, ready to try again when things have cooled off? Where did he go?'

'You might not believe me when I tell you that I don't know. Probably back to his hotel.'

'I will find him. In the meantime, Miss Walsh will remain with me until her godmother returns from France.'

Sofia straightened her shoulders and glared at him with defiance, while something that might have been desperation twisted her features as she realised that Lucy might truly have slipped from her grasp.

'I think you forget that her father made me her guardian. Lucy is my responsibility. You cannot simply take her away.'

'I didn't. She chose to run away.'

'Nevertheless, you must return her to my care, which was what her father wanted. I must insist.'

Christopher smiled with the ingrained arrogance of a true aristocrat. 'Insist all you like, Mrs Walsh. Although whatever her father was thinking, he should have known better than to give his daughter in marriage to a man of Barrington's character. If it is true that he gave you guardianship over her—which I very much doubt—then you forfeited that right when you stood aside and allowed Barrington to enter her bedroom to rape her.'

Sofia paled and her hand rose to clutch her throat. 'He—didn't.'

'No. Thank God she was desperate enough and had the presence of mind to fight back. You failed in your duty to protect her—in fact, I would go as far as to say you colluded with that blackguard to do what he did. Once ruined, she would have no choice but to marry him. When you see him, remind him that he owes me money, that I have documents in my possession that could send him to gaol for several years—and considering your nefarious dealings with Miss Walsh I could have you both thrown into goal.'

His voice took on a steely edge. 'Barrington has done harm to me in the past and I let it go unchallenged, but now I would gladly run the blackguard through with my sword or see him ruined and hanging from the end of a rope, so do not think for one minute that any threat of mine is idly voiced.'

Turning on his heel, he strode to the door, where he stopped and looked back. 'See that Miss Walsh's clothes are packed and sent to my address in Hanover Square. She will not be returning to this house.'

After a troubled night's sleep Lucy awakened. Looking round the unfamiliar room, at first she could not remember where she was, but then the horrific events of the night closed in on her. She felt groggy and her whole body ached as though she had been beaten, from struggling with Mr Barrington and her

own tension as she tried to fight him off. Mrs Ward
had tended the wound on her shoulder and rubbed
witch hazel on the bruises she had acquired. No matter how hard she tried, she could not dispel the disturbing memories from her mind of Mr Barrington's
attack and her flight to Hanover Square in the middle
of the night. The vision of him lying across the bed
with blood oozing from his wound tormented her. Was
he dead? Had she killed him—however accidentally it
had been, she had done it. She was to blame.

She was still in bed when Christopher returned
from visiting Sofia.

'Christopher! I—I did not expect to see you.'

'I'm glad to see you are awake. I hope you have
been comfortable.'

'Yes, thank you. Everyone has been very kind.
As you see I am still abed and wondering where my
clothes have got to.'

Approaching the bed, he took a moment to observe
her and savour the delicate lines of her face. A light
flush mantled her cheeks and her eyes from between
the thick fan of lashes watched him keenly as she
pulled the bedclothes up to her chin.

'Mrs Ward will have taken them. I'm sure she'll
return them shortly. I've just come from seeing your
stepmother—I've instructed her to have your clothes
packed up and sent here.'

Lucy paled. 'Oh—you have? And—and did she say
anything about Mr Barrington?'

'You can cease worrying. You did not kill him. He

soon recovered from the blow you inflicted on him. He's very much alive and has disappeared to goodness knows where.'

Lucy's relief was obvious. 'Thank goodness. I do not like him, but I would not like to be hanged for his murder. What will happen to him? How will you handle it if you find him? He—he won't be killed, will he?'

'Lucy!' Christopher sounded shocked by her words. 'I don't understand you. I don't think you have any idea what we are dealing with. He is a gambler, a seducer and a thief. He is unscrupulous and diabolically cunning. It is a profession he has chosen. But you sound as if you actually feel sorry for him.'

'I—I just do not like violence.' She sighed deeply. 'I have put you to a lot of trouble I am sure you could do without.'

'I'm relieved you felt able to come to me and I reproach myself most severely for not coming to your aid sooner. I should have found some way to remove you from that house, but I did not think he would act as he has done.'

'You have nothing to reproach yourself for. Since leaving the academy I have needed a friend, someone I can trust and talk frankly to. I wonder where he is?'

'He's left his hotel—I went there after leaving your stepmother. I'd like to say he has gone for good and that he will not be troubling you any further, but I can't do that. I have no illusions with regard to his character. He is a dangerous man who has managed to survive despite everything. He's not to be trusted and even now he will be planning what form his revenge will take.'

'Do you think he will have left London?'

He shook his head. 'My guess is that he'll be lying low somewhere. I will take you somewhere where I know you will be safe. While ever you are living here with me your reputation is at risk.'

'What? More than it is already? You must have seen the papers. You must know that according to the *ton* I am not fit to keep the company of the young ladies of polite society. And to add to the shame that we were seen on the terrace together in an intimate embrace, everyone has surmised that we are indulging in a liaison. In other words, I am blacklisted from every society event before I have even started. It makes me furious to find myself caught up in a chain of circumstances over which I have no control.'

'I'm sorry, Lucy. It is my fault,' he said with contrition. 'I've heard the gossip and I am mortified. Please forgive me for my unbecoming conduct. I took advantage of you and it was wrong of me. There is no excuse.'

'And did you have to do that at the ball?'

'Do what?'

'Kiss my hand the way you did.'

'I had no idea we were observed.'

'We were—by those who were leaving the card room at the time. It provoked Mr Barrington even further.'

His smile twisted with a self-derisive motion. 'You were fortunate. Had I done what I was tempted to do and kissed you on the lips, that would have provoked an even bigger scandal.'

'Thank goodness you didn't. How did you do it—win, I mean?'

'You are asking me if I cheated?'

'I suppose I am.'

'Then the answer is no. No one knows what card is given until it is turned up. It might be the ace of hearts or the ace of clubs or diamonds or any other card. It's knowing what to do with them that counts and being able to read your opponent. There's a lot of luck in cards as there is in life. You have to believe in luck to get it.'

'But there has to be skill.'

'That, too.' He grinned suddenly. 'With time to kill on board ship I spent many hours perfecting that skill. It certainly paid off when I took Barrington on at the tables. I believe he'd been gambling without success for a long time—that he'd lost his touch. For one success there can be a thousand failures.'

Lucy sighed, relaxing back into the pillows. 'It seems to me that whatever you and Mr Barrington have in your past that is so terrible, you will not be content until you have destroyed each other. After that disastrous ball I came to a decision, but unfortunately Mr Barrington showed his hand before I could act on it.'

'And what was that?'

'When I came to England my father made me an allowance, which he reviews every year. I have enough to pay for my passage to Paris. Because there are dangers of a young woman travelling alone—especially in a foreign country—I had no wish to travel alone, which was why I approached you. However, yesterday I made up my mind to do just that. I think it's time I took my life in my own hands. I will also write to my father. I would like to know what he has to say concerning his decision to marry me off to Mr Barrington.'

'Mark Barrington is not unknown here in London. His flamboyant life style and charm and exuberance for life has always been appreciated—although he's seen as something of a loner, which is why it is such a surprise to everyone for him to suddenly appear betrothed to you. From what you have told me, Aspendale is one of Louisiana's thriving ranches. As your father's heir and with the expectation of coming into a handsome fortune, if Barrington married you he would have complete control over your affairs. After his performance at the tables at Skeffington House, he has clearly lost his touch. As an alternative scheme he has decided to marry his way to a fortune—which would not be the first time. But I feel there is more at the back of all this. My concern is for your father.'

'Yes—mine, too.'

'I would advise you to do nothing until you have spoken to your godmother. I believe you are still in danger and I will continue to protect you until she returns to London.'

'That is considerate of you, but I am sure you have more important matters that concern you without protecting me.'

Lucy's troubles and her very presence were in danger of making him forget his reason for being in London—mainly selling his beloved ship, the *Sea Nymph*, and coming to terms with taking on a dukedom. And he knew it would be bound to create a stir of curiosity should it be known she was staying in his house unchaperoned.

'I feel I must dissuade you from travelling to Paris alone. You are right. The dangers that could beset a young woman travelling along are many and to be avoided.'

'There is nothing else for it. I will not go back to that house.'

'No, of course not. I will take you somewhere where you will be safe. I promise you.'

Tilting her head to one side, Lucy eyed him curiously. 'You are a very mysterious man, Viscount Rockley. Why are you in London? Why are you suddenly selling off your assets—your ship and your father's shipping business in Charleston? What secrets are you hiding?'

'There are no secrets—just some matters I prefer to keep to myself.'

'Of course, and I wouldn't want to pry. But how should I address you—as Captain Wilding or Lord Rockley? I'm not sure, you see, how one should address a viscount, never having met one before.'

'I'm only just getting used to it myself. Christopher will do nicely.'

'And one day you will be a duke?'

'I will on my grandfather's demise—which I hope

is many years away. And what of you? Do you have any other names?'

'As a matter of fact Lucy is short for Luciana. As you know my mother was Spanish. I was baptised Luciana Gabriella. I prefer to be called Lucy. And since you have appointed yourself as my protector, may I ask where you are taking me?'

Christopher went to sit on the bed, facing her. He dearly wanted to protect her, but he knew that despite all his best intentions, there was a danger that he would do her harm. After a moment's thought he said, 'I will take you to stay at Rockwood Park in Surrey— my grandfather lives there. I have to go there shortly and you will accompany me—at least until your godmother returns. You will be perfectly safe there.'

'Won't your grandfather mind?'

'Not when I explain the circumstances. I'll leave a message at Lady Sutton's house telling her where you are. I also thought we would call at the academy on the way down to take a look at that letter from your father—if indeed it was sent by your father. You would recognise his handwriting?'

'Yes, of course I would. Do you think it might have forged by Mr Barrington or Sofia?'

'It is highly probable. Although Miss Brody obviously didn't think there was anything suspicious about the letter.'

'If the letter had been written on a piece of my father's personal stationary, she would have no way of knowing he hadn't penned it himself.' Lucy rested back on the pillow, her hair a dark halo about her face. 'Do you have other members of your family in England?'

'I'm the last in the line of Wildings—which is why my grandfather was keen for me not to turn my back on my heritage.'

'What would happen if you did?'

'The estate and title would pass on to some watered-down member of the family—a far-flung cousin that no one has heard of.'

'Did your grandfather have reason to think you would turn your back on it?'

'My father did—when he married my mother. She wasn't suitable, you see.'

'I'm sorry. Why wasn't she suitable?'

'The Wildings are a family of aristocratic lineage—until my father married my mother, Grace Tully, the daughter of a poor clergyman. It was a union my grandfather didn't approve of.'

'I see. Do you have other siblings?'

His eyes darkened and his mouth tightened when he thought of his sister. 'I have a sister, Amelia.'

'Is she here—in England?'

He nodded. 'She is at Rockwood Park—with my grandfather.'

'Tell me about her. What's she like?'

'Seven years younger than me and she is adorable.' His voice was low and husky with emotion as he directed his gaze beyond Lucy. 'Everyone loves her. She has dark hair and brown eyes. She is beautiful and quietly spoken with a big, generous heart and a large capacity for love.' Reaching out and taking

Lucy's hand, he looked down, studying it as if it was something very precious. 'Like you, Lucy, just over three years ago she became involved with Barrington.'

Lucy stared at him. Her mind was stunned by his revelation. 'How? I—I mean, how could she?'

'My mother died. I was in the West Indies but set sail as soon as I got the message. Amelia was without a woman's guidance and my father was distracted by his work. She met Barrington in Charleston and became besotted. My father died of a fever a few months after my mother, which meant she was alone for a whole month before I could get there. Barrington took advantage of her lonely state and her grief and ruined her. As soon as I arrived on the scene and saw what he was doing, knowing of his reputation as a gambler and given to every kind of indulgence known to man, I ordered him off the premises, threatening to shoot him if he as much as came anywhere near Amelia again. He hotfooted it out of Charleston.'

There was a note in his voice Lucy had not heard before. Gazing at him through the thick fringe of her lashes, she met the piercing eyes. Inwardly she shivered, seeing something ruthless in that controlled, hard silver gaze. She kept perfectly still and tense. 'What happened to her?'

'Amelia tried to take her own life,' he answered quietly, 'in the lake close to our home.'

He fell silent, looking ahead, wrestling with his troubled thoughts.

'Please don't feel you have to explain anything to me.'

'I want to. It's just that it's difficult to know where to begin. I managed to get to her in time. A gently bred young woman without a care in the world doesn't suddenly decide to kill herself. She was with child—Barrington's child. I was relieved my parents were no longer alive to see what had happened to her. I knew that one day when I got my hands on Barrington I would make him wish he had never been born.'

Looking at his proud, lean face, moved by the pain that edged his voice, feeling momentarily at a loss to know what to say, how to comfort this suffering man, Lucy said, 'I'm so sorry, Christopher. What a dreadful thing to have happened to her. It must have been awful for you. What happened to her and the child.?

'What she did that day caused her to lose the child. She has never forgiven herself. I often think that if I hadn't sent Barrington away she would never have tried to take her life.'

'You mustn't torture yourself. Considering Mr Barrington's reputation, you did what you thought was right. But what would you have done had you known Amelia was with child before ordering Mr Barrington to leave? Would you then have insisted that he do the right thing and marry her?'

'I've asked myself that many times. It was all such a mess at the time. The answer is I suppose I would have done—if that's what she wanted—despite the fact that he would have made her miserable and no doubt left her when he found out there was no money. Although had she come into a fortune he would have married her and rid himself of her once he'd got his hands on it. It was seeing Amelia's fragile state that persuaded me to come to England to take up my inheritance. I was responsible for her. I knew she would recover here. Sadly, what happened to her could not be healed overnight. Three years on and she still can't forget what happened.'

'Did Amelia blame you?'

'No. She isn't like that. Until she met Barrington she had gone through life happy because she could not see the unpleasantness all around her. She always believed in the goodness of others. She saw no evil and therefore there was no evil.'

'I can see you have carried the hurt and bitterness round your neck like a millstone since it happened.'

Christopher's smile was one of cynicism. 'Does it show all that much?'

'Sometimes. But you cannot go back through the years and change what has come to pass.'

'I know, but there are some things, Lucy, that cannot easily be put aside. Amelia is still traumatised by what happened to her. Later, I came to realise the deep love she felt for Barrington—a love that was not reciprocated. He saw her as a means to an end and nothing more.'

'You must think of your life now—and Amelia. Don't throw it away in trying to repay someone for what happened a long time ago.'

'After what you have been through recently you, more than any other person I know, should understand how difficult that would be.'

'Yes, I do. I'm not afraid of Mr Barrington, only of what he might do.'

'It is sensible to remain wary. Hopefully after what occurred at the ball and the wound to his head following your assault with the candlestick, with any luck he will realise nothing can come of his plans to marry you and will move on to someone else.'

'I hope not. I hate to think of someone else having to go through what I—and your sister—suffered at his hands. I can't think why he would want me, never having set eyes on me.'

'Can't you?' Christopher said softly. 'I can. You have spirit and you're very lovely, Lucy—and clever—like a beautiful jewel he wanted to own.'

'He won't—not ever. I hate him and I hope never to set eyes on him again. Thank you for telling me about Amelia. I suspect it's not something you are comfortable speaking about, that it is still too raw and painful. Among the many emotions you must be feeling I know how angry and hurt you must feel. I cannot blame you for that. I understand perfectly.'

Christopher's eyes searched her face with something like wonder in his silver eyes. 'What a wise young woman you are.'

'If I were wise, I would have come to terms with everything that has happened to me since Mr Barrington entered my life, but I am finding it difficult. That is a millstone round my neck I have to bear.' Lucy shook her head and sighed with sympathy for their mutual plight. 'So apart from your grandfather, you don't have any family either.'

He shook his head, meeting her candid gaze. 'That's right. At least we have that in common.'

'What will happen to Sofia?'

'Does it matter?'

'I think she is in love with Mr Barrington—but I also believe she is afraid of him. I—would like to see her, talk to her.'

'If you think anything can be achieved in doing so, then of course.'

Christopher was far less concerned with Lucy's stepmother's fate than with protecting the woman who had been brutally attacked. Lucy had endured enough. He would not have her become the subject of unpleasant rumours if it were discovered Barrington had attempted to rape her.

As much as he was against Lucy visiting her stepmother, he knew she would not be content until she had seen her.

Sofia admitted them to the house herself. It was clear she was expecting them. Lucy looked at her without affection or kindness. She could not forgive her for turning a deaf ear when Mr Barrington had entered her room to rape her.

'I could not let this pass without seeing you, Sofia. You must see that what you have done is beyond all forms of decency.'

Sofia took a deep breath and nodded. 'I understand how angry and abused you must feel, Lucy, and for what it's worth I am sorry.'

'You should be. No doubt you thought I was too young and simple to fight you, that without Aunt Caroline I would be at your mercy. You sent the letter to the academy, didn't you, Sofia?'

She nodded. 'Mark insisted on it.'

'And—and my father?'

Clearly emotional suddenly, Sofia looked at Lucy then down at her lap. 'I'm sorry, Lucy. Your father is dead. He—he died three months ago. I should have told you but—but Mark…'

Lucy stared at her, unable to comprehend what she had said. 'Dead? But—but he can't be. How…?' She stopped a gasp with her hand, unable to take in what she said. 'But—how? Why didn't you tell me?'

'I—Mark—we were playing for time. I already knew Mark—had done for some time—but I was never unfaithful to your father.'

That was some consolation, at least, but the disgust Lucy was feeling and the heartbreak that would come later on from losing her beloved father showed clearly on her face. 'But why was I not informed? His lawyers would surely have written.'

'I told them that being so far away, with no one close, I didn't want you to be upset, that it would be better if I came to London to tell you myself.'

'But I had Aunt Caroline.'

'Who, according to your father before he died, was on an extensive tour of the Continent.'

Lucy looked at her with loathing. 'You had it all planned out, didn't you, Sofia? With Aunt Caroline not expected to arrive back in London for at least six weeks, it was enough time for the wedding to take place and to return to America, secure in the knowledge that Mark Barrington was the new owner of Aspendale and my wealth—as is the custom. You began the affair with Mr Barrington soon after Father died,' she accused angrily. 'How could you do that?'

'Your father became ill all of a sudden—his heart, the doctor said.'

Bright tears filled Lucy's eyes. She swallowed and held herself very erect. 'I wish I had known. You should have told me. I would have gone to him.'

Sofia shook her head. 'It wouldn't have done any good. His passing was quick. You couldn't have got to Aspendale in time. You must write to his lawyer. He will explain your father's last will and testament to you. He left me a small allowance. Everything else he left to you.'

'Which you and Mr Barrington colluded to get for yourselves by forcing me into a marriage with him. He wanted to marry me to get his hands on the ranch.'

'It was Mark's idea. Everything he had lost at the gaming tables he could get back if he married you.'

'And much more besides. You thought I would be truly at your mercy when you devised a clever plan to get your hands on my inheritance. How could you do that?'

Sofia raised her head and looked directly at her. 'Because I loved him. I still do, so nothing is changed. There, it's as simple as that.'

As the full implication of what Sofia was telling her began to sink in, Lucy saw the truth at last, along with the full horror if it. 'And what would you have done had I married him? Would you have been content seeing me as his wife—or did you plan to have me removed permanently?'

Sofia blanched. 'No, Lucy. You must never think that. I might be many things, but I am not a murderer.'

'You might not be, but I wouldn't put it past Mr Barrington.'

'I'm sorry for what he did to you. After losing so much money to you, sir,' Sofia said, glancing at Christopher, who stood rigid, his face expressionless, 'he had to find a way to recoup his losses, which meant bringing forward his marriage you, Lucy—'

'And getting his hands on my fortune,' Lucy retorted. 'Which was why he decided to compromise me.' Sofia hung her head. In a strange way Lucy felt sorry for her. All her arrogance had been wiped away. There was only fear, and no one to turn to for help. 'After the Skeffington ball he became desperate, didn't he? So he thought to force the issue by seducing me, leaving me with little choice but to marry him or endure the shame of it. You thought he loved you, didn't you, Sofia? When all the time he treated you no better than me. He saw you as a means to an end and nothing more.' She would have liked to say more, but there was something more than ordinarily pathetic about the arrogant when they are brought low. Lucy was looking at a worried woman as well she might be. 'So, what are your plans? Do you know where he is?'

'No, and that is the truth. I intend to return to Louisiana for the time being. Should you need to contact me your father's lawyer will inform you where I can be reached.'

Not until they were in the carriage taking them back to Hanover Square did Lucy give way to her grief and anguish in a sea of tears and emotion. Christopher gathered her in his arms and let her weep, silently and sorrowfully, as though her heart was breaking, hoping that by doing so it would help to ease her loss and would cleanse her soul of all the ugliness that had defiled it by her association with Mark Barrington.

Chapter Six

Rockwood Park, three storeys high, was a house of peace and dignity. Set in a vast deer park, it was built of stone, which had mellowed into a beauty that was ethereal. Ancient trees stood about the house and the lawned gardens which produced an explosion of colour in the summer. Dotted here and there were stone sculptures and rockeries and a fountain spouting water into the air. The house overlooked a lake with a boat house at one end, almost hidden in the trees.

Christopher felt an odd sensation of unreality as the carriage passed through the wrought-iron gates. The drive wound through the neatly tended park, crossing an ornate stone bridge that spanned the upper reaches of the lake and offered a splendid view of the grand and impressive sprawling mansion. When the carriage came to a halt they stepped out, then entered the house. The hall was large, the ceiling high and vaulted, and long-dead Wildings hung on the walls. Over the huge stone fireplace the family tree stretched out in all directions.

A small army of green and gold liveried footmen and housemaids seemed to be lurking about, ostensibly going about their work. As Christopher looked around him, with his mind on getting cleaned up before his meeting with his grandfather, he was oblivious to the searching scrutiny he was receiving.

Lambert, the butler, a lean, dignified man with a shock of white hair and a poker face, stepped forward. 'Good afternoon, my lord,' he intoned formally. 'And might I say how good it is to have you home at Rockwood Park.'

'Good afternoon, Lambert. It's good to be back. This is Miss Walsh. I sent word ahead to have rooms made ready for her. She will be staying with us for a while.'

'Of course. A maid has been appointed to her.'

Christopher turned to Lucy, aware of the effect the house was having on her. 'You like the house, Lucy?'

'It—it's quite splendid.'

'That's exactly how I felt when I first arrived. I suppose those who live here are inclined to take it all for granted. Mrs Edwards will show you to your room. I will see you at dinner.'

'If you would prefer to dine with your grandfather and sister alone, I can eat in my room. I have no wish to intrude.'

'I wouldn't hear of it. You are a guest in this house. You must feel that you can come and go as you please. Besides, I know my grandfather will be delighted to meet you—as will Amelia. She spends her days quietly with her maid as her companion. She spends time with Grandfather. They get on very well—which is a relief.'

Nothing had prepared Lucy for the exquisite splendour of Rockwood Park. Her godmother had told her about the grand country houses the English nobility lived in, but never had she envisaged anything as lovely as this. Rockwood Park was certainly not a house of modest proportions. At a glance as the housekeeper escorted her to her room up the ornately carved oak staircase, she became aware of the rich trappings of the interior, the sumptuous carpets and wainscoted walls. The opulence and elegance of the muted cream and green room into which she was shown took her breath away. The bed was huge over which was a dome upheld by four columns, the hangings of green velvet.

'Oh, what a lovely room, Mrs Edwards,' she enthused with delight.

'You will see it offers a splendid view of the park. It also faces south and has an abundant supply of sunshine—especially during the summer months.'

A fresh-faced young woman with dark curls escaping from beneath a mob cap appeared from what Lucy would find out was a dressing room. She bobbed a respectful curtsy, her face split with a broad smile. Lucy thought she was probably just a little older than herself.

'This is Ruby. She is to be your maid while you are here.'

'It's lovely to meet you, Ruby. I'm sure we'll get along just fine.'

* * *

Later, having taken great care over her appearance, Lucy entered the dining room, nervous about meeting Christopher's grandfather.

The Duke of Rockwood, tall and silver haired, possessed a commanding presence. He had the poise and regal bearing of a man who had lived a thoroughly privileged life. He looked cool and contained in his charcoal-grey suit and pristine white stock. She saw at once that Christopher bore a striking resemblance to him. A chandelier suspended above the table filled the room with flickering light, reflecting the large, ornate silver pieces set on the mahogany sideboard, where the two gentlemen stood drinking wine.

Breaking off his discussion with his grandfather, Christopher placed his glass on the sideboard and came to meet her, his eyes warm with admiration as they swept over her. Taking into account that she was in mourning, but reluctant to wear black, she had settled on a plain dark blue gown to wear with a high neck, which made her look prim and proper. Apart from her face and slender hands not an inch of flesh was exposed. In the soft light her face was like a cameo, all hollows and shadows. There was a purity about her, something so endearingly young and innocent that reminded Christopher of a sparrow.

'You look lovely, Lucy,' he said, taking her hand and drawing her towards his grandfather.

'I do hope I'm not late.'

'No, and try not to look so nervous. Grandfather, may I introduce Miss Lucy Walsh.'

Lucy dropped a graceful curtsy, aware that the Duke's eyes were studying her with an unnerving intensity.

'This is a most unexpected pleasure. I'm very pleased to meet you, Miss Walsh, and welcome you to Rockwood Park. I hope that the rooms are to your liking?'

Lucy smiled. There was an unmistakable nobility etched on his features, but the light grey eyes held a kindness that instantly eased her tension. 'They are, thank you, Your Grace,' she said, taking the glass of wine Christopher handed to her. 'Rockwood Park is a beautiful house.'

'I think so, too—but then I am an old man and allowed to be biased. I suppose we who live here are inclined to take it all for granted.' He gave her a warm smile. 'Christopher has told me a little of your situation and that you are from Louisiana?'

'Yes—between Baton Rouge and New Orleans. My father sent me to England for my education.'

'I imagine that was a wrench—to leave your home.'

'It was. When my mother died, my father thought it would be for the best for me to receive an English education. I haven't been back to Louisiana since.'

'I offer my heartfelt sympathies for your loss. It must have come as a shock, losing your father like that.'

'Yes, it was. I wish I had been with him. I am just sad that I didn't see him one last time.'

'I can understand that.'

'Now come and meet Amelia,' Christopher said, taking her arm and escorting her to where a young woman sat on a sofa. She rose when Lucy approached and bobbed a small curtsy.

Amelia was older than Lucy, but looked the younger of the two. She looked very young, in fact, and very shy and there was a nervous, lost look about her.

'Amelia, this is Miss Walsh,' Christopher said, 'the young lady I told you about. She is to stay with us for a few days.'

'How do you do, Miss Walsh,' Amelia said. 'I am so happy to meet you.'

The words were spoken as though she had rehearsed them many times. Knowing what she did about her, Lucy felt sorry for her and understood Christopher's need to protect her.

Lucy smiled at her. 'I am well and delighted to meet you, too.'

Amelia was very pretty with a clear, creamy complexion and large soulful brown eyes. Her dark hair was her crowning glory.

'Now come and sit down,' Christopher said. 'The food is ready to be served. It's been a long time since you've eaten. You must be hungry.'

He pulled out her chair at the damask-covered table decorated with orchids from Rockwood Park's hothouse. Lucy slipped into it, taking a sip of wine while taking in the grandeur of the room. The long table shone with silver and crystal ware and up above was a magnificent stuccoed ceiling. Gilt-framed paintings of hunting scenes adorned the walls and the white marble mantelpiece was supported by Roman figures.

It was a simple, lovely meal, excellently cooked and

served by the aloof footmen who came and went. Unfortunately, having little appetite, Lucy was unable to do it justice and toyed with her food, too nervous to eat. Her stomach was all aflutter.

'You must eat something,' Christopher urged. 'You will do none of us any good if you die of starvation—and the cook is extremely temperamental and takes it as a personal criticism if anyone refuses to eat.'

'Then I will endeavour to do the food justice, but really, Christopher, you are beginning to behave like a mother hen,' she said and even as she spoke she scooped some trout with her fork and methodically consumed the rest of it with an unconscious grace under his watchful eye.

Christopher and his grandfather talked amiably about Rockwood Park and the surrounding countryside, giving Lucy a brief insight of the people who lived and worked in and around the village of Rockwood, just one mile from the house.

As soon as Amelia had finished her dessert she expressed her wish to retire. 'You will come and talk to me over the coming days, won't you?' she said to Lucy as Christopher stood up to escort her from the room.

'Of course. I would be delighted.' Amelia smiled and Lucy was pleased because she could see that the apprehension she had clearly felt on meeting her was already receding. After a few minutes Lucy followed Amelia.

'Would you like some coffee before you leave?' the Duke asked.

'No—thank you. I'm rather tired and coffee might keep me awake.'

'I would very much like to show you around, Miss Walsh,' the Duke said, having risen from his chair and placed his napkin on the table. 'It would give me great pleasure to have you join me in my carriage—and,' he added, a mischievous twinkle in his eye, 'it will give the neighbourhood something to gossip about. It's a long time since I entertained such a charming young lady.'

Lucy laughed. 'I would like that. Thank you.'

Christopher accompanied her to the door, opening it for her. 'Are you sure you wouldn't like a nightcap before you retire? Can I not tempt you?'

Meeting his gaze, his heavy lids half veiling those gleaming silver-grey eyes, she felt her flesh grow warm from his nearness and the look in his eyes, which had grown darker and was far too bold to allow even a small measure of comfort. The impact of his closeness and potent masculine virility was making her feel altogether too vulnerable.

'No—thank you. Perhaps another night.'

'As you wish.' Seeing the uncertainties of innocence in her gaze, telling Christopher that the sudden panic he saw there was not in the least feigned, he smiled. 'I hope you sleep well. I must warn you that I have been told that the old timbers creak and groan, so don't be alarmed if you hear anything untoward during the night.'

Lucy felt a sudden quiver run through her as she slipped away from him, a sudden quickening within as if something came to life, something that had been asleep before. She went up the stairs in awed bewilderment, feeling his eyes burning holes into her back as she went.

Lucy had been eager to be taken by the Duke on a grand tour of the Rockwood estate. When she had suggested that Amelia accompanied them, she'd been pleased when she appeared to welcome the outing. Lucy often sat with Amelia. Sometimes they would walk in the garden. There was a camaraderie between them, probably because of their similar backgrounds. They talked of things in general—about America mainly. Often Amelia would laugh, which was something Lucy thought she didn't do very often. They never mentioned what had befallen them at Mr Barrington's hands. It was like an unspoken rule between them. Lucy was moved by the care the Duke showed his granddaughter and that he was all attentive concern.

He reigned supreme over the surrounding villages. The Wildings were the most important family in the neighbourhood, the benefactors on whom so many depended. People stood respectfully at the side of the road while the carriage, emblazoned with the majestic Rockwood arms, drove past, the men touching their forelocks and the women bobbing their deferential curtsies. The land around the house was extensive and stretched as far as the eye could see, with fields and forests and a lake stocked with fish.

But it was the times she was with Christopher that

she enjoyed the most when he drove her in the carriage. It was clear to her that he loved his ancestral home. Today was a lovely summer's day and she felt at ease. He was relaxed and fell into reminiscing about his early life and the sadness that the rift between his father and grandfather had caused both himself and Amelia.

'They never became reconciled which I deeply regret,' he said, unable to hide the aching wound he could not entirely disguise, though his face remained in stoic lines. His defences had been honed to grim perfection over the years. 'It's a consolation knowing that my father had a good life and that my grandfather produced a son to be proud of despite their differences.'

'That is very sad,' Lucy said sympathetically. 'I imagine something died in your grandfather at his separation from his son.'

'Where my father was concerned, I believe what he did was for the best—for myself there were times when it was difficult, torn between the two, which was the case when I came to England for my education. Grandfather knew he had made a grievous mistake and tried to make amends, to sow the seeds of forgiveness, but it was too late. I know that if he could undo what he did all those years ago he would do it. He's spent many sleepless nights worrying about Rockwood Park—even more so recently as he's got older and his health continues to fail. His hope was that where I was concerned and knowing I was torn between my loyalty to my parents and my grandfather, in time he would gain my respect, if not my forgiveness.'

'Correct me if I'm wrong, Christopher, but I suspect he has your respect—and I have observed when the two of you are together how fond you are of him.'

He nodded. 'Yes—he has both.' He laughed softy. 'I was born with the same proud arrogance and indomitable will as all the Wilding men who have gone before—so it took some time, I admit. I always knew what he expected of me, but like my father I fought against it—for different reasons. I felt that to accept my inheritance I would in some way be betraying my father—and my mother, who was the gentlest of women. When I returned to Charleston I didn't see my grandfather again until after my father died. He knows how losing my parents so close together and what happened to Amelia affected me. He could not have been more supportive.'

'And Amelia? How did he take what happened to her?'

He fell silent for a moment, deep in thought, and then he said, 'He was upset—and angry. He insisted that I brought her here to heal her wounds. He has become fond of Amelia—spends time with her. He could not have been more understanding.'

Lucy's heart squeezed with sympathy. 'Yes. They seem close.'

'He knows that to some extent I blame myself for what happened. He has told me that it was not my fault that Amelia attempted to take her own life, but I know she would never have become involved with Barrington had I not been at sea.'

'What happened to your sister was a tragedy, but

it was not your fault, Christopher. That is too heavy a burden for you to bear. You should not punish yourself.'

'That's easy to say. I still hold myself responsible.' He smiled across at her. 'I'm a complicated person, Lucy, and it takes an exceptional woman to understand me.'

Lucy felt a lump of constricting sorrow in her chest, deeply moved by what he had revealed to her, which went a long way to helping her understand Christopher and the demons inside his mind. She saw the pain in his eyes and her whole heart went out to him. He needed someone to love—and someone to love him unconditionally in return. Whoever that woman turned out to be, she hoped he would learn to love because only then would he be released from the past.

Determined that Christopher, who had spent many years at sea, would be well prepared to step into his shoes when he was gone and knowing that running an estate the size of Rockwood Park was all so new to him, the Duke was teaching him all there was to know about the estate and the many business ventures he was involved with. Fortunately Christopher had a good head for figures and finance and he developed a passion for the land and Rockwood Park.

Determined to know all there was to know, he poured over the ledgers and accounts most nights into the early hours. It took a large staff to run Rockwood Park and they were all devoted to the Duke, who was well loved. He felt a huge responsibility to them all.

* * *

Having been ensconced in the study with his grandfather and his lawyer, going over family business, legalities, documents to be drawn up, signing papers and having explained to him what would be expected of him in the future, with the business of the day concluded to everyone's satisfaction, he glanced through the window, saw Lucy strolling alone in the gardens and excused himself.

As Christopher stepped out on to the terrace she seemed to sense his presence and looked towards him. He smiled as he feasted his eyes on her and, stepping down from the terrace, strode towards where she stood. The gardens were a summer paradise, the flowers and shrubs alive with colour. Christopher sensed as he watched her breathe the potpourri of wonderful scents all about her that she was deeply affected by the beauty of the garden and the feelings that the house were unfolding within her.

Attired in a plain charcoal-grey mourning dress, the starkness of it emphasised the perfect oval of her lovely face. His breath caught in his throat at the sight of her. The morning sunlight shimmered on her glorious wealth of hair and warmed the delicate creaminess of her features.

He had appeared too suddenly for her to prepare herself, so the heady surge of pleasure she experienced on seeing him was clearly evident, stamped like an unbidden confession on her lovely face. For the time it took him to reach her they held each other with their eyes, savouring the moment, aware of the powerful current that fizzed between them.

'Christopher! I did not expect you.'

'The meeting ended sooner than I expected. I saw you from the window so I thought I'd join you.'

'The gardens are so beautiful I couldn't resist coming outside to explore,' she said as they strolled along a winding path that ended at a stone summer house on a rise, built there so anyone inside could take in the wonderful vista. There was a light summer breeze and her skirts billowed about her leg. There was also the scent of mown grass and somewhere not far away a cow lowed. Lucy was content to walk beside Christopher and feel his warmth and strength, his body lean and long, moving slowly in long, lazy strides. 'This place is beautiful, magical. You must be proud of your ancestors.'

He grinned. 'I am, but we did have our share of sinners along the way—it might be better not to enquire. Although in a family such as ours, we know something of those who went before. People are all different. Those who appear so virtuous often have their secrets.'

'And I suppose villains might possess a little goodness.'

'Exactly.'

'It's so peaceful here.'

'It wasn't always so. My father used to talk of all kinds of entertaining, of brilliant balls and elegant banquets and hunting parties.'

'It must have been exciting. Will you be able to put

your adventuring behind you to spend your days running an estate and lead a placid life?'

'I hope so. I do not take my position for granted, I assure you. I had to do a lot of soul searching before I came here. I cannot escape the fact that I have my roots firmly fixed in the past and it is obligatory in the family to carry on. I fully understand and appreciate how the fortune of birth has given me all the opportunities and physical comforts of life, enabling me to choose which path to take, but I find I have to shoulder responsibilities I never thought to have. I'm not comfortable with them. I wasn't raised to the task. But I mean to make the best of it.'

'I can see how fortunate you have been. And now you have a place in the world. You know what it is and where you belong. That is a very comforting thing. I can comprehend how it feels to have roots that tie you to a place and give you purpose. That is how I feel about Aspendale. Whether I go back or remain in England, it will always be my home.'

Her sudden intensity startled Christopher. She was clearly a person of deep feeling. 'That was how my father felt. He grew up here and it was a terrible wrench to him when he left mainly because it had always been his home. But he always felt stifled by it all. From an early age he was made aware of family obligations. He had been brought up to regard them as all important.'

'He must have been deeply troubled by the rift between him and his father. Why did you go to sea? Why didn't you go into business with your father?'

'He never encouraged me to do that—although I

became involved in transporting his cargoes to their destination. My father was of the opinion that a man should choose his own way in life the way he had done, that it should not be dictated by the past. He realised he didn't want to go on doing things in the same old way they had been done for generations. He wanted his freedom. He had a carefree attitude to life—unfortunately, he didn't have much of a head for business. When he died I realised I'd inherited a mountain of debts and unfortunately the creditors weren't going to let me off the hook. I managed to pay them off when I sold the business.'

'Is that when you decided to come here—to Rockwood Park?'

He nodded. 'Amelia, who is the most important thing in my life, needed taking care of. I couldn't do that unless I sold up and came to Rockwood Park. It has turned out to be her salvation.'

'Your grandfather told me how happy he is to have you both here.'

'He is. Growing up in Charleston, I was always interested in the sea and ships. I learned first-hand about all things nautical and about the lands that could be reached. The letters from my grandfather kept on coming and I found I could no longer ignore them or what was mine by right. Where Amelia was concerned, I had to get her away from Charleston, to make sure her position was secure. She had lost everything—our parents, the man she thought she loved and her child. She believed she had nothing else to live for and I was afraid she would try ending her life again. Eventually

I brought her here and left her in the care of my grand-father. Afterwards I returned to Charleston. There was a great deal I had to do there that could not be done overnight. Afterwards I set sail for England for good.'

'And I have been a distraction you could have done without.'

'A beautiful distraction, Lucy. Thankfully, with patience and loving care, Amelia is slowly coming back to life and becoming more like her old self. But there are times when she thinks of Barrington. I can see it in her eyes.'

'Such experiences are bound to have left their mark. What you did was a huge undertaking on your part, I can see that.' Lucy felt a wave of pity for Christopher, but she also felt admiration for him. None of the situation he had faced had been his doing and everything he had done afterwards had been for his sister's good. She could imagine the carefree young man who, with his father's blessing, had gone to sea. After all that had happened to him, these days he was anything but carefree.

She found herself wondering what kind of woman his mother had been to have made his father love her so much he had forfeited his inheritance. She had to have been a very special woman for him to have done that. 'Is this what your father would have wanted for you?'

'He always told me that it would be my decision and mine alone. He might have turned his back on his inheritance but by the laws of English entailment he still held the title until he died, when it was passed on to me.'

'And did you not choose to use it?'

'No. It was of little use to me in Charleston. My business associates were more interested in the amount of their merchandise I could ship than what title I hold in England. I am not impressed by titles and the pretences of society.'

Having reached the summer house, they went inside and sat looking out over the parkland, watching a herd of deer grazing among the trees.

'I suppose now you've decided to accept your inheritance you'll spend most of your time here at Rockwood Park,' Lucy commented, letting her eyes wander over the rich rural landscape. 'Although you'll have to go London sometimes.'

'I will? And why is that?'

'To enter Parliament. Isn't that what peers of the realm do—enter Parliament as they do university and gentlemen's clubs? It all seems very grand to me.' She turned her head and smiled up at him. 'We learned all about it at the academy.'

'Did you? And what else did they teach you at the academy?'

'That King George III has lapsed into incurable madness and his son, the Prince of Wales, the Regent, leads a profligate life. Miss Brody explained that George III and his Queen set a standard of decorum and domestic virtue, but that their court was a very dull place to be—much different to that of their son's.'

Christopher smiled broadly. 'Miss Brody was

right—although I'm amazed such things were discussed so openly. As soon as the old King was struck down with madness and fastened into his strait waistcoat, the Prince of Wales took to wearing corsets and the ladies to shedding their petticoats. There are those who say the country is falling into a decline in moral standards—if not the onset of national decadence.'

'I was of the opinion that the English aristocracy has always been a profligate lot, who has indulged in loose living and has never ceased to do what it likes and cares only for its own whims. Why—after listening to the loose comments bandied about at the Skeffington ball, and the occasional comment uttered by the servants when I stayed at your house, it would appear you enjoy a certain reputation yourself,' she said teasingly, glancing up at him obliquely.

Christopher's mouth curved in a smile, his eyes warm as he gazed down at her from beneath hooded lids. 'If, during the occasions I have been in London, I have acquired a certain reputation, I did not look for it and certainly did not enjoy it.'

Lucy shrugged, swallowing down a giggle. 'Whatever the case, I am sure at some time that you have kept a mistress. All men seem to do that as it it's the fashionable thing to do.'

Christopher's gaze narrowed and slid to her seemingly innocent face. 'You are well informed, Lucy, about gentlemen's behaviour. Did Miss Brody tell you that, too?'

Her eyes opened wide, mischief dancing in their dark depths. 'Of course not. Miss Brody is too much of a lady to indulge in tittle-tattle. But I do have ears and when a lot of girls are thrown together, then they talk about such things. But it is no secret that gentlemen have mistresses. Do you like children, Christopher?'

He hesitated a fraction of a second, perplexed by her question. 'In all honesty I've given them little thought. Why do you ask?'

'Because since you are the last in line, don't you think you should? I mean, should anything happen to you and there's no one to come after you, this place that has belonged to the Wildings for generations would have to be sold off, wouldn't it? It would be a great shame if that happened.'

Standing up, Christopher leaned his arm against the wall and looked out at his domain. 'That's what would happen.'

Lucy went to stand beside him. 'Look at it, Christopher. This is yours. You can't let that happen. Your ancestors would rise up and condemn you for it—or turn in their graves, whatever it is they do.'

Turning his head and looking down at her, he said with mild amusement, 'You're putting the horse before the cart, Lucy. Before I consider any offspring, I have to find myself a wife.'

'Of course you do,' she said, a puckish smile touching her lips. 'Why not marry one of your mistresses?'

Christopher stifled a grin at the complete absence of guile on her lovely, upturned face. 'Gentlemen do not marry their mistresses, Lucy.'

'Why—I cannot for the life of me see why not. If a man considers a woman suitable to take to his bed, why not marry her?' She laughed outright when he looked at her as if he couldn't believe his ears, staring at her in amused amazement.

'Forgive me if I decline to answer your question, young lady. I think we will drop the subject.'

'Oh, dear,' she retorted, continuing to smile. 'In which case I am beginning to think you are a lost cause.'

Thinking she was quite incorrigible, Christopher relaxed and smiled down her, a teasing light in his eyes as he turned the tables on her. 'Why, what is this, Lucy? Are you offering by any chance?' She was really only an American miss with no more knowledge of the world and of men than a schoolgirl.

Completely flustered by his question, Lucy laughed nervously. 'Why—I—of course not.' She studied him intently, her eyes alight with curiosity and caution, and the dawning of understanding. 'If you weren't the Duke of Rockwood in waiting, I would say that in other words you are married to your ship.'

He grinned. 'And I would say you are quite right. I've spent many days and nights alone at sea, with just my crew for company, and it was a sad day when I had to let it go. What would you like to do with the rest of your life, Lucy, if you were not awaiting your godmother to come and whisk you away to goodness knows where?'

'What can a woman do with her life? Men can do whatever they want, but if women are not wives, if they are without means, then what are their hopes? Domestic service is the only thing open to them.'

'You're quite wrong there, Lucy. A clever woman can do almost anything she likes. Women as well as men can be as free as they choose to be.'

'In an ideal world, perhaps, but this is not an ideal world.'

'Sadly, no, but you do not have to worry about that. I imagine your inheritance is quite substantial.'

'Yes, I imagine it will be. I find it hard to forgive what Sofia did to me—and Mr Barrington. The easing of the fear that has held me since Mr Barrington's attack has lessened, but it has not gone away.'

'He cannot reach you here, Lucy.'

'I know. He has no claim on me now. I intend to put it behind me and get on with my life, but I can't run from it.'

Christopher noted the anxiety in her eyes which told him she was more worried than she had led him to believe. A cold chill spread through his body. She looked so young and fragile. Tilting her chin up to his face, he looked down at her with gravity.

'I cannot blame you for being fearful, Lucy. It is not irrational, but it can be overcome if you try. You cannot keep looking over your shoulder.'

'No, but I won't always have you to protect me.' She spoke quietly, with feeling.

His finger was still beneath her chin, her eyes large and luminous as they held his.

'You will soon have your godmother's protection, but until then you have me.'

'Yes,' she breathed, moving closer to him, turning her face up to his, her lips moist and partly open.

Unable to resist doing so, Christopher's mouth settled on hers. Her lips opened like a flower beneath his own, her warm, sweet breath entering his mouth. He kissed her tenderly, but then his senses started to flee and his breathing quickened and he deepened his kiss. Dear Lord, what was he doing? Kissing her and loving it. It had to stop.

With great effort he released her lips. Her eyes were half closed, slumberous, her lips moist and full. It would be so easy to take advantage of her, here in this summer house, to lay her down and make love to her. But he couldn't—it would make him no better that Barrington. On that thought he took her hand and kissed it.

'Come, we'd better get back to the house. It will soon be lunch time and Grandfather is a stickler for punctuality.'

They walked together, neither of them having much to say after their kiss, but Christopher was very much aware of her presence, very much aware that the kiss had brought about a subtle change in their relationship. Because she was not the kind of sophisticated, worldly woman he usually made love to it made her more alluring, more desirable. She was nothing like the glamorous, experienced women who knew how to please him, women who were mercenary and hellbent on self-gratification, whose beds he sought only to leave the moment his ardour was spent. Lucy was not yet awakened to the ways of men.

He recognised something in her expression, something joyous, yet reverent. Her gaze was warm and gentle, at the same time vivid and urgent. Her feelings shone luminously from her smiling face, and her mouth moved and lifted in its desire to be about something of which she was scarcely aware of. But Christopher knew and his heart lurched with the pain of it. He began to question his feelings for her, to take them apart and weigh them. He liked being with her, enjoying her immense enjoyment of every single moment of the time they spent together. She was fresh and alive and he was amazed by the gracious ease with which she conducted herself with ease with Amelia and the way she had effortlessly charmed his grandfather. Despite her youth, there was a natural sophistication about her that came from a lively wit and an active mind.

He was beginning to discover the whole tenor of his life was changing with his new status and with Lucy in it. Vivid beauty was moulded into every aspect of her face and there was something deep within her that made her glow like a flawless gem. Constant awareness of her presence kept him in a perpetual state of delightful confusion and he caught himself up short. Now was not the time for him to indulge in youthful dreams. It could not continue. The time had come for him to put some distance between the two of them, but how to do it without hurting her?

Chapter Seven

Lucy was in a state of enchantment, lost in the blissful and blessed state into which Christopher had cast her when he had kissed her in the garden. Nothing could steal the joy, the silent glow of rapture, which had been with her ever since. He was responsible for putting the roses in her cheeks and the stars in her eyes. Though Christopher had not yet said the words, it would lead, she knew, to the fulfilment of every thought and dream she had had of him since they had met. She could hardly believe that a worldly and sophisticated man should see qualities in her he found admirable. He enchanted her to the point where she could not think of anything else and she waited with fast-beating heart and anticipation for the day when he would tell her he felt the same.

He had come as close to admitting that he cared for her as he dared without putting himself in a position where she might expect him to make a choice. But she wanted him, all of him, and she could not be-

lieve her good fortune that he should find her worthwhile, for was that not a sign of his respect? He had
taken no further liberties with her other than the kiss,
which was right and proper with a woman he intended,
surely, to marry. He had talked of her going away
when her godmother came, but she didn't want to go,
not now, not ever. She must convince him how much
he meant to her. She would use all her wiles and tac-
tics to keep him.

Climbing out of bed and loosely slipping her robe
over her nightdress, she left her room, flitting along
the corridors like a sprite until she came to Christopher's door. Casting a surreptitious glance along the
corridor to make sure no one was observing her, then
taking a deep breath, she swallowed her reserve and
her pride, and with an unsteady hand she knocked
gently on the door.

It was opened almost immediately. 'What is it…?'
Attired in breeches, his shirt open to the waist, Christopher stopped abruptly, arrested in midsentence.
'Sweet heaven! Lucy! What are you doing here?' He
breathed the words as he stood there, staring at her.

'I—I wanted to see you.'

For the space of half a dozen heartbeats, he didn't
move. Then slowly he stood aside and allowed her to
pass through before closing the door and propping his
shoulder against the door frame, as if he needed the
support. It was a long moment before he slowly let out
his breath. 'I suppose,' he said softly, 'you're going to
tell me what this is all about.'

Lucy returned his gaze, wide-eyed and uncertain.

This was going to be much harder than she had expected. 'I—I have come to keep you company.' She could feel herself flushing. 'When you said you were too much alone when you were on your ship with just your crew for company, I thought you might be in need of some—female company.'

Christopher took a moment to digest her words, his eyes never leaving her face. 'Let me see if I've got this right. You are here to provide me with your company—for how long?'

His bold scrutiny caused Lucy's modesty to chafe. With her heart thumping in her breast and fighting to quell her rising panic because she knew she'd made a gross mistake in coming to his room, her colour deepened, but she was committed now. She could not retreat. 'Why—as—as long as you like.'

'And how do you propose we pass the time?'

'I don't know. I was hoping you would tell me.' She bit her lip in consternation. She was making a terrible mess of this and Christopher wasn't helping her. Her gaze went past him to a dresser across the room, on which stood a decanter of what she presumed was brandy and an empty glass. 'Perhaps you would let me pour you a brandy.' She went to the dresser. She could feel his eyes following her. When she had poured him a full measure of the brandy, she carried the glass to him.

He accepted her offering silently and raised it to his lips, drinking deep and watching her all the while.

'Will you not join me? It's impolite to let a man drink alone.'

'No—thank you. I don't like brandy.'

'But I insist.'

Uncertain what to do next, Lucy looked up at hm, searching his features. There was a strange light in his eyes. It was not amusement she saw, nor was it anger. It was a coldness, she thought, and she wondered why.

Ignoring her remark that she disliked brandy, he held the glass to her lips and murmured, 'Now it is your turn.'

She stubbornly took a quick sip of the brandy, realising he had expected her to refuse. The potent liquor burned a fiery trail all the way down to her stomach. Stepping away from him she shuddered, partly because of the unaccustomed spirits, mostly because of Christopher's nearness.

Incredulous, Christopher continued to stare at her. She was oblivious to the sight she presented to him. The pure, sweet bliss of having her close spurred his heart. She was too damned lovely to be true. Her cheeks were a delectable pink and her hair formed a torrent of dark silk tresses, with adorable tendrils clinging and curling around her face. The very sight of her here in his rooms wrenched his vitals in a painful knot and the urge to pull her into his arms savaged his restraint. If she knew the full force of that emotion he held in check, she would tremble and seek the sanctuary of her room.

He lowered his gaze to her mouth, watching as she ran the tip of her tongue over her moist, parted lips. Lust hit him with such unexpected force that he could not move. He tried to say something, anything, but he made the mistake of looking down. She was wearing nothing but her flimsy nightdress beneath her open robe, her body visible beneath the fine fabric. She seemed blissfully unaware of the view he had of her, the delicate curve of her breasts, the slenderness of her waist and the gentle swell of her hips.

He tore his gaze away from her body and looked at her face as he strove to regain control. Normally he would deny himself nothing he could take without hurting others, but that was not the case with Lucy. A stolen kiss was harmless, but he was not fool enough to interfere with the innocent and inexperienced body of a girl he had befriended and protected from the moment she had turned to him for help.

'You little fool,' Christopher said furiously, seeking refuge in anger to quell his burgeoning thoughts. 'Suppose someone other than me had opened the door— what do you think would happen?'

'I don't know. I never thought...' she answered, trying to brazen it out. 'I suppose they would ask me to leave.'

Christopher's eyes dropped once more to her semi-clad body, following the line of her throat down to her tantalising swell of flesh exposed to his view above her chemise, emphasising the undeniable fact that she was an alluring young woman and not the child he had tried to convince himself she was.

'I doubt very much they would do that.' Shrugging himself away from the door, he moved to stand in front of her. 'I will show you what would happen,' he snapped, pulling her toward him none too gently. 'But first I'd like to know how brandy tastes on your lips. Would you like me to kiss you, Lucy? You did not seem to mind earlier,' he breathed, pushing the hair back from her face.

'Yes,' she murmured, 'I—I would like you to.'

He bent his head, yet to Lucy's surprise he didn't kiss her right away. His mouth hovered just above hers, heating her lips, caressing them with his breath and the heady fumes of brandy. His gaze dropped to her breasts straining beneath her nightdress, scrutinising them intently as he slowly curved his fingers around the tender flesh swelling out of the bodice. He felt her entire body tense. The tips of her breasts hardened under his warm fingers and, as much as he wanted to continue touching her there, he moved his hands away and drew her into his arms, his lips finding hers, parting them in a deep, languorous kiss.

'You're very lovely, Lucy,' he murmured as his hands boldly caressed her back, one settling in her nape to press her head close to his, capturing her lips once more, his mouth hard, his tongue plundering the softness of her mouth. As if sensing something was wrong, Lucy squirmed against him, trying to drag her mouth away from his and break free. Her struggle only seemed to make his arms tighten about her and he deepened the kiss, his lips moving on hers with hungry ardour, insistently shaping her lips to his own. At last he released her and thrust her away. She staggered back.

'Why did you do that?' she asked, her eyes wide

and bewildered. 'I suppose it was my fault for coming to your room.'

'When a woman comes to a man's bedroom at this time of night, scantily clad, it can mean only one thing. You should not be here.'

'I know,' she whispered. 'But...'

'Don't say anything else, Lucy.' His voice was soft, but the stern note of authority underlying it brought the silence he had requested. His eyes continued to study her and when he spoke again his voice was gentler. 'It was a mistake for you to come here, I grant you. This one was mine. Next time you decide to visit a gentleman in his rooms, you must consider the consequences. Consider yourself fortunate that I am not in the habit of seducing naive innocents.'

Lucy stood unmoving. Christopher's silver eyes were narrowed on her body, reflecting the glint of the candlelight. 'I—I don't know what to do,' she said in a small voice, feeling undressed, naked, even, though she was partially clad.

'Don't you? Then let me tell you,' he said, taking the hanging ties of her robe and drawing it tightly about her delectably body and concealing those delicious breasts from his line of vision. His desire for her was hard driven, but he couldn't overstep the mark. 'You will return to your room and we will forget this ever happened. Do you understand, Lucy?'

She nodded. 'I'm sorry if I disturbed you.' She clung on to her dignity as she backed away, her hair spilling over her shoulders. 'You are right. I shouldn't have come, I know that now,' she whispered, her voice shaking with her emotions as she tried to maintain her self-control. 'Please don't be angry.'

Her straightforward, ungrudging apology caught Christopher completely off guard. 'I'm not. However, I am truly sorry if I scared you just now. Despite how it might have felt, it was never my intention to hurt you.'

'You didn't, but don't ever kiss me like that again.'

Turning from him, she went to the door. Christopher followed, halting her by catching hold of her arm and speaking close to her ear from behind. 'Of course you must leave, but before you do, Lucy, I will give you a warning. Just one,' he enunciated harshly. 'Call it advice, if you prefer. I don't normally receive guests in my bedroom—and should it become known, then your reputation will be beyond salvaging. Remember that.'

'You seem to have forgotten that I've been in your bedroom once before—not too long ago—when I ran to you for help and you took me there yourself.'

'That's true, but the circumstances were entirely different.'

'Then why did you kiss me? Was it a desire to humiliate me for having the audacity to come to your room? If so, I will never forgive you for that. Please don't touch me again.'

Her words scorched Christopher's soul with its fierce, despairing passion. 'You won't fight me, Lucy. I know you. I know how you feel.'

'No, you don't,' she cried, her cheeks and eyes blazing, her fists tightly clenched as she struggled to contain her rioting emotions. 'No one knows how or what I feel. No one.'

Trying desperately to control her raging emotions, in helpless misery Lucy opened the door and slipped out, closing it quietly behind her while wondering what on earth had possessed her to come to his room in the first place. Now she could only feel the pain and humiliation of what she took to be a form of rejection. The tight tension of regret was beginning to form in her chest that she had dared to come here. This wasn't what she had wanted when she had sought him out. This wasn't the same man who had kissed her before with so much tender passion that she had wanted him to go on kissing her for ever.

The pleasure they had taken in each other suddenly seemed fragile, like thin ice, too easily shattered. Why must happiness always carry with it the burden of doubt—that it cannot last? Despite her foolishness in going to his bedchamber and their bitter altercation, she wanted him to hold her, to seek his comfort and reassurance, but already, insidiously, she had started to feel within herself the beginnings of anxiety and apprehension, and a kind of sadness. Her godmother would be here soon. Where before it had seemed to be of no consequence, now it appeared she had not enough time left at Rockwood Park.

Christopher's room felt surprisingly empty now Lucy had gone. When she had opened the door, helplessly he had stretched out his hand to stay her, but she had gone. He longed to go after her, to take her in his arms and slide his knuckles over her soft, silken cheek, but it was too late. Lifting the glass holding the remains of the brandy, he drank it in one swallow to dull the ache inside him, filling it up when it was empty. Combing his fingers through his hair, he threw himself into a chair, disgusted with himself and contrite.

Angrily he attacked his sentimental thoughts until they cowered in meek submission, but they refused to die down. His attraction to Lucy was disquieting—in fact, it was damned annoying. If he wanted an affair or diversion of any kind, he had a string of some of the most beautiful women in London to choose from—so why should he feel this insanely wild attraction for an eighteen-year-old girl who had hardly left the schoolroom?

He tried to put her from his mind, but failed miserably in the effort. The sweet fragrance of her perfume lingered everywhere, drifting through his senses, and the throbbing hunger began anew. He cursed with silent frustration, seized by a strong desire to go after her and cauterise his need by holding her close and clamping his lips on hers. But common sense told him that now was not the time for either of them to even contemplate forming any kind of union.

Hard logic and cold reason had always conquered his lust—with Lucy it was different. She was too much of a disruption. He had to purge her out of his mind before he was completely beaten—and if she were to remain living close to him then he would lose the battle. He was in danger of losing his heart to her and he would not permit that. The stakes were too high.

The solution to his dilemma produced itself in the form of Lady Caroline Sutton. Lucy had been at Rockwood Park two weeks when she arrived mid-morning.

A tall attractive woman with light brown hair and bright blue eyes, not only was Lady Caroline Sutton highly respected among society, but her late husband had been a skilled politician who could claim the friendship of some of the most powerful men at home and abroad.

His grandfather had taken Lucy on yet another guided tour of the estate in his carriage so Christopher had the pleasure of receiving her alone.

'I have been in Milan. When I returned to Paris I found Lucy's letter waiting for me. I cannot tell you how alarmed I was when I read the contents and I came as soon as I could. There was also another letter—from America.'

Christopher looked at her sharply. 'Her father?'

'It was from her father's lawyer. As Lucy's guardian he wrote to me to break the news of her father's death—these three months past.'

'Lucy already knows. Sofia told her prior to her coming down here.'

Lady Sutton was surprised. 'Oh, I see. Lucy mentioned in her letter that Sofia was in London. She must have set sail as soon as her husband died.'

'I imagine she did—along with a companion by the name of Mark Barrington. I'm afraid the pair schemed to get their hands on Lucy's inheritance. Barrington's closeness to Sofia Walsh and her husband's death was an unexpected windfall that they were both swift to use to their advantage. Lucy was devastated when Sofia told her about her father.'

'I imagine she would be. She has only seen him once since he sent her to England for her education. They were very close. He came three years ago. That was the last time she saw him. I must thank you for taking care of her. London is a dangerous place for an innocent.'

'I couldn't agree more, which is why I took the liberty of bringing her down here.'

'Before Lucy comes back from her walk, I would like you to tell me exactly what happened and just how it will affect her future. How badly has she been compromised?'

With the minimum of fuss Christopher explained all that had occurred since the day he had met Lucy. He also told her about Barrington's connection to his own family. Lady Sutton listened in silence.

'That is a terrible story. I am so very sorry that your sister was driven to do what she did. So in different ways both you and Lucy have been touched by the evils of Mr Barrington.'

'Yes. He makes his living out of dishonesty and deceiving people. With Barrington still out there it will be sensible to take her away. I believe he still poses a danger.'

'You think he might try to contact her or—heaven forbid!—that he might try to kidnap her?'

'Believe me, Lady Sutton, that man is capable of anything—but I believe he will move on to some other unsuspecting rich young woman to try to get his hands on her cash.'

'Whatever his intentions, I will not let her out of my sight. Since Lucy came into her inheritance she has become a very wealthy young woman—and a desirable one, but I fear it will be for the wrong reasons. You say she has been compromised by her association with Mr Barrington. How dare he announce their engagement to all and sundry at the ball. How dare he do that to Lucy.'

'My sentiments exactly. Where I am concerned, the last thing I wanted to do was compromise her in any way. I find it hard to understand why so much ill feeling was directed at Lucy instead of Barrington after he was ruined at the card tables.'

'Which was down to you.' She sighed. 'It is a terrible situation. We will leave for France as soon as it can be arranged—quietly and with no one any the wiser.'

'If it will help, I will put the word out that she has left for Louisiana.'

'Yes, I think that would be for the best. I do not want her to be worried by all of this. She will be in mourning for her father for a while yet, so some time out of the public eye will be sensible, but eventually I want her to enjoy herself as a young woman should. The mere thought of people pointing fingers at her, gossip that will follow her around for ever, horrifies me. It was not what her father wanted when he asked me to take care of her. And it must be put out that she rejected Mr Barrington—not the other way round. I will not have it said that she was jilted by that—that blackguard. She has already endured the shame of being betrothed to him and assaulted by him. I will not have her being a source of scandal among the elite.'

'I agree,' Christopher replied, becoming thoughtful, not for the first time thinking that, in his determination to protect her, he had actually managed to do her harm. 'We will both do what we can to rectify any damage done to her reputation.'

'You have been very kind to Lucy, Lord Rockley. Without your protection I dread to think what might have happened to her. I regret that she has been exposed to society already and it is unfortunate that she has already been compromised by association with Mr Barrington—and residing for a short time in your house, but don't worry. I'm not going to insist that you do the honourable thing and marry her. She is still young and I want her to experience everything a young woman of her age should before she settles down. But what about Mr Barrington? If you have reason to fear for Lucy, you must think he's still in London.'

'I have people looking out for him. They will keep me informed. When he is located I will have him kept under surveillance.'

'And if he's fled back to America?'

'I've put word out among the captains of vessels in the pool. They will inform me if anyone tries to buy a passage who resembles him. I have spent years commanding my own vessel, Lady Sutton, not as a gentleman of leisure. I possess an awareness that is only found among men forced to live by their wits and their cunning.'

'I am so sorry—and I am deeply sorry for what happened to your sister. I hope I can be introduced before I leave.'

'I will make a point of it. Amelia has warmed to Lucy's presence and is more relaxed and approachable than she was when she first came here. However, she still has some way to go before she is back to what she was before.'

'That man has much to answer for. But it only confirms my fears concerning Lucy's future. She is a lovely young woman and, because of the way she looks and the large fortune she has inherited, she is vulnerable to fortune hunters. I promised her father when he was last here that if he should die, then I would see her introduced into English society and see her suitably wed. Lucy is like a daughter to me—the child I never had. Her mother and I were close. I spent some time in Louisiana when I was growing up—that was how we came to meet. When I met my husband I came to England. I am impatient to see Lucy.'

Ever since the night Lucy had sought Christopher out in his room there was tension between them that she had tried to pretend didn't exist. His handsome face held a forbidding look that kept her at a distance. She was determined that he should not see how she agonised inside herself and took refuge behind cool politeness, her mask of reserve slipping only when he smiled, only to be put back in place when she saw the smile was not for her. He was deliberately reminding her that the time was fast approaching when she would have to leave Rockwood Park.

When she arrived back at the house she was delighted to be told that Aunt Caroline had arrived. Lucy was to her godmother the child she had never had. It worked well. Lucy loved her dearly and there was no doubt whatever that Aunt Caroline loved her. It was to her loving arms that she went in moments of crisis, the arms she had longed for when Sofia and Mr Barrington had arrived to take her away from the academy.

When she entered the drawing room, Lady Sutton rose to her feet in one sinuous movement to glide across the carpet with her arms outstretched.

'Lucy, my dear, at last.' She embraced her goddaughter in a cloud of expensive perfume. 'Why, just look at you,' she said, holding her at arm's length, gazing at her fondly. 'No longer the schoolgirl, but a fashionable young lady. Now come and sit beside me and tell me what you have been doing. I'm so sorry I wasn't here for you,' she said, drawing Lucy down on the sofa beside her. 'When Lord Rockley told me of all you have suffered at your stepmother's hands—and that truly awful Mr Barrington—I was horrified. I never met either of them, but I can imagine how they used your dear father's death to draw you into their web of deceit. I want you to know that if I had been home I would not have allowed it.'

'You weren't to know, Aunt Caroline.'

'But I should have. You were on the point of leaving the academy and I should have been here, but I had no idea you would leave so soon. It was arranged that you remain at the academy until I retuned or sent someone to chaperon you to Paris.'

'I had no say in the matter when Sofia arrived and I was allowed to leave sooner than the other girls.'

'Nevertheless, I was supposed to protect you and I failed miserably. I am only thankful that Lord Rockley was on hand to look after you. I intend to do everything in my power to make it up to you. I promise you.'

'I am just happy to see you. I have missed you.'

'As I have missed you. I believe Mr Barrington actually introduced you as his betrothed?'

'That is so.'

'It will be announced that the engagement is over.'

'According to the gossip, which I have read in the newspapers, it has been reported that because of my unladylike behaviour at the Skeffington ball, Mr Barrington broke off the engagement—which, knowing how society always likes to believe the worst of a person, will go against me in the future.'

'Hopefully in no time at all it will be forgotten.'

'I sincerely hope so. I'm not going to sit about and wait for acceptance. I've decided to return to Louisiana. I have to decide what to do with Aspendale. It is mine by right.'

'No one can dispute that. But we must think about what is to be done, Lucy. There is nothing in Louisiana for you any more.'

'There will be papers to sign.'

'That can be dealt with by a lawyer. You don't have to go all the way to Louisiana to do that. If you decide to sell Aspendale, then we will notify your father's lawyer to set things in motion.'

'Are you to remain in London, Lady Sutton?' Christopher asked.

'For the time being. I have to consider Lucy's future. I'm sure you realise that Lucy is not the worldly, sophisticated sort of female you will be used to. She could very easily be hurt.'

'I might be young, Aunt Caroline, but I am not stupid.'

Hearing the indignation in Lucy's tone, Lady Sutton laughed. 'Of course you're not—far from it, my dear.'

'You were telling me you have plans for her future?' Christopher said.

She nodded. 'There is no hurry for her to land a husband. I would like to take her travelling—to see Europe. She is in mourning, but I see no reason why we can't do that. Would you like to do that, Lucy?'

'Yes—I mean…' She glanced at Christopher, deeply disappointed that she would have to leave him and wishing he would give some indication that he didn't want her to leave. 'I would like to think about it.'

'By the time we return from the Continent all this unpleasantness will have been forgotten. If, at that time, you still want to go to Louisiana, then that is what we'll do. But at this point in time we will leave for London right away. You must prepare to leave, Lucy.'

Disappointment and a deep despair that she was to

be whisked away from Rockwood Park—and Christopher—overwhelmed Lucy. Her world tilted crazily. There was no room in her sights for anyone except him. Her future stretched before her in a kaleidoscope of disbelief, misery and loneliness. How was she going to bear it?

While she had been walking with his grandfather Christopher had changed into black breeches and a plain grey waistcoat over a white shirt. The severe style emphasised the hard perfection of his body and attractive features. She took one look at him and had a feeling of longing and need so strong that she felt faint. He was so unbearably handsome, so splendid, that she wanted to fling herself against him and beg him to let her stay. She beheld the faint widening of his eyes as they turned on her, but his expression was as inscrutable as a marble mask. She found it difficult to endure his gaze, but she did, his words regarding her future in which he would have no part sounding inside her head like a death knell.

Seeing her disappointment, with a pained expression Lady Sutton moved to her side. 'It is for the best, Lucy.'

'Would you mind if I spoke to Christopher alone?'

'Of course not. I think it's as well that you do.' She got to her feet. 'I believe I saw your grandfather in the garden, Lord Rockley, with a young lady I assume is your sister. I'll go and sit with them for a while.'

Not until Aunt Caroline was out of earshot did Lucy get to her feet, the better to challenge Christopher.

'Why are you doing this?' she demanded heatedly. 'Why are you sending me away? Are you deliberately trying to be cruel?'

'If it seems that way, then you are mistaken. The last thing I want is to hurt you. Lady Sutton is right to take you away, to let what has happened die down.'

'I suppose it would be naive of me to believe that would happen if I didn't go.'

'Yes, I'm afraid it would,' he replied quietly but firmly. 'I'm sorry if that hurts, Lucy, but it's best you know how society will behave. What everyone saw at Skeffington House was a man who was down on his luck at the card tables—an everyday occurrence, I'm afraid. But what they also saw was a young woman that gentleman was betrothed to playing fast and loose with another.'

Indignation flashed in Lucy's eyes. 'I most certainly was not.'

'Nevertheless, that is how it looked to them and, eager for some fresh gossip to titillate their mundane lives, you became the focal point of their interest. Barrington committed a crime against you, but it is you who will pay for that crime if you remain in London.'

'So I will be ostracised by everyone and not looked upon favourably as marriage material for any one of their precious sons lest I corrupt them.'

'That is nonsense.'

'No, it isn't. It's how it is. It is hard to believe and quite ridiculous that two men battled it out over a game of cards, that one of them was ruined, and before that there were people who witnessed our interlude on the terrace, yet I am the one being focused on and condemned. I hate having to obey society's laws which seem totally absurd to me.'

'Never having had to obey such rules and regulations myself I agree with you. But that's the way of things, Lucy. You are young and exceedingly pretty. Prepare yourself for new experiences. Hopefully by the time you return to London, a dozen or more such incidents will have occurred to keep their tongues busy and you will have been forgotten. There will be a veritable army of young men on the Continent who will be more than happy to marry you.'

'But I don't want any of that. You have kissed me on occasion. Did that mean nothing to you at all?' She wished she hadn't mentioned that. A kiss was often as good as a declaration, a kiss with witnesses was sometimes enough to compel two people to marry.

'Of course I remember and, yes, it meant a great deal to me—more than you will ever know. But it should not have happened and I am sorry. You are very lovely, Lucy, very sweet.' He sighed. 'I am a man with many weaknesses and there have been times when I have been unable to resist you—when I should have exerted more determination to do just that. I know that is no excuse.'

'Sweet?' She was indignant. 'There was nothing *sweet* about the kiss you gave me when I went to your bedroom. You do not care for me at all, then?'

'What do you want, Lucy? Do you want me to say I love you? Is that it?'

He said the word as if it were an offence to love

someone. She should have been angry at him, but all she felt was an emptiness inside her. She was also saddened that he didn't say he loved her, but she felt a flicker of hope for he hadn't said he didn't love her. 'I don't ask that of you. Love is an emotion you have to feel.'

'Lucy, you are a very beautiful young woman. How could any man not be moved when they set eyes on you? But I think that night at the Skeffington ball we were both carried away by the music and the night. As much as I wanted to repeat the offence, I told myself that it would not happen again—but it did, I know.'

'Offence? I did not consider either of the kisses you gave me an offence,' she said, knowing that she was beginning to sound irrational and unreasonable, but she couldn't help it. 'When you kissed me at the ball it was my first kiss. Yes, I will remember it always, but you should have known better.'

'Yes, I should. You'll forget it soon enough when you get to Paris and all those romantic cities Lady Sutton is to whisk you away to and you have every young fop trailing after you.'

This was no consolation for Lucy. How gullible she had been. Why did he adopt this cold, remote attitude with her? Was it possible he was ashamed of the way he had behaved towards her and was impatient to get her off his hands, or was his hunger for her so great that he couldn't bear to be close to her? She hoped it was the latter, but the way he was looking at her made her discount it. Another thought suddenly occurred to her that was far more disturbing than that. He was

Viscount Rockley, heir to a dukedom. How could he possibly form a serious attachment to a woman whose reputation was so tarnished? Her eyes met his proudly.

'You really think that as soon as the rakes and fops on the Continent begin paying me attention and whispering sweet nonsense in my ear, I will be silly and weak enough to fall at their feet?'

'Not at all. I credit you with more sense than that. You are a beautiful young woman, Lucy. You will not go unnoticed.'

His easy dismissal of her from his life raised Lucy's ire. But it was the way he retained his arrogant superiority that was hard for her to take, when she wanted nothing more than for him to reach out and draw her to his chest and hold her, the way he had when he had comforted her when she'd been told her father had died, when he had soothed and petted her tears. Displaying a calm she did not feel, she managed with a painful effort to dominate her disappointment and accept the slap fate had dealt her. She must blot from her mind the events of the days since she had met him, the exquisite sweetness of his kiss and the overwhelming emotions he had managed to awake in her. Jerking her mind from such weakening thoughts, she looked at him.

'Do you mind telling me why you are dismissing me as though I were an untouchable?' She knew the answer, but wanted to hear him say it. 'What have I done that makes you treat me so indifferently?'

'Nothing,' he said, 'and I cannot be accused of in-difference where you are concerned. At least not intentionally. Too much has happened to you in so short a time. It's time you faced the truth. It's time we were honest with each other. I can't make any promises.'

'I haven't asked you to do that.'

'Lucy, a wonderful vista is opening up before you. An adventurous life. You should grasp it with both hands.'

Lucy could hear the absolute finality in his voice that told her it would be futile to argue. There was a time not so very long ago when she had been so excited about the future Aunt Caroline had mapped out for her—seeing as much of Europe and meeting new, exciting people. It was everything she had dreamed of—but that was before she had gone to the fair and met a handsome sea captain who had stolen her heart.

'I will, Christopher. I will do just that. And now there is nothing more to be said except thank you for all you have done for me. I really do not know what I would have done without you.' Her words were of resignation, not defiance.

Suddenly Christopher looked at her with unexpected softness. Surprised by the change in his expression, she opened her mouth to speak, but he stopped her by reaching out and tilting her chin with the tip of his finger. Looking reverently down into her eyes, he said gently, 'I hope the man you eventually fall in love with is worthy of you. I hope he is a man who will have your head spinning and your legs turning to jelly.'

For an endless moment Lucy searched his features and for a moment her world seemed safe and secure again and warm. 'I think,' she whispered softly, 'that it will be more a question of whether I will be worthy of him after all that has happened. I am also troublesome and opinionated, which might not be tolerated. But I've never talked to a man like I can talk to you. I'm beginning to think you are different and the only man who can understand me.'

Christopher stared down at her, then abruptly turned, shoving his hands into his pockets and staring out of the windows into the garden, where Lady Sutton was seated on a bench in quiet conversation with his grandfather and Amelia. Uncertain of his mood, Lucy remained silent. His profile was harsh. He looked like a man in the throes of some deep, internal battle. She remembered the times when they had been close, when he had held her and comforted her and kissed her—she held that memory like a talisman against her doubts.

'Thank you once again for what you have done for me, Christopher,' she said when some time had passed and his silence became unsettling.

Christopher turned and looked at her. 'It was my pleasure.'

Beneath the heavy fringe of her dark lashes, her eyes were mesmerising in their lack of guile. 'I will never forget it,' she said softly, her words sincere and heartfelt. He was looking at her intently and suddenly she wanted to show her appreciation in the way she had done before when he had taken her in his arms and kissed her. Taking her courage in both hands, she raised herself on tiptoe and placed her mouth on his.

She felt his initial surprise, his withdrawal, but she

kept her lips on his, feeling him respond. Gently he took her arms and drew her towards him. His lips began to move on hers. But then he raised his head and pushed her back.

'No, Lucy. This has to stop. It is wrong.'

She stared at him, her lovely face mirroring her bewilderment at his abrupt change. 'But—I don't understand. Why did you kiss me before and yet now you say it is wrong?'

'Because it was wrong. You are young. You have your whole future before you. You have to go. I want you to go. There are some things you cannot understand.'

'I'm sorry. I acted without thinking, but I am confused—*you* confuse me. It is clear to me now that I read too much into our friendship. I'll know better next time.'

Christopher's eyes narrowed on her face. 'Of course you will. But there won't be a next time.'

Angry and humiliated beyond anything she had known in her life, Lucy flinched from the sting of his tone. She looked at his hard, handsome face, at the cynicism that was part of him. His eyes were chilled and unyielding. There was a certain air of impatience about him, as if he couldn't wait for her to be gone. She was no more than a silly young girl, his attitude seemed to say to her. She did not understand him. She could not penetrate the complex masculine depths of him.

'You know, Christopher, I didn't ask for any of this,' she said in an attempt to ease the tension vibrating between them. 'By my behaviour I have been stupid and naive and gullible. And now I have learned my lesson. You told me that I will attract the attention of other gentlemen and marry well. The advice was well intentioned, but I shudder at the thought of trading my body for security. You forget that I have an inheritance of my own and I intend to use it to my own advantage—to eventually establish my own household,' she said, her voice quiet but filled with an unshakeable dignity. 'I will never depend on a man for either comfort or security.'

Christopher arched one dark eyebrow. 'A woman of independent means. A woman of worth.'

Something in Lucy snapped then, something small and rebellious. He was the first male in maturity she had known and she was weak in her ignorance, but there was no mistaking, however, the wounded fury that flashed in her magnificent eyes or the stiffening of her spine as she took an instinctive step forward. 'That's right. Exactly the kind of woman who attracts fortune hunters—like Mr Barrington. And now I really don't think there is anything left to say—at least, nothing you want to hear.'

'No.' He stood still, taut, fierce tension marking his mouth.

Lucy heard the absolute finality of that word. She would not stay to argue. She had too much pride to allow her raw, aching emotions to be exposed further. 'I'll go and help Ruby to pack my things. If we are to return to London before dark, we must be away.'

Offering him a glare that cut like a dagger, Lucy

gathered her small reserve of strength and turned her back on Christopher Wilding, whom she loved and hated with every instinct that was in her, crossing to the door on legs that shook, trying to retreat from a predicament into which she should never have put herself in the first place. Never in all her life had she felt so humiliated. She was chilled to the marrow. Even now, when she was desperate with the thought of being parted from him, she had to ask herself why it should hurt so much and to question what was in her heart.

She was surprised when, as she opened the door, Christopher was behind her.

'Wait. We cannot part like this.'

Standing with her back to him, she swallowed. 'You mean there is more you have to say to me?'

'There is,' he said on a softer note. 'I think there is something I should say to you before you leave and I want you to listen to me very carefully.'

Lucy stood, holding her breath for what was to come. She felt his eyes on her, burning into the back of her neck like a physical force.

'I want you to know how much I both like and admire you. I think you are a very beautiful young woman and very brave—you've had more to contend with recently than most girls and you have coped magnificently. There have been times when I forgot how old you are. If I have treated you as if you were a great deal older, led you on and given you reason to think there could ever be anything between us, then that was very wrong of me and I am sorry. We both have things to do before our own personal feelings can be considered.' He smiled. 'I forget how grown up girls are in this new age—how much they know.'

'We were encouraged to learn as much as we could at the academy.' she said quietly. 'I know a good deal more that you imagine.'

'I imagine you do. Having said all that, I admit I am attracted to you and it's been one of the hardest things I've ever done to resist you. But that's where it must end. The last thing I want is for you to feel rejected, spurned and humiliated. You are very special to me. I like and respect you too much. You do understand, don't you?'

She nodded. The only thing she was aware of was that he was sending her away, ripping her heart apart. The pain inside her was terrible and it was going to get worse with every bitter moment of their parting. 'Yes,' she said. 'Perfectly.'

'And I haven't made things worse?'

'Not at all,' she said, turning round to face him, feeling a little better suddenly, no longer stupid and embarrassed. Yet she was confused. What had she expected from him? What had she wanted? He didn't feel the same as she did about him. She was a young girl who had thought she was in love, with all those charming mannerisms such a state imposed. Why had she let herself be swayed too much by her emotions and her own desires? He was going to be a duke, for heaven's sake, and way beyond her in social class.

She saw this with a new clarity of mind. Of course he wouldn't commit to her—the daughter of a Louisiana planter. Men of his distinction married ladies from their own sphere. But it didn't alter the way she still felt about him and made her wish she was a good deal older. Even his companionship was to be denied her in the days and months ahead. He had fulfilled his obligation and now he was doing his utmost to distance himself from her. His next words proved this.

'Whatever sentiment I have created, you have deceived yourself. Many women have made that mistake and regretted it. I made no promises, Lucy. So go with you godmother to the Continent and enjoy your parties and balls—you might find a husband, even, which is what it is all about.'

Lucy laughed with derision and, for sheer defiance, she gave her head a toss, determined to make herself anything but meek and sad. 'You may stop there, Christopher. I understand perfectly. I am quite happy with my single state—which is probably a good thing. You are not entirely blameless when it comes to the damage done to my reputation. You really should have known better than to take advantage of a girl fresh out of school with no experience of the world at large and gentlemen with seduction on their mind. I have only recently finished my education and I shall enjoy testing the water, so to speak. It's all very exciting.'

Summoning all the dignity she could muster, she turned from him and walked out with her spine ramrod straight and her chin held high.

Chapter Eight

Christopher steeled himself to let her go. He emitted a low groan with the gnawing hunger she had aroused in him, for he had never felt anything quite so stimulating as that moment when she had turned from him and he had pressed his body close to hers. He had been tempted to slide his arm around her waist and pull her back to him, to forget all logic and sweep her away and make love to her. Recollecting himself, he was prone to wonder if he was having some kind of lewd fantasy involving the precocious young woman and it came as no surprise to him that she had once again awakened his manly cravings like none other before. At that moment he was torn between an impulse not to go after her and prolong their goodbye, and another to offer her some sort of comfort. The latter impulse was the stronger, but it was the first that won out.

He watched her go and, despite her coolness, knew how upset she must be feeling and his conscience tore at him. His rejection had hurt her, but he'd done it because he had to, he reminded himself. But he hoped his parting words had reached her and taken away the hurt—although her own parting words had cut him to the core and she was right. Along with Barrington, he was equally to blame for the damage done to her reputation.

Lucy was young—her godmother was taking her on a grand tour of Europe, where she would meet all kinds of sophisticated young men who would sweep her off her feet. Their friendship had to end. He couldn't let her waste one moment of her precious life believing she was in love with him.

He had thought this would solve the problem of this lovely young woman, but his plight somehow only became more unbearable at the thought of being parted from her. He watched her leave with Lady Sutton, determined to follow his standard policy of never looking back where females were concerned, but Lucy Walsh was not to be so easily forgotten.

Having left Rockwood Park behind, Lucy was aware of her aunt looking at her with some concern.

'You have come to rely on Viscount Rockley perhaps too much, Lucy.'

'He has been very kind and considerate to my situation, which, strangely, is linked to his own.'

'I do realise that. How do you feel about him?'

Lucy sighed, remembering how he had looked when the carriage had pulled away from the house. She could almost imagine the look in his eyes was asking her to stay—but perhaps that was only because she wanted to see it. Whatever it had meant, it was too late.

'I like him, of course, and he has been very kind to me.'

'He has certainly been there for you when you needed someone and I am grateful. But—how important is he to you?'

'I suppose he is—important. He will become very powerful in his new position.'

'That isn't quite what I meant.'

'Then what did you mean?'

'I think he is not indifferent to you. He is very handsome and he possesses that fascinating allure that is so fatal to a young girl's heart. Your heart is still intact, I hope, Lucy?' she asked, watching her goddaughter's face closely.

Lucy lifted her chin, Christopher's words still raw in her mind. She was not so sure whether she was in love with him. She was very much a novice when it came to falling in love. And yet why should she feel angry and hurt that he had turned from her? She had feelings for him, yes, but love? Was it just infatuation? How would she know, never having experienced either emotion? She was fresh out of the schoolroom, so how could she know? Perhaps she had been flattered by his attentions and finding in him a certain sensuality which kindled in herself.

'Yes, it is,' she replied, not at all sure that it was.

'He's a lot older than you, darling, you know that, don't you, and far too experienced.'

'I know, but…'

'…but you like him just the same.' She smiled sympathetically. 'You'll soon put what happened behind you. You have your whole future ahead of you.'

Aunt Caroline was right, of course. Tormenting herself about something that had happened and could not be changed would do her no good. 'I know and I plan to enjoy every moment of it. You and I are going to Europe. I expect that by the time we return he will be married. Don't worry about me, Aunt Caroline. Christopher Wilding is well and truly in the past.'

Lucy sighed and looked out at the passing scenery. She was returning to London and a new life. She had not been alone with Christopher since he had dismissed her so casually—and what had seemed to her brutally—from his life. After she had said goodbye to Amelia in her room, they had partaken of a light meal before setting off and she had heard nothing of the conversation between Aunt Caroline, Christopher and the Duke as they said their farewells. She had, in fact, not seen or heard anything since the incredibly strong arms of Christopher Wilding had pulled her out of the path of a runaway horse. But she was another person since that day, when she had taken part in the excitement of the fair and her enjoyed her newfound maturity of leaving the academy and embarking on a whole new and exciting future.

But she was deeply troubled by the recollection of her time at Rockwood Park, which she carried in her softly pledged young heart—the one that she had given without thought and, she was certain, irrevocably to Christopher Wilding because she had found herself defenceless against the sheer magnetism and vitality of the man, the man who had struck at her heart, leaving a great emptiness inside her. But she would not spend her life nursing unrequited love. She knew that in time she would forget him…no, not forget him, but at least her heart wouldn't ache when she thought of him.

The time following Lucy's departure from his life was a time of adjustment in Christopher's life. But, by God, how he missed her. He had felt out of sorts ever since she'd left. He threw himself into his work to try to forget her, but it was no use. Her lovely face had a habit of popping up in his mind like a mischievous sprite when he least expected it. In the silence of the night he would lay awake, his chest aching with wanting her, remembering her laughing her musical laughter, holding out her arms to him, how it had felt to kiss her sweet, soft lips. He had a habit of conjuring up her image and concentrating on it, tracing every delectable curve of her face in his mind. Even as the weeks faded into months, the memories of their brief time together did not fade and suddenly the year of waiting for her to return seemed like a lifetime away.

Taking the cross-Channel packet from Portsmouth, Lucy kept her eyes on the receding English coastline, wondering what the next twelve months would bring. She was determined to put the past few weeks behind her once and for all. She had hated leaving Rockwood

Park and she felt a pang of loss at leaving Amelia, but it was offset by the thought of the exciting prospect of seeing Europe.

Accompanied by her maid, Aunt Caroline had a full schedule, beginning in Paris. Lucy thought Paris was heaven. Throbbing to its own frenetic rhythm, in her opinion it was the most wonderful, invigorating city on earth. The days were long and relaxed. Aunt Caroline was an extremely likable, socially ambitious woman for whom fashion and society newspapers and magazines satisfied all her literary requirements, whereas Lucy tried desperately to banish all thoughts of Christopher by losing herself in literature written by popular authors of the time.

Eventually they travelled on to the south of France where they stayed in fashionable hotels or homes of Aunt Caroline's friends. When the heat was not so intense they would visit local places of interest or simply sit around on sunny terraces beneath trailing bracts of tropical bougainvillaea, surrounded by blood-red geraniums in terracotta pots, drinking cool lemonade. When Lucy could manage it, she dipped her feet in the turquoise waters of the Mediterranean Sea.

And then it was on to Italy. Lucy fell in love with Florence. Here there was no shortage of young men to dance attendance on her—French, Italian and English gentlemen doing the Grand Tour. But she could not find elsewhere that certain exhilaration she had felt when she had been with Christopher Wilding. Her moods were like quicksilver and unpredictable, but whether she was aloof and frosty or wickedly appealing, she drew men to her side almost without conscious effort. Those who fell victim to her potent magnetism soon learned to their cost that the fascinating Miss Walsh was not so easily caught.

All too soon it was time to return to England. Lady Sutton considered that enough time had passed since Lucy's unfortunate association with Mark Barrington and that it was time for her to be reintroduced into English society. Much to Lucy's amusement her aunt could think of little but the coming Season and how she would revel in bringing her out. She was certain that her beautiful goddaughter would be the debutante of the Season. Remembering how it had been when she had left London, Lucy wasn't convinced.

Her affairs in Louisiana had been settled. As an extremely wealthy young woman, with nothing there for her any more but childhood memories, she had sold the Aspendale ranch. No word had been heard of Sofia and, after what she had done, Lucy wasn't too concerned about her.

Lady Sutton's London home was a large residence on Curzon Street, tastefully furnished and filled with art. She was high up in the social scale and normally a constant stream of friends would visit when she was at home and she entertained on a regular basis, but this did not happen. This did not worry her unduly for she surmised her return had not been circulated. They were having tea in the drawing room. Surrounded by recent newspapers and magazines, Lady Sutton sifted through the invitation cards that had been delivered for various functions. She did note and comment on the fact that they were for minor events and fewer than she had anticipated. She did so wish for Lucy to make what she called a brilliant match and to do that she would vet closely all Lucy's suitors.

Pleading her case—and contrary to Aunt Caroline's decision for her to marry as soon as a suitable beau could be found because, having enjoyed her time in France, where she had loved attending the many social functions continually held in the nation's capital and had looked forward to attending the same in London—Lucy was in no hurry to wed and didn't want to look too far into the future. She wanted to delight in the finery and revel in the admiration and the flattery of those who found her appealing, giving no indication to her aunt that at the heart of her resistance were the feelings she still carried in her heart for Christopher Wilding.

Why did she keep tormenting herself with memories that were better forgotten? Christopher had promised her nothing, given her no assurances beyond the fact that he wanted her. She had tried to force him from her mind since leaving him that day at Rockwood Park. His life did not impinge on hers. But now they were back in London he was the only man she wanted to see. Just the thought of him made her stomach churn and she was amazed that he could still do that to her. She wondered if he ever thought of her. She doubted it.

'I am so looking forward to reintroducing you into

society,' Lady Sutton said, scrutinising one particular gold embossed card that pleased her and gave her hope that things might not be as dire as she had surmised. 'We can only hope that everyone's memory regarding your association with that unpleasant Barrington man was of short duration. I wonder what happened to him—where he disappeared to. No doubt Lord Rockley will know since he put him under surveillance. Fortunately you didn't remain long enough in London to see if you were the topic of any scandal.'

Lucy was aware how concerned her aunt was, even though she tried to hide it behind a smiling face and encouraging words. 'I was exposed for just the one night at Lord and Lady Skeffington's ball—indeed, I still have the scars to show for it—but it was so eventful that I fear it will still be remembered and my reappearance will resurrect the scandal—not that there won't have been others in the meantime, but society does seem to thrive on gossip. Perhaps that's the reason why your visitors are few.'

'Lady Beckwith indicated as much when she came to call, being the inquisitive sort, hoping to get a glimpse of this flighty young woman who'd garnered so much interest on her first outing into society— betrothed to one man and seen kissing another—so she could spread the gossip. I made a point of avoiding her. It was my hope that what happened that night would have been forgotten. It would appear that it has not, so I shall have to suffer the slights of society's narrow-minded hypocrisy. But how dare they presume to criticise me when their own lives are dripping with indiscretions?'

'It might not be as bad as you imagine, Lucy.'

'I truly hope not—for your sake. I am not unaware of the upset that unfortunate affair has caused you, Aunt Caroline, but none of it was of my doing. The guilty parties appear to have escaped without as much as a blemish, whereas I have been left to shoulder the blame. But I intend to enjoy myself and I will snap my fingers at those who show their disapproval of me.'

'I agree. There is nothing to be done about that, but you have the spirit to endure what they will put you through if they have a mind. I am determined that before the Season is over you will be engaged to a marquess or a duke.'

'You set your stakes high, Aunt Caroline.'

'Of course. I have high standards. None but the highest in the land for my beautiful goddaughter.'

'I would rather be happy with a pauper than miserable married to a marquess.'

'I would not see you marry anyone you cannot love, Lucy. I see we have an invitation to attend the Wilmingtons' ball in two weeks so things might not be as dire as we thought. Lord and Lady Wilmington's affairs are always popular. Everyone who is important will be there so it will be a complete crush, which might be to our advantage.'

To alleviate the tedium of the days leading up to the Wilmington ball, they often drove through Hyde Park, which was a rendezvous for fashion and beauty.

Lucy was a new distraction, drawing the admiring, hopeful eyes of several dashing young males displaying their prowess on high-spirited horses, but few approached her. Today the park seemed to glow with light and gaiety and vibrant colour. They halted the carriage to greet an acquaintance of Aunt Caroline, an elderly lady shielding her face from the sun with a gaily painted parasol. Lucy was introduced and Aunt Caroline left the carriage to sit with her to exchange pleasantries. Left alone, Lucy let her eyes stray beyond the carriage and alight on a lady and gentleman riding into the park.

The smile faded from her lips as she recognised Christopher. Seeing him again, she found he disturbed her. When they had been apart he had intruded into her thoughts more than she liked to admit and seeing him again seemed more disturbing than ever. She had resolved not to be tempted by him, but already her defences were being sorely tested.

Whatever it was that had caught his attention he looked her way, halting his horse. Across the distance their eyes locked—and those silver-grey orbs struck her to her heart, eyes that had not so long ago melted her. She clutched at her memories as recognition flashed between them at the speed of light. There was no change in his expression, nor did he make any attempt to approach her.

She stared at him, feeling her heart rate increase, and the sounds of the park muted. Colour flushed her cheeks. It was not caused by the heat of the day, but rather the uneasiness and tension within herself. She realised her feelings towards Christopher had not changed. She still loved the flesh and bone of the man and whatever it was that made him the way he was. But she could not allow this to blind her to the fact that he had hurt her once and she would not give him the opportunity to do so again.

Aware that his attention was directed elsewhere, his companion followed the line of his vision and her face broke into a broad smile. Lucy's did likewise when she recognised Amelia. Turning to her brother, Amelia said something to him and then she was riding in Lucy's direction. Lucy noted the dramatic changes in her and wondered a little apprehensively if what had happened to her in the past had left scars that went too deep to be put right. But bringing her horse to a halt at the side of the carriage, Amelia widened her smile.

'Lucy! I cannot believe it is you! You have returned from Europe, I see.' Her voice was filled with pure delight.

'We returned a week ago.'

'Then you must come and visit us. Christopher is always away on some business or other and I am left alone, craving company.'

'Thank you. I would like that.'

Urging her horse closer, Amelia launched into a torrent of questions. 'What was Europe like? I mean to go there one day. How long are you staying in London? I do so hope your aunt is not going to whisk you away again.'

Lucy laughed. 'We are done travelling for a while, Amelia, and will be content to remain in London indefinitely.' Lucy noted the dramatic changes in Amelia in the past year, thinking how elegant she looked attired in a sapphire riding habit, her dark curls exposed from beneath a matching hat set at a jaunty angle. She looked different. There was a certain transformation in her face and she possessed an air of confidence that had been sadly missing when they had met at Rockwood Park.

Amelia turned and looked at her brother, who was approaching at a slower pace than his sister had done. 'See, Christopher. Lucy has returned from abroad. Isn't that splendid? I'll leave you to catch up while I go and speak to Lady Sutton. Our meeting was brief when she came to Rockwood Park and I would like to become better acquainted.'

Lucy watched Christopher come closer, her gaze absorbing the sheer male beauty of him. Suddenly she felt the time they had been apart fall away. It was like a dam wall that had contained all the water behind it bursting in a flood and all the feelings she had kept tight inside her burst forth. His bottle-green riding coat clung to wide shoulders that were broader and more muscular than she remembered, and his thick dark hair beneath his tall hat was almost black. His face had an arrogant handsomeness and she noticed the cynicism in those silver-grey eyes and the ruthless set to his jaw that she had obviously been too young to notice before. Elegant, virile and as beautiful as a demigod, he looked into her eyes and gave her a polite bow.

'Lucy.'

The intimate caress when he said her name sent a

tremor down her spine she could not repress. A world of meaning passed between them. But she was increasingly aware of his presence and of the barely leashed tautness she had sensed in him when they had looked at one another across the park. All she could think about just then was being in his presence again and how happy that made her. He was darkly bronzed from the sun and, in contrast, his silver-grey eyes seemed to shine like bright jewels. Just when she had thought she might get over him, that he no longer affected her, he appeared and all her carefully tended illusions were cruelly shattered. He edged his horse closer and looked down at her, frowning, as if uncertain what to say or do next. Lucy drew a deep breath, steadying her nerves and her heart which had started to beat far too fast.

'Hello, Christopher. How are you?' She was amazed that her voice sounded calm when she was trembling inside.

'I am doing nicely. You look exceedingly well. You enjoyed Europe?'

'Yes—enormously. I was sorry to leave. Our travels were quite extensive and we visited all the conventional places.'

'Tell me what you thought of Italy—Florence is a place I've always wanted to visit. It sounds fascinating.'

'There are many who would agree with you. We strolled along the Arno—where Dante met Beatrice and fell hopelessly in love with her. We also visited Pisa, with its leaning tower, and Rome before returning to England. And you? You have become settled at Rockwood Park?'

He nodded. 'If one comes from such a family as mine, then one is expected to uphold tradition.'

'Why, you poor thing,' she uttered with mock sympathy, 'but somehow I do not think you find it such a trial.'

He laughed. 'I dare say I deserve my fate. I have done my adventuring—made mistakes along the way.'

'I think that is not uncommon with most of us.'

He looked at her with a doubtful frown. 'I cannot imagine you have made any.'

She raised her eyebrows and laughed. 'I am certain I have, but nothing major. I suppose everyone looks back on their lives and thinks—if only.'

'What a perceptive young woman you have become. Your time abroad has suited you well.'

'Yes, I did enjoy it, but I suppose it was ineffectual. Nothing that has gone before can be changed.'

'And would you?'

'Oh, yes. I would have seen what Sofia was up to when she arrived at the academy to take me away. I should have looked at the letter my father was supposed to have sent. I would probably have seen it was not his handwriting and everything would have been different. Is it business that brings you to London?'

'I do have business affairs to take care of, but they do not absorb me so much than I cannot find time to escort Amelia to this and that and visits to the theatre to see popular melodramas which she cannot get enough of.'

The tone of his voice was as natural as if they had met the day before and nothing untoward had passed between them. Its very ordinariness struck at Lucy's heart. His eyes remained fixed on her. It unsettled her, for she had not forgotten how brilliant and clear they were. In a strange, magical way they seemed capable of stripping her soul bare. Every inch of her cried out for him, but her betrayed spirit rebelled.

'Amelia looks very well,' Lucy said, observing how Christopher's sister was chatting animatedly to Aunt Caroline.

'Yes, she is.'

'She is very beautiful.'

'I think so. Since I brought her to Rockwood Park her life has taken on another dimension and she is happy. I fear for her sometimes, but she has weathered what happened to her and is stronger because of it.'

'You have heard nothing of Mr Barrington?'

He shook his head. 'The man remains elusive, but I watch and wait. I'm sure he'll emerge from wherever it is he's hiding eventually. There is a warrant out for his arrest and I still have men looking for him. There's always a chance that someone will see him and recognise him.'

'I remember him saying to you that it wasn't over, that he'd be seeing you again.'

'If he said that, then it will more than likely turn into a point of pride with him to make good on his boast.'

'I don't think he was boasting—more a statement of fact. Perhaps he'll change his mind—he might think it's too great a risk to take to seek you out for whatever evil purpose. If he should reappear, what will you do?'

'Unless he can settle his debts to me, I shall have him arrested.'

'I remember that night at the Skeffington ball so clearly. From my own observations I know what happened is not forgotten and that I am likely to be ostracised when I attend my first society event—the Wilmington ball, as a matter of fact. Aunt Caroline has high hopes for me and is quite determined to make me a success. She will not be satisfied unless the King himself proposes marriage.'

'Then she must remember that the King has been declared mad and his son, the Prince Regent, has a wife—although he is not averse to the odd mistress or two,' he said with some amusement. 'As for you being ostracised—I can't say since I don't listen to gossip, although I sincerely hope it is forgotten. What happened was not your fault.'

'No, it was not, although those who witnessed that unfortunate game of cards didn't think so—or the fact that we were observed on the terrace earlier.'

Christopher frowned, his expression serious. 'I know that and because of the harm it did you, I deeply regret it. What else can I say?'

She shrugged. 'There is nothing you can say. One thing I have learned is that society is neither discerning nor kind. I was branded a woman of easy virtue. When my aunt launches me into society I shall be at the mercy of the *ton*. If my indiscretion is remembered and I am censured, my reputation will be in shreds and everyone will cut me dead. If that happens, then

I can see nothing for it but to leave London and live in shamed seclusion in the country.'

'I very much doubt that will happen. If I happen to be present, then you can rest assured that I will do the gentlemanly thing and come to your rescue.'

'That's reassuring, but I'm used to using my head and fighting my own battles. Although why life should be plagued by gossips puzzles me. The gossips are like vultures. They watch everything one does, take note and remember it and embellish it and feed off it for evermore.'

'Which seems grossly unfair that you will be ostracised while the unprincipled reprobate who brought so much censure should have walked away scot-free.'

'Is it Mr Barrington you are referring to or yourself?'

'Both, I suppose. We neither of us did you any favours that night. I sincerely hope it is all forgotten.'

'My thoughts exactly, although heaven preserve me from such scrutiny. Aunt Caroline has been walking on air since our return—but I know she is concerned about how my reappearance into the ranks will be received. They really might decide to give me the cut direct. I have not set my hopes too high that all is forgotten. I should hate them to be disappointed.'

'That won't happen.'

'It might.'

'Don't tempt fate.'

'I have a sneaking feeling that fate likes to be tempted.'

'That's just your opinion.'

'I dare say it is, but then I never did care for the opinions of others. I am a realist, an individualist, and I will defy those who try to discredit me. So you see, Christopher, here I am, fresh from my travels, all grown up at last and prepared to do battle with whatever is amusingly called polite society throws at me.'

'And full of common sense.'

She smiled. 'Not as much as you appear to think.'

'I am sure you are.'

'You have not seen me for a whole year. How can you think that?'

'Because I know a good deal about you. You told me, remember.'

'I was fresh out of school then—still a child in many ways.'

'That may be, but you have never been far from my thoughts while you have been away.'

Lucy laughed. 'How gallant you are, Christopher.'

'Not at all. When I first saw you I had never met anyone like you.'

'I certainly had never met anyone like you—but then I wouldn't, would I, being fresh out of the schoolroom?' She paused and looked at him steadily. 'The truth is that I have thought of you also. It is hard not to think of someone who has saved one's life.'

'Now you exaggerate.'

'Indeed I do not. Remember the horse that nearly ran me down on our first meeting—and you were the one I ran to when I needed a friend. I had no one else and you sustained me during those days. I will be eternally grateful to you for that—and you were right to send me away, telling me to live life to the full—although I didn't think so at the time.' She thought back to that moment when he had sent her away. He hadn't wanted her then. Why would he do so now? Her pride brought her head up high and she looked him directly in the eye. 'So you see, in a way you did me a favour.'

'I did?'

'Yes. And I must thank you for being so frank with me.' Lucy watched his dark brows lift in surprise at her bluntness, and she could not suppress a hint of satisfaction.

His expression softened. 'That didn't stop me missing you.'

Something in his voice made her pause. What was it she heard? Longing? Emotion? Regret? Trying to imply that she was indifferent to him was no easy matter, but she was resolved to keep him at arm's length. She would not humble herself at his feet and pride—abused, stubborn pride—straightened her back and brought her head up high as she met his steady gaze. But she noted that as they talked, she could feel an extraordinary lassitude creeping over her. She was unsure what it meant, except that it was a warning. She ought to put an end to it quickly.

Christopher made a choked sound that sounded suspiciously like a laugh and Lucy's sense of satisfaction evaporated. She had wanted her words to sting.

'I see you have not lost your tongue, Lucy,' he commented, a wry note in his voice.

'I was not aware that I had,' she answered at once. 'To my knowledge my tongue has always remained firmly in my mouth and I am not likely to curb it for your sake.'

He laughed outright. 'Heaven forbid you would do that. I would not wish it.'

'Then I won't. Now tell me, have you managed to sell your ship?'

He nodded. 'Shortly after you left for France.'

'And how is your grandfather—in good health, I trust?'

'He does remarkably well and takes comfort in having Amelia around. Speaking of which,' he said, pulling his horse further away from the carriage when his sister joined him, 'here she is.' He turned his attention to Lady Sutton, who had climbed back into the carriage and taken her seat across from Lucy. 'I am happy to meet you again, Lady Sutton. I was just enquiring of Lucy if you enjoyed your travels abroad.'

'We had a splendid time—did we not, Lucy? There was so much to see—so many friends to meet and to be introduced to Lucy. And here we are, back in London and ready to enjoy what is left of the Season.'

'And you must,' Amelia said enthusiastically. 'You must also visit Rockwood Park again soon. I know Grandfather would be delighted if you would.'

'Thank you,' Lucy replied by way of being polite, but knowing that as things stood between her and Christopher it was unlikely to happen. But she was immediately transported back to the time she had spent there and the happy memories that crowded into her mind, memories of a time when she had temporarily put aside her fears.

They talked some more of inconsequential things before they had to move on since their carriage was causing an obstruction, but not before Amelia had said how she was looking forward to seeing them at the Wilmington ball the following week.

Christopher stared after the carriage with a firestorm of emotions erupting from his heart, searing their way through every vein and artery. He could not believe the change in her. Could the stylish goddess of a creature, as breathtakingly elegant as a fashion picture, with her gleaming dark hair swept back and up in a perfect chignon beneath an adorable little hat, be Lucy Walsh? This was a different Lucy Walsh from the one he had known before. There was an unspoken message about her now that said, *Don't come too close.*

He had hardly recognised her. She looked stunning. When she had been at Rockwood Park one year ago, he had told himself that their relationship was over and done with. But it was not as simple as that. She might have disappeared from his sight, but he had been unable to banish her from his heart and mind, and he resented her for having the power and the ability to do that. Although he had not seen her for so many months, the image of her had remained fixed in his mind as if carved in stone. Ever since he had known her she had stirred his baser instincts and during her absence he had found himself beset by visions of her. As much as she ensnared his thoughts, he found his dreams daunting to his manly pride, for she flitted through them like some puckish sprite.

* * *

The evening of the Wilmington ball arrived. Having sat for what seemed like hours in front of the dressing table mirror, watching as her maid painstakingly arranged her hair into an elegant coiffure, Lucy turned her attention to the gown she was to wear. It was a vibrant, off-the-shoulder peacock silk which brought out the bronze lights in her rich dark hair. It set off her figure to perfection and Lucy turned this way and that in front of the cheval mirror to survey her reflection.

'What do you think, Aunt Caroline? Will I do?'

Lady Sutton stood back to take a good look. Lucy was already beautiful, but tonight she looked positively breathtaking, daring, elegant and special. 'Indeed you will. Any man who sees you tonight, looking as you do, will surely be unable to take his eyes off you. Here,' she said, producing a narrow box and opening it to reveal a necklace, a single row of diamonds with an oval-shaped pendant, and matching drop earrings. 'I would like you to wear these. My husband gave them to me as a wedding present. I would like you to wear them tonight. They will complement your gown and your hair.'

Lucy fingered them at her throat. They were hard and cold and exquisite in their beauty. The earrings brushed her cheeks and the pendant rested just above her breasts.

'They're lovely, Aunt Caroline. Thank you.'

She smiled. 'Nothing but the best for you tonight, Lucy. Nothing but the best.'

Chapter Nine

Waiting for Amelia, who had disappeared into the ladies' retiring room to adjust her gown, promising him that she wouldn't be long, Christopher lounged against a pillar at the top of the stairs, idly watching the arrival of the glittering cream of London society into the hall below. Raising a lazy brow on seeing Lady Sutton enter, his eyes slid to the young woman by her side. On recognising Lucy he slowly drew himself upright. A cool vision of poised womanhood, attired in a peacock-blue dress and glittering diamonds, and undeniably the most magnificent woman he had seen, though it was not the way she looked that drew his eye, since the distance between them was too great for him to see her features clearly. It was the way she tossed her imperious head, the challenging set to her shoulders and the defiant stare that did not see those about her.

Smiling to himself, he stood and watched her as she walked beside Lady Sutton—though walked

hardly described the way she moved, for she seemed
to glide effortlessly, her body eternally female in its
fluid movements, her slippered feet barely touching
the ground.

Less than half an hour in the crowded ballroom,
Lucy was painfully aware of the extent of her disgrace.
She could feel everyone looking at her, talking about
her. She chose to ignore the stares and whispers of impropriety, but it was a long way from Paris and Italy
when she had been surrounded by admiring beaux.
Those friends and acquaintances who did not wish
to distance themselves from Lady Sutton were polite
and courteous, but didn't hesitate to ignore Lucy even
though, unbeknown to her, some had a grudging admiration for the way she had come tonight.

Before she had stepped down from the carriage
Lucy had already declared war on those who still held
her in contempt. The days leading up to tonight and
the painstaking efforts she'd made in order to look
her best, had set her nerves on edge and she was in no
mood to back down when faced with their unaccept-
able attitude which continued to provoke her. She had
entered the ballroom with an air of cool composure
and when their eyes rested on her for only an instant
before sliding away with a kind of contemptuous dis-
regard, even though she kept her head high and her
shoulders straight, something was dying inside her.
She wanted to run from the house, but she would not
give these strangers, these brittle, sophisticated strangers who resented her intrusion into their select soci-

ety, the satisfaction of seeing how affected she was by their censure.

Lady Sutton moved closer to her side. 'It's very much as you thought it would be, Lucy. How are you bearing up?'

'I'm fine, Aunt Caroline,' she replied in a voice that belied her calm expression and made it obvious to her godmother that she was deeply affected by the cruelty directed at her.

The minutes dragged by. There was the same exchange of polite inanities, of pointless bursts of laughter and the fluttering of fans as ladies cooled their flushed faces in the heat generated by so many bodies crowded together and the warmth of the night. The large ballroom, adorned with huge banks of flowers, glittered at its most brilliant in the light of the immense crystal chandeliers ablaze with innumerable candles. Her eyes were drawn to Christopher's tall, urbane figure in a plain, but perfectly cut black coat. His shoulders were squared with rigid hauteur, his hands clasped behind his back, the candlelight gleaming on his dark hair. His face was expressionless and for a brief moment their eyes met. He lifted his eyebrow and she was certain his lips quirked in the merest of smiles. He did not approach her—she suspected this was because he had no wish to draw attention to the two of them being seeing together, but his presence was reassuring.

'I think I will just go to the ladies' retiring room, Aunt Caroline. Excuse me.' She moved away, threading her way thought the throng in the entrance to the ballroom. Nothing penetrated her thoughts, for her mind was turning like a disembodied wraith through everything but the quandaries which she faced.

The Duke of Rockwood had been highly thought of and respected in his day and in their eyes this handsome grandson of his who had appeared within the midst of London society over a year ago—a rich and worthy prospect for mothers with unmarried daughters—could do no wrong. As far as Miss Walsh was concerned—an unknown American girl, an upstart who was of no consequence as far as English society was concerned, especially those who had been present at the Skeffington ball and who was, in their opinion, sadly lacking in moral standards—she was the guilty party. The only thing that saved her from being cut completely was that Lady Sutton was well liked and respected within society and she had a reputation for being both fair and honest in her dealings with others.

Christopher knew all this. From across the room, having witnessed her humiliation, he watched Lucy leave. Assured that Amelia was all right as she was twirled about the floor in the arms of an attentive beau, he made his way to Lady Sutton.

'How is she?'

'How do you think she is? This is worse than I expected. Everyone is whispering about how infamously wanton she was a year ago and now here she is again, tainting good society with her indecency. Lucy is going through the motions and behaving as if nothing untoward is happening, while all the time she is drowning in humiliation.'

'She is a courageous young woman for putting herself through this.'

'Yes—especially when you—along with Mr Barrington—had a hand in her downfall. She has certainly been fed to the wolves by coming here tonight.'

Christopher flinched. He said nothing to defend himself for what she said was true. Thoughts of his mother came to mind when she had sought to share her wisdom she had gained from her own experiences, teaching her son not merely with words but through example. Above all she had shown him the true meaning of duty and honour, which Christopher had put into practice many times in his daily life—the same duty and honour that had been absent in his treatment of Lucy when he had left her to shoulder this damning situation. It had been remiss of him and he reproached himself most severely, but he had hoped everything would have been forgotten.

'I really should have known better,' Lady Sutton said. 'I could not have been more wrong. I should not have taken it upon myself to defy the whole *ton* and introduce her back into the ranks. There is no lack of beaux here tonight, but not one will partner her.'

'I have done her a great disservice and I have no choice but to rescue her from what she is suffering now.'

'And how do you propose to do that?'

'If I am to make things right for her it is important to play out a charade and appear casual. Since I can't stop the gossip about what happened that night, I have to set out to turn it about, to ensure the attention is directed in the way I want it directed.'

Lady Sudden looked perplexed. 'I haven't the faintest idea what you are talking about.'

'The time has come to stem the gossip, to dispel this nonsense that is in danger of ruining Lucy completely. Leave it with me.'

Lucy was just leaving the ladies rest room when she met Amelia coming in.

'Lucy! How lovely it is to see you. You mentioned you were coming when we met in the park. Is this your first ball since arriving back in London?'

'It is—although I'm beginning to wish I'd remained at home.'

'Why do you say that? Oh—is everyone still harping on about that unfortunate affair at the Skeffington ball?'

'I'm afraid so.'

'After a whole year it's a pity they have nothing better to talk about—Christopher told me about it. You know all about me—I know. Christopher told me that as well.'

'Yes, I do.'

'I'm glad. When you came to Rockwood Park I was still all mixed up—about what I had tried to do—but I'm not any more. Christopher told me about you and Mark Barrington. I hope you don't mind.'

'No. Why should I? It's no secret. What he did in collusion with my stepmother was unforgivable. If I had not had Christopher to turn to, I shudder to think what might have happened to me.'

'I'm glad you managed to get away from him. I cannot forget or forgive his offences against me. He did me a great wrong. When he came to Charleston I fell in love with him as soon as I saw him. He was a popular man about town who had all the eligible ladies setting their caps at him—and he chose me. What I did when he left me was a terrible thing which I deeply regret. I hadn't told him about the child and I often wonder if things would have been different if I had.

'When Christopher brought me to England I had to accept that that part of my life was over, but for some strange reason I feel as if it is incomplete, not quite done with—and it will always be so unless I see him again and ask him why he left me. I know what Christopher believes, that he wanted me for any money that would come my way from my grandfather, but there were times when we were so close that I cannot believe that was the only reason he was with me. In spite of everything it is difficult not to remember.'

'But you have recovered from it, I hope.'

'Yes, I think so. I've decided not to wallow in self-pity any longer. Life is meant to be enjoyed. There should be laughter and pleasure.'

Lucy stared at her. She had changed, grown up suddenly, and looked so lovely in her dusky pink gown.

'At first I blamed Christopher for sending Mark away, but when he told me about the blackness of his character, I realised that what I had done was very foolish and irresponsible and that Christopher had acted in my best interest. When Mark left me I truly thought I had nothing left to live for—but I'm better now.'

'I'm happy to hear that, Amelia. You've had a traumatic time.'

'So have you. I can only hope that he's not doing it to someone else. Have you spoken to Christopher tonight?'

'No—I thought I saw him earlier.'

'No doubt he will seek you out before long. Let's try to meet up at supper, shall we?'

'Yes, let's do that.'

Lucy made her way back to her Aunt Caroline, not at all sure she would still be here for supper.

When Lucy returned to Lady Sutton, Christopher knew everyone was watching them both, positively bursting for a first-hand *on dit* about his relationship with her. After the Skeffington ball a year ago, everyone believed that in the wake of being ruined by his rival at cards and the young lady's affections, Mr Barrington had thrown her over and hotfooted it back to America. Christopher was determined to turn things around. It did cross his mind that he should have done this before, but at the time there had been so much going on in his life and Lucy was leaving for the Continent that he had pushed it to the back of his mind. He should have known better, he realised that now.

He mingled with the throng, giving a nod here and pausing now and then to shake hands and speak with an acquaintance, but all the while never losing sight of Lucy. A friend from his schooldays, Lord Timothy Cawthorn, came to have a word, having noted the situation and asking if he could be of assistance. Christopher smiled, deciding to make the most of the offer.

A waltz was starting when Lord Cawthorn suddenly appeared by Lucy's side and, with the permission of Lady Sutton, led her on to the floor, dancing her into the midst of the twirling couples. The fact that Lord Cawthorn was championing her was immediately remarked upon. Christopher breathed a sigh of relief. She was safe for the time being.

Mingling with a group of flamboyant young lords whose tongues had been loosened by drink, he accepted a glass of wine from a tray and joined in the frivolity. One of them, having glanced with interest to where Lucy was dancing with Lord Cawthorn, turned to Christopher, commenting on her beauty and with a leer and a nudge remarking that he would know, wouldn't he, having been caught in a passionate embrace with the said young lady at the Skeffington ball. Showing his lack of polish—and also his inability to hold his drink—he gave Christopher another nudge and a wink and remarked that he had heard that Christopher knew her intimately.

'Do I?' he uttered in an amused tone.

'By all accounts you do—don't you?'

Christopher laughed. 'Not in the way you imply.' Then he automatically added a proviso to forestall further gossip. 'However, Miss Walsh should count herself fortunate that I was there that night.'

The young lord noted that with some surprise.

'She should? What are you saying? I thought you two were…'

Christopher lifted his eyebrows with some amusement. 'Were what? Lovers? I should be so fortunate and all the rumours about that night are just lamentable nonsense and people should learn to separate the rubbish from the truth. It was nothing but a gross misunderstanding.'

'But—are you saying you did not compromise Miss Walsh?'

'That is exactly what I am saying. When I arrived at Skeffington House I couldn't believe my eyes when I saw an old sparring partner of mine, Mark Barrington, a man who made his living seducing wealthy young ladies in order to get his hands on their money—which was exactly what he was about to do to Miss Walsh and she just fresh out of the schoolroom and her father dead three months past. When I managed to draw her away from him I informed her of his character, telling her the man was a charlatan. It's fortunate I was there that night otherwise she would have found herself married to Barrington—although it wouldn't have lasted.'

'It wouldn't?'

Christopher shook his head. 'He would have absconded with her money. Naturally she was relieved to know the truth and immensely grateful to me.'

'And Miss Walsh was innocent in the whole affair.'

'Absolutely. The lady is a paragon of virtue and a finer example of refinement you couldn't hope to meet. Seeing her here tonight, I intend to renew our acquaintance and hope she will look on me with favour.'

Christopher almost felt sorry for the young man. He'd taken everything in like a hungry dog eager to set about a meaty bone, but Christopher had other things on his mind and was in no mood to indulge in further conversation. Draining his glass he walked away, leaving the young man to impart this new bit of information to his friends, that the beautiful Miss Walsh had been saved from a terrible fate by Viscount Rockley. He was confident that what he had disclosed would filter through the gathered guests like quicksilver.

Seeking out his sister, who was breathless from so much dancing and taking a moment to cool herself with a long, cold drink, he watched with satisfaction as the story he had imparted to the eager youth was circulated and in no time at all male heads turned to look at Lucy with renewed interest and speculation. It wasn't long before several presented themselves to Lady Sutton and requested she introduce them to Miss Walsh. Glancing across the room to where Christopher stood, he gave her a knowing smile, leaving her in no doubt that it was his doing. More than happy with this new direction, Lady Sutton was delighted to oblige.

From a distance Christopher watched a group of young bloods with flirtatious grins and with furious persistence toadying around this gorgeous creature who had suddenly appeared in their midst. They were effusive in their compliments and attentions, requesting introductions and dances with her, vying for her attention. He noted how, without a qualm, she happily

used all her ability at flirtation—no doubt this was
how she had been on her year abroad. She smiled happily, allowing first one and then another to lead her
into the dance, clinging on to their arms and hanging
on to their every word, carrying it all off with aplomb.
Christopher stood watching from the sidelines, his
face a veneer of bland sophistication, while inside he
wanted to stride out on to the dance floor and drag
her from their arms.

Satisfied that everything was going to plan, he
casually shrugged himself away from the pillar and
left the ballroom by the French doors to the terrace.
Thankfully the gardens were quiet.

At first Lucy was bewildered by all this sudden attention, but she was so relieved that she was no longer
being ignored that she said not a word as one young
beau followed by another led her on to the floor to
dance. She danced with Lord Cawthorn again and
laughed when he danced her through the open French
doors on to the terrace, where he released her. Looking
at him with a good deal of confusion, she was about
to ask him what he was about when he laughed and
bowed his head before slipping back inside.

And then she knew. Christopher was responsible
for the sudden change in everyone's attitude towards
her.

'At last,' Christopher said. 'I was wondering when
I would get you alone.'

Lucy froze at the sound of his voice, her shoulders

tense. Christopher moved from the shadows to stand being her. After a long moment she at last turned.

'I take it you are responsible for this about-turn. My coming here tonight has turned into a nightmare. Have I not been humiliated enough without you adding to it? What did you do to get them to dance with me—bribe them?'

'Of course not, but I did the best I could to change people's opinion. Those men wanted to dance with you. They are not nearly as malicious as their female counterparts and were looking for any excuse to lead you on to the floor. I provided them with the opportunity.'

She laughed, which was not without a ring of bitterness. 'My, my, Christopher. Not only were you an accomplished captain on the high seas, you also appear to have a gift for strategy and subtlety on the dance floor, too.'

'I do my best,' he replied, ignoring her sarcasm.

'You must have seen what was happening to me in there. They might as well have strapped me to a ducking stool and dropped me in the Thames.'

At any other time Christopher would have laughed at the image her words conjured up in his mind, but now he would not insult her by doing so, for the strain of what she had gone through—was still going through—was there on her lovely, troubled face for him to see.'

'I did see, Lucy. You have done nothing to deserve that and I wanted to repair the damage. I merely thought it was time to put an end to the scandal.'

'And how did you manage that? By telling them what really happened before I left for France? How it was not my fault and that the two men who ruined my reputation had escaped being vilified?'

'Something on those lines—which is the truth. I started a rumour—which soon spread like wildfire—to blacken Barrington's name, of the cunning and villainy he used to get his hands on the fortune of a vulnerable young woman.'

'And everyone actually believes that?'

'That you have been wrongly maligned? Yes. It might gratify you to know that I did not exonerate myself either, freely admitting that some of the blame was mine and that I hold myself accountable. I made it known that I had designs on you myself and that you evaded all my advances. I have no doubt they admired your good sense in steering clear of me. Personally I don't care a damn what people think of me, but no matter what you think, it is not my wish to cause more gossip that will hurt you.'

'And now here we are—in a similar situation as we were that night at the Skeffington ball—whereas this time you arranged to have your friend bring me on to the terrace. If we are seen, then everyone will believe we are starting it up again.'

'Let them. Following your rejection of me at the Skeffington ball, they'll think I'm trying to repair my damaged male pride. That is what I want them to believe.'

'You do? I'm not sure I do.'

'I am heir to a dukedom, Lucy—dukes are few and

far between. Since acquiring a title and wealth is like
a holy crusade for most of them, they'll admire and
envy you all the more for it.'

Lucy's face was working with the strength of her
emotions, which had, for the moment, got the better of
her. Reluctantly she gazed up at him. His eyes glowed
with the reflected light of the lanterns hanging from
the trees as he watched her unrelentingly, heightening
Lucy's tensions until she could hardly stand the suspense. Two more couples stepped out on to the terrace.

'I think I should go back inside.'

'Walk with me in the garden. I would appreciate
your company, Lucy.'

On a sigh she nodded, reluctant to return to the
dancing.

She did not object when he took her hand and led
her down the terrace steps to the garden below, then
tucked her hand in the crook of his arm. They sauntered along a path lined with marble statues. Neither of
them spoke until they turned a corner into a leafy arbour. Stillness was all around them and music drifted
over the garden. Grateful he'd sought some privacy for
them, breathing in the scented night air, Lucy turned
to face him, gazing at his handsome face with its stern,
sensual mouth and hard jaw, and in the moment that
followed she felt once more that wild surge of excitement and anticipation when she remembered being
in his arms.

'Why have you brought me here?'

'Because I wanted to be alone with you.'

'I see.' Horrified at the possibility that he'd somehow known what thoughts had been running through her mind on the terrace, she said uneasily, 'Why should you think I want to be alone with you? What are you going to do?'

Moving until he was only inches from her, Christopher regarded her from beneath hooded lids.

'Actually, I would like to kiss you—to see if it's as pleasurable as I remember. You are a desirable woman, Lucy, and I am a man who possesses a fine appreciation for such beauty.'

'Really? You do surprise me, Christopher. Is your memory so lacking that, not satisfied with compromising me a year ago, you are about to do the same again?'

He chuckled softly. 'I'm willing to risk it if you are.'

She sucked in a deep breath, the scent of his warm, clear skin, assaulting her senses and making her body tremble with awareness. She could not deny a dark fascination as she watched his beautiful features twist with what appeared to be intense pleasure at the idea of kissing her, a pleasure that she'd briefly tasted as his lips had captured hers in the past.

It was one thing to want to be kissed by him before, but here, with absolute privacy and nothing to prevent him from taking all sorts of liberties, it was another matter entirely and far more dangerous. And based on that other time when she'd wanted him to kiss her, she couldn't blame him for thinking she'd be willing now. Struggling desperately to ignore the sensual pull he was exerting on her, she drew a long, shaky breath.

'I'm surprised that you want to kiss me again after the last time. I seem to recall you telling me that you regretted doing so—because of my age, I suppose,' she said softly. 'I, too, had regrets—about the fact that I behaved like a shameless wanton for letting you. We both should have known better and not allowed our—weakness to get the better of us.'

His voice was heavy with irony. 'Weakness? Is that what you put it down to? It had nothing to do with the fact that we were attracted to each other, that I could think of nothing other than dragging you off somewhere even more private to make love to you? Or that I had scruples enough to ignore that ignoble impulse? I wanted you then, Lucy. I want you now.'

Lucy made the mistake of looking at him and his eyes captured hers against her will, holding them imprisoned. 'It was a year ago, Christopher. We—have changed.'

'Neither of us has anything to gain by pretending that what we felt then is over,' he said bluntly. 'Seeing you again has proved that it isn't.'

Lucy wanted to deny it, but she sensed that if she did he would hate her for her deceit. She raised her chin, unable to tear her gaze from his. 'All right,' she said softly. 'I've never forgotten you. How could I?'

He smiled and his voice gentled to soft velvet. 'Thank you for not denying it. Now I would like to kiss you again—if you are willing, that is. I will not force you to do anything against your will because I do not want you waking up tomorrow and saying it should not have happened.'

Some small, insidious voice in her mind urged her to do as he asked, reminding her that after the public contempt she'd had to endure this very night she was entitled to experience again the passion that had consumed her before.

His smouldering gaze dropped to her lips, riveting there. Taking her silence for consent, he placed his hands on her upper arms and drew her close. Lucy was breathing too fast so that she was almost dizzy and knew she would not be able to bear it if he released her now. There were certain times when certain actions seemed natural. Christopher placed his finger beneath her chin and tilted her head back. Perhaps he could read in her face what she could see in his— wonder and hunger. Then he kissed her, with a passion that was like an explosion, stunning them both.

Lucy felt the sturdy trunk of a tree against her back and his body against hers as she pressed herself closer to him with a shameless ardour she would not have believed herself capable of. They kissed with a passion and Lucy pressed the palms of her hands against his chest. His mouth moved urgently against hers and she began to match his pagan kiss, lost in the heated magic of the moment. A shudder shook his powerful frame as she fitted herself to him and his lips pressed down on hers, parting them with a hungry urgency before becoming gentle and caressing. Lost in the heated magic of the moment, Lucy touched her tongue to his lips and felt the gasp of his breath against her mouth. She could not have denied her longing for him any more than she could have commanded herself to stop breathing.

An eternity later he lifted his head and looked down

at her lovely face upturned to his. 'Until now I have managed to convince myself that my memory of our kisses, of the passion that erupted between us, was exaggerated. But that kiss surpassed my imaginings.'

Lucy was silent as her breathing evened out and the sounds of the night began penetrating her senses. Sudden female laughter coming from just beyond the arbour broke caused them to move apart.

'I think we should go inside,' Lucy whispered. 'Aunt Caroline will be wondering where I've got to.'

'I think Lady Sutton will be happy to know you are with me. However, we will return to the dancing and I would very much like it if you would dance with me.'

'Do you think that would be wise?'

He raised his brows and smiled wryly. 'Nothing you and I have done has been wise, Lucy. Let the gossip begin. They'll see how weak you are and see you can no longer evade my manly charms.'

Beginning to walk away, she glanced at him coolly. 'Don't flatter yourself—and remember that now that my reputation has been redeemed, there are other beaux impatient to dance with me.'

'You will dance with me first.' He held out his hand. 'I insist. I happen to have worked very hard to-night on your behalf—the least you can do is dance with me. Let everyone see us together and you will see how easily most minds can be manipulated. It might give the gossip a turn of direction, one they have not expected.'

Lucy relented and placed her hand in his. As they walked into the ballroom, heads turned as one, every eye focused on them, some filled with curiosity, some with puzzlement. They stepped on to the dance floor, where Lucy walked into Christopher's arms and felt his right arm slide about her waist like a band of steel, bringing her close against the solid strength of his body. His left hand closed around her fingers and suddenly she was being whirled gently around in the arms of a man who danced the waltz as thought he had danced it a million times before.

'A whole year has passed since I last held you in my arms. It's as if we have scaled some invisible wall that has kept us apart and now there is no need for impatience. We will wait and let matters run their course.' Lowering his head to hers, Christopher murmured, 'Lift up your head, smile at me, look as though you've never enjoyed a dance more.' His eyes twinkled wickedly. 'You might even flirt with me if you like.'

Lucy drew a shaking breath and a smile curved her lips. 'I can smile, Christopher, but flirting is definitely out. Look where it got me before when you danced me out on to the terrace and kissed me.'

'How can I possibly forget? The kiss has been repeated and I am already impatient to repeat the experience.'

'You sound very sure that I will let you.'

'You will,' he said, twirling her about. 'Now relax. Your aunt and Amelia appear to have found each other. They have their heads together and are watching us closely.'

'I am relaxed.'

'Your body tells me something different.'

'My body is my own affair.' She was acutely aware of his hand against her waist and she had a sudden impulse to shy away.

'I would like to know what your body looks like, Lucy.' His eyelids were lowered over his eyes as he looked down at her upturned face, gently flushed by his remark. 'I would like to know everything about you, every curve, every hollow and every inviting, secret place.' He grinned at the shock that registered in her eyes and spun her round more vigorously than the dance required. 'I am going to be a duke after all.'

Lucy scowled up at him, seeing sparkling humour in his eyes. 'You're loving this, aren't you?'

'Every minute,' he admitted shamelessly. Scowling when he saw her glance towards the edge of the dance floor and smile at a group of young beaux who stood in a group watching her, impatient to ask her to dance, he spun her in the opposite direction. 'You don't have to smile at every man you come into contact with.'

'Why not?' she replied, her look one of complete innocence. 'I was only being polite.' She laughed lightly. 'Why, what's this, Christopher? Are you jealous by any chance?'

With his lips close to her cheek his voice was hunky and warm, his eyes devouring her with a hunger he did not try to conceal. 'I am jealous of your every word, thought and feeling that is not about me. I want you, Lucy. It is my dearest wish to make you mine. Don't waste your time on those young cockscombs. They're not worth it.'

Trying to ignore what she saw in his eyes, his lips

hovering just above her own, Lucy tried to still her rapidly beating heart. 'And what of you, Christopher?' she asked, breathing heavily. 'Are you worth it? You say you want me. If I were to yield myself to you, would you honour me?'

'Until death,' he breathed. 'I have been plagued with thoughts of you since you left. Don't you know how much of a temptation you are to me—how much I missed you when you were away?'

'How did you miss me, Christopher? Tell me?'

'I missed everything about you. I missed your bright smile, your high spirits and the wild sweetness of you that I have never found in anyone else. I missed *you*.'

Her mind reeling over the shock of what he was saying, Lucy could only stare at him as a torrent of emotions overwhelmed her.

'I want you, Lucy,' he murmured. 'There is a chemistry between us—has been from the start.'

'But—'

'And I must point out that a young lady should never, under any circumstances, contradict a duke.'

'I wasn't going to.'

'Not even when I ask you to marry me.'

Unable to believe what he had said, Lucy felt her surroundings melt into a haze. She was amazed that she carried on dancing. The heady, intoxicating joy that flooded through her body was nearly her undoing. She wanted to say yes, despite her bold determination to become a woman of independence, but she hesitated. His gaze had moved to her mouth, lingering there. He wasn't smiling any more, his face having taken on a serious expression. After a moment, unable to work out where the proposal had come from, amazed that her voice sounded so calm and controlled, she said, 'This is all so sudden, Christopher.'

'Yes, I know.'

'Couldn't you have asked me somewhere else instead of the middle of a dance floor?'

'You have less chance of running away from me here. It would be sure to start another scandal and that is the last thing you want.'

'True.'

'It is not the way I intended to propose, but the truth of the matter is that I have precious little experience when it comes to asking a woman to be my wife.' He gazed down at her. 'Have you nothing to say?'

Lucy had plenty to say, but not while she was dancing a waltz. Besides, it did not take a great deal of intelligence to realise that, considering all that had happened, he felt obliged to offer for her. An awkward silence descended until she at last said, 'You don't have to do this, Christopher.'

'What? Ask you to be my wife?'

'Because of what has happened, I suspect you feel obliged to propose to me. It is not necessary to feel that way. I did not expect it.'

'What occurred is in the past and has nothing to do with my proposal. You are in my blood, Lucy. I care for you deeply and I want you in my life.'

A heady burst of heat flooded through Lucy's body. It was more than she had ever hoped for, but she was cautious. 'I might be in your blood, Christopher,' she said, unable to completely disguise her doubts. 'That is so very different from wanting me to be your wife. Marriage is important and serious and not something to be undertaken lightly. Forgive me, Christopher, but I'm reluctant to commit myself to you or anyone else just now. Aunt Caroline has gone to an awful lot of trouble in making me a debutante and I want to savour the opportunity a little longer.'

Christopher's expression hardened. 'And to look over other eligible suitors before you settle on a husband.'

Lucy smiled up at him obliquely. 'Oh, don't be too despondent, Christopher. I promise to consider your proposal along with any other I might receive. You sent me away, remember, and now you say you want to marry me. Pardon me if I appear confused.'

'Yes, I sent you away—but you will never know the strength of will it took to do that. I had to do it. You were young. It wouldn't have been right to ask you to commit yourself then. I had only recently come to England to accept my inheritance, which was a massive undertaking for me. And I had a duty to Amelia, who, as you saw for yourself, was still deeply affected by what Barrington had done to her.'

'Yes. She's come through it remarkably well.'

With a smile he spun her once more as the waltz came to an end. 'She has—and you are determined to make this difficult for me. I don't expect you to answer right away—but in the meantime,' he said, a wicked smiled curving his lips, 'I will do my utmost to persuade you and enjoy every minute of it. I'm not noted for my patience, Lucy, as well you know,' he said, looking at her with that all-absorbing attention Lucy had come to know. 'The die is cast. You will be mine in the end.'

They were met by Amelia and Lady Sutton, who looked from one to the other.

'I'm so happy everything has been resolved, Lucy,' Amelia said sincerely. She looked at her brother. 'I think I would like to leave now, Christopher—if you would order the carriage. I'm quite fatigued with all the dancing.' She turned to Lucy. 'On Wednesday of next week, Christopher has promised to take me in a boat on the river and a picnic at Greenwich—he's so busy that we have to plan these things in advance, you understand.' She turned to her brother, smiling in anticipation that he would agree to what she had to suggest. 'Why don't we all go? It would be such fun. Do you not agree, Christopher?'

Lucy began to stammer a polite refusal, but Christopher would have none of it.

'That is a splendid suggestion, Amelia. If you would care to join us,' he said, 'we would be delighted.'

'Oh—but I don't think…' Lucy said.

'I refuse to take no for an answer. It would be such fun,' Amelia said, beaming. Lucy agreed. 'Splendid. Then that is settled.'

They talked some more and arrangements were made for Christopher and Amelia to collect them in their carriage four days hence at ten o'clock.

They parted company then, Lucy and Christopher

trying to give the impression that what had passed between them was nothing more than a friendly meeting. It was a poor pretence. They could not pretend the feelings they had for each other did not exist. But that's what they did as they went their separate ways.

Chapter Ten

'Well,' Lady Sutton said when they were in the coach. 'It turned out to be an enjoyable evening after all. Now, don't keep me in suspense, Lucy. You and Viscount Rockley spent a great deal of the evening together after everything was sorted out.'

'We have him to thank for that—although I think you already know that. If you really want to know, Aunt Caroline, he asked me to marry him.'

Lady Sutton was rendered speechless and then she smiled, well pleased with the way everything had turned out. 'Well—that is good, isn't it?'

'Is it? I'm not so certain.'

'I might be a bit longer in tooth than you are, Lucy but I am not entirely blind. It is obvious to me that you love Christopher.'

Lucy could no longer evade the truth. For all her pretended indifference, even the most mindless person could deduce she was utterly and completely and hopelessly in love with Christopher Wilding.

'Yes—I do love him.'

Lady Sutton tilted her head to a puzzled angle. 'Then why did you not give him an answer?'

Lucy shrugged. 'Because I'm not sure of his intentions. Because of what happened I don't want him to feel obligated to marry me and I fear he might come to regret his impulsive proposal.'

'Impulsive? He's had a whole year to think about it. It's evident that he is a gentleman who appreciates having to fight for what he desires, and, my dear Lucy, it is evident that he very much desires you.'

Lucy's heart gave a powerful jolt. 'His desire for me is something I have never doubted, but it is not his desire that I want, it is his heart that I seek.'

Lady Sutton gave a slow nod of her head. 'Ah—I see. Well—this is all so sudden. Of course I had hoped that you would have had more time to enjoy what is left of the Season which so many other girls enjoy and, perhaps, consider more proposals and be courted. But none will come with a higher title than Viscount Rockley's.'

'I'm not interested in titles, Aunt Caroline—only the man.'

After Lucy's first appearance in society, the house on Curzon Street was deluged with callers and there followed an intense three days of social functions. Escorted to all the stylish gatherings by Lady Sutton, Lucy's popularity had increased considerably and she found herself revelling in the fun of it. But the period between the ball and the trip on river was also a time of serious deliberation and heart searching before deciding that, for better or worse, she would become Christopher's wife. Unable to come to a decision and reluctant to face him again until she was more certain of herself, she tried to find an excuse to get out of the excursion on the river, but Aunt Caroline would not hear of it. The more Lucy was seen in the company of Viscount Rockley the better.

The morning of the excursion dawned sunny and warm—perfect conditions for a trip to the river, Lady Sutton proclaimed, before taking to her bed with a raging headache. Lucy was all concern, telling her she would send a note of apology to Christopher's address. They would have to turn down the invitation. But Aunt Caroline, determined not to disappoint Amelia, wouldn't hear of it and was adamant that Lucy should go. Besides, a picnic basket had been prepared. It would be silly to waste it. Lucy had no time to argue for Christopher and Amelia arrived, Christopher looking very elegant in his dark blue coat and matching waistcoat and Amelia looking summery in a lemon dress trimmed with white lace.

'I'm afraid Aunt Caroline isn't very well—she has developed a headache and taken to her bed.' She smiled weakly at them both. 'It looks as though I will have to forgo the trip on the river and a picnic.'

'I'm sorry to hear that,' Amelia said, frowning with concern. 'Is there anything we can do?'

'No, thank you, Amelia. She has taken to her bed, I'm afraid. She might feel better when she's had a sleep. I think I should stay with her. Besides, I hate to intrude on your day out.'

A sudden gleam entered Christopher's eyes. 'You aren't. We wouldn't have invited you if we thought that. Besides, the food is prepared. It would be a shame to waste it.'

Lucy felt her cheeks warm. 'But—I have no wish to impose on your time.'

His smile broadened into a grin. 'It's no imposition. We insist you come with us. Is that not so, Amelia?'

'Yes. We insist.'

'Good. Now that is settled, fetch your cloak. It might be cool on the river. I cannot tell you how much pleasure it will give me having two beautiful young ladies to escort.'

Lucy searched his bold visage. 'Your persistence really does amaze me, Christopher. I'm only thankful that Amelia didn't go down with something that would have caused her to cancel her presence on the outing.'

He chuckled, smiling a wicked smile. 'Why? We might both have enjoyed the outing. However, I promise to be on my best behaviour and as charming as my nature will allow.'

Lucy cast Amelia a smile. 'We shall see, won't we, Amelia?'

'We certainly will. It should prove to be an interesting afternoon.'

'It will be what we make it,' Christopher said. 'Now come along. We are wasting time.'

The housekeeper appeared carrying the picnic basket and handed it to Lucy, happy that all the work she'd put into it wouldn't be wasted after all. Seated in the Wilding carriage, with its grey upholstery and the hood down, Lucy experienced a strange exhilaration as they headed for the river.

When they reached the river they left the driver with the carriage to while away the afternoon. Christopher hired a boat and helped Lucy and Amelia in. There was a slight breeze and the water lapped the sides of the boat, but fortunately it was warm and Lucy decided against her cloak. Then he picked up the oars and they were away, moving at a steady speed. They were soon past the Tower of London and on their way to Greenwich.

The rippling silvered river was busy with every kind of craft—ferries, lightermen and a string of barges heading upstream, the movement keeping the water constantly on the swell. There were lots of people in pleasure boats, all enjoying the warm weather, laughing and calling to each other. Amelia's mood was carefree and she joined in the fun, waving happily to others when they waved to them.

Lucy watched Christopher, impressed how easy rowing a boat was for him. 'I imagine you must feel quite at home on the water, Christopher.'

'Can you smell it?'

'What?' Lucy asked.

'The salt on the incoming tide.'

Breathing deep, Lucy could detect a tang on the air—the smell of salt and what she thought might be tar. When Lucy looked at Christopher she saw he was watching them both, a smile curving his lips.

'What is it that makes you smile?'

'I was thinking how adorable you both are, with your pink cheeks and shining eyes. You put me in mind of two children opening their presents at Christmas. Are you enjoying yourselves?'

'I am most certainly,' Lucy replied.

'And are you glad you came?'

'Yes. I've never been on the river before.'

'It will be quieter at Greenwich—the perfect place for a picnic.'

The boat drew up at some stairs. Christopher climbed out and secured it, before helping his companions out. Carrying the picnic baskets and rug, they climbed the embankment and eventually found a secluded place beneath some tall trees and not far from the water's edge. Here the quietness could not be denied. The breeze was fresh, but seasonably warm, rustling the leaves in the trees and dappling the shade.

Christopher spread out the rug and settled on it, his back propped against a tree, content to watch as Lucy and Amelia busied themselves emptying the baskets of food and wine. Totally relaxed, they talked and laughed easily together, and watched the world sail by, and all the while Lucy was aware of Christopher's appreciative gaze on her animated face.

In all it proved to be an enchanting afternoon and Lucy experienced a twinge of regret that it would have to end.

When some ducks left the bankside and waded

into the water, half a dozen ducklings following in their wake, Amelia couldn't resist taking some left-over bread to feed them, walking away from Lucy and Christopher.

'She looks quite radiant,' Lucy commented softly, resting on her knees. 'I can't believe she is the same young woman I saw at Rockwood Park.'

Stretching out on his side, Christopher leaned on a forearm and studied her profile from beneath hooded lids. 'You are a strange young woman, Lucy Walsh,' he murmured, focusing his eyes on a wisp of hair against her cheek.

Without thinking, he reached out and tucked it behind her ear, feeling the velvety softness of her skin against his fingers. She did not move away as he ran the tip of his finger down the column of her throat, along the line of her chin to her collar and the cameo brooch at her throat.

'You are a fascinating young woman, Lucy. I find myself wanting to know everything there is to know about you.'

'You already know a great deal about me—more than anyone else.'

'I have learned some things, I grant you. I have also realised since we kissed at the ball that you have matured into a lovely young woman. There is little sign of the schoolgirl I met at the fair—or the young lady I kissed and who returned my kiss with such fervour before you left for France.'

'Christopher, please!' Resting back on her heels, Lucy gave him a reproachful look. 'Stop it now,' she retorted, her face heating. 'That was a year ago. We neither of us are the same people.'

'No? Are you saying that you didn't enjoy kissing me?' He reached into the basket for an iced cake and slowly began to eat.'

'No—yes… Oh, behave yourself. I was hoping you would.'

Christopher was by no means done with her yet. He grinned. 'Have you kissed anyone else while you have been away? They say the Italians are a passionate race—that few ladies can resist their charms.'

Lucy's cheeks flamed with indignation. 'No—and if I had it is none of your business. Now will you please stop tormenting me about my—slip of propriety when I let you kiss me.'

His grin widened at her embarrassment, then he gave a shout of laughter. 'I like reminding you. I enjoy seeing you get all flushed and flustered and hot under the collar.'

She glowered at him. 'Will you please stop making fun of me? Amelia will notice and wonder what we are talking about.'

'I know—but I doubt she will be shocked. I have a feeling that she knows how I feel about you and is tactfully keeping out of the way—hence her sudden desire to feed the ducks.'

Unable to stay cross with him—knowing he was teasing anyway—Lucy laughed, waving to Amelia who had heard her brother's loud laughter and was looking their way as she continued to throw bread for the gathering, greedy ducks.

Christopher lay back, linking his hands behind his head and looking up at the trees. 'I like to hear you laugh, Lucy. I'm happy that you still can. You have a beautiful laugh.'

Hearing the sensuous huskiness that deepened his voice, Lucy could feel her pulse increase its beat. 'You are only saying that to placate me.'

'Do you need placating?'

She sighed, shifting her position and wrapping her arms round her drawn-up knees. 'No. I'm having too nice a time to be cross.'

'That's a relief.'

When he closed his eyes, Lucy let her gaze wander over the smooth, thick lock of hair that dipped over his brow and the authority and strength in every line of his handsome face. She let her gaze travel the full length of the superbly fit, muscled body stretched out beside her. How well she remembered being held in his arms, how he had exuded raw power and a potent virility that had held her in thrall.

As if he could feel her eyes studying him, without opening his eyes, he quirked the mobile line of his mouth in a half-smile. 'I hope you like what you see.' He sighed. 'You can kiss me if you want to, Lucy.'

Lucy's eyes opened wide in astonishment, then she laughed. 'I really cannot believe your arrogance, Christopher. I most certainly will not,' she objected, slapping him playfully on the chest with her napkin.

With no warning he reared up. His hands shot out and, gripping her upper arms, he pulled her down on to her back. 'If you won't kiss me, do you mind if I kiss you?' His voice was low pitched and sensual, his face only inches from her own.

'Yes, I do, now—please stop it. Amelia will see. What will she think?'

'She's too busy feeding the ducks to notice.' He smiled, then, and it was a wonderful smile, the kind of smile that would melt any woman's heart. It curled beautifully on those chiselled lips and his silver eyes were full of amusement as he gazed down at her. 'Are you not curious to find out if it will be as good as when I kissed you at the ball?' His heavy-lidded gaze dropped to the inviting fullness of her lips, lingering there. 'Have I told you how much I've missed you, Lucy?'

'No, I don't believe you have. Should I believe you?'

He did not even blink at her sceptical look. 'I speak truly, for the year has dragged by. It was cruel to keep me on tenterhooks for twelve whole months and I was beginning to lose hope of you ever coming back.'

'It was never my intent to cause you such suspense,' she countered. 'It was you who told me to go away and enjoy myself and partake of all the pleasures Europe had to offer—which I did, by the way, to the full.'

'Yes, I did and I soon came to regret it. Sometimes things happen at the wrong time, Lucy. That was the wrong time for us. But words cannot express how happy I was to see you returned.'

'Happy?' she countered. 'I was hoping your feelings would take on a different direction—toward futility rather than happiness since you couldn't wait for me to be gone.'

'Not at all. I really have missed you and I aim to convince you that I shall live for any favour and attention you care to cast my way.'

Lucy wriggled to sit up, forcing him to roll away from her. 'Will you please stop this, Christopher? Your compliments and lavish expressions of sentiment fall on deaf ears.'

'They do?' he said, sitting close beside her and absently trailing his finger over her wrist. 'And why is that, pray?'

'Because it smacks of insincerity—and it's unlike you and flowery speeches don't suit you.'

'I am being honest—and I have often complimented you on your lovely eyes and beautiful face in the past. I suppose hundreds have told you how beautiful you are on your travels.'

'I never believed them. I keep remembering that naive young girl fresh out of the academy.'

'You were beautiful then. You were the most captivating young woman I had ever seen, gentle and graceful and totally unaware of your beauty.'

'And now?'

'You're even lovelier.'

'You just want to marry me,' she accused lightly.

'That's true. I remember how pleasurable it was to dance with you, how warm your skin was to the touch and how adorable you looked when you blushed—how sweet your lips.'

Lucy rolled her eyes and began picking up the remains of their picnic and placing them in the baskets. 'Oh, please, Christopher, do not disappoint me by resorting to flattery, for I know very well what I look like.'

He chuckled. 'Dear Lord, Lucy! Will nothing I say please you? A man tries to be polite and complementary and gets told off for it. But I cannot forget you are female.'

'Will you please stop this? You are talking nonsense. You will make me cross when I don't want to be.'

'This,' he said with mock indignation, 'from the woman who threw a napkin at me is cross? I do not believe it. I am the injured party.'

'I did not throw it, I hit you with it,' she reminded him. 'You deserved it. Now see—Amelia is coming back so behave yourself and make yourself useful.' She paused and looked at him, holding his gaze and allowing a smile to curve her lips. 'Did I really blush?'

'Delightfully so.'

'How embarrassing.' Her smile broadened. 'Thank you, Christopher, for inviting me today. I've had a lovely day. Truly. I don't know how to thank you.'

His heavy-lidded gaze fixed meaningfully on her lips. A dangerous light entered his eyes and a smile tempted his lips. His voice was low with a husky rasp. 'How about agreeing to be my wife?'

'Not yet. I would like to give your proposal serious consideration,' she said, folding a tablecloth and placing it in the basket.

'Keep me dangling, more like—and enjoying every minute of it.'

'It serves you right for sending me away.'

'It was necessary at the time, you know that. Have you any objections to me as a husband?'

'No, of course not.'

Placing his hand under her chin, he tilted her to face to his, wanting more than anything else to eradicate the hesitation he saw in her eyes. 'I have never asked any woman to marry me before. I've had mistresses, yes—but it is you that I offer marriage to. No other woman has been able to get that close. What I know is that when you were away from me you were never far from my deepest thoughts. You suit me better than any woman I have ever known. You amuse, delight and frustrate me to the point where I don't know whether to throttle you or make love to you. You test my patience and my sanity beyond the limits of my endurance. And yet, despite all this, I still want you for my wife. Will you do me the honour of accepting my proposal—and become my wife?'

'I—I would like a little more time.'

'Of course, but don't take too long thinking about,' he murmured softly. 'I'm not noted for my patience.'

Lucy looked directly into his face, feeling herself respond to the dark intimacy in his voice. His expression was gentle, understanding and soft. And there, plain for her to see, was the sincerity of his words. 'Have you told Amelia?'

He shook his head. 'Not yet. I'll do that when I have good news to impart.'

'And you're sure there will be?'

'Absolutely.'

'Has it not entered that arrogant head of yours that I might refuse to marry you?'

Christopher looked at her for a long moment with those magnificent silver-grey eyes, then he smiled. 'We'll see about that,' he told her.

That was the moment when Lucy knew that she would be his wife. She was in love with him—shamelessly, recklessly in love—and the knowledge left her strangely weak. She could hardly believe how deep her feelings were running and the joy coursing through her body melted the very core of her heart. The feeling was so strong there was no room for anything else. She could not resist these new emotions that were compelling and held her in thrall and moved her towards her destiny, for she was destined to love this man and she knew it would be futile to resist.

They left Greenwich and started back up river, slowly. Tired and happy, Lucy and Amelia were quiet, content to let the river ripple by. Lucy didn't care how long it took. She was with Christopher and the knowledge that she had decided to marry him after all was light and lovely inside her, a wonderful effervescent feeling as though she had imbibed the finest champagne.

On reaching the house, after saying farewell to Amelia with the promise to call on her very soon, accompanied by Christopher she walked to the door where she paused.

'I will call on you shortly, Lucy, for your answer,

ahead of the throng of suitors who will soon be queuing up at your door—although you will probably accuse me of arrogance to assume you might prefer me to any of your other suitors.'

'You don't have to do that,' she said, her expression serious as she looked up at him. Her feelings for him could no longer be denied.

One dark eyebrow rose as he gave her a sceptical look. 'I don't? Are you going to tell me you reject my suit after all the…?'

She laid her fingers gently over his lips, silencing him. 'No, I am not. Quite the opposite, in fact. I love you, Christopher,' she said softly. 'I want you to know. And if your offer still stands…' she hesitated, hopeful as she peered into his eyes '… I would be most honoured to become your wife.'

He stared at her with astonishment. 'You love me?'

She nodded, a gentle flush mantling her cheeks.

'And you will marry me, Lucy? You're sure?'

'I won't change my mind. I know exactly what I want. I've never been more certain of anything in my life. There has never been anyone else for me, Christopher, and there never will be. When I give my heart away I do it only once. Please take care of it.'

With a deep sigh of relief and absolute joy, he gathered her into his arms and held her close. 'I promise and thank you,' he murmured, his lips against her hair. 'Thank the Lord you have decided to wed me at last. I cannot believe this is happening. I hoped and prayed…' Holding her away from him, he tilted her face to his, looking deep into her eyes, searching for proof of her words and seeing the truth. 'You are sure about this, aren't you, Lucy? You will promise to love…'

'And honour.'

'And obey?'

She laughed, wrapping her arms about his waist and kissing his lips. 'We'll discuss that at a later date.'

'As we will our wedding. Now before I leave we will seal our bond with a kiss.'

'What? On the doorstep?'

'On the doorstep where everyone can see and be either scandalised or share in our joy.' Taking her face between his hands, he looked into her eyes. 'I love you, Lucy Walsh, and there is nothing that I want more than to make you my wife.'

'You do?' Her heart soared.

His smile was filled with tenderness. 'If you don't believe anything else I've ever said to you, at least believe that.'

So saying he swept her in his arms and placed his lips on the soft curve of her cheek, before moving gently, exquisitely to her lips and assaulting her senses before raising his head and releasing her. 'Now go inside and give Lady Sutton the good news. It is my hope that we will be married soon.'

Lucy let herself into the house in a happy state of euphoria. She could not believe what was happening to her. When he kissed her he made his feelings known, leaving her in no doubt that he was sincere when he said he loved her.

* * *

Everyone was delighted at the way things had turned out. When the betrothal was officially announced in the *Post*, it was received with considerable surprise, although, since Viscount Rockley's attentiveness towards Miss Lucy Walsh had been duly noted, word was already getting out that she had won the heart of London's most eligible bachelor.

It was arranged that they would be married at St George's Church in Hanover Square four weeks hence. In a flap, Lady Sutton declared that it was too soon, that there was so much to be done to arrange a wedding on a scale that befit the heir of the Duke of Rockwood in a month. A guest list had to be drawn up before wedding invitations could be sent out, there were florists to be consulted and the bride's dress to be made. But all her protestations fell on deaf ears. Both Christopher and Lucy were adamant that they did not want a lavish affair with a grand banquet and reception and that a long delay seemed pointless. There were to be few guests and one bridesmaid—Amelia, who was so happy by the whole affair that anyone who didn't know would think she was the bride.

The Duke of Rockwood could not have been more delighted about the wedding and knew Lucy would make his grandson an excellent wife. He also made no secret of his immense pride in his grandson. He had made a rare visit to town for the wedding and when Lucy walked down the aisle wearing an ivory silk gown of incredible beauty and extravagant expense on his arm in the church bearing a spray of orchids picked from the hothouses at Rockwood Park, all the radiance in the world was shining from her large eyes, which were drawn irresistibly to the man who was waiting for her at the front of the church.

As the wedding ceremony progressed and Lucy had just repeated the vicar's words—for richer or poorer, in sickness and in health—from the corner of her eye she exchanged a fond look with her godmother and smiled as she watched her wipe a tear from her eye. And then the ceremony was over, they were pronounced man and wife and Christopher could kiss the bride.

With a wicked glow in his eyes, but behaving with admirable restraint, taking her hand he drew her close and placed a somewhat brief but heartfelt kiss to her lips. After signing the documents that made their union legal in the eyes of the law as well as God, with broad smiles and the sound of congratulations ringing in their ears, Christopher led his bride down the aisle and out of the church.

As Lucy was about to climb into the coach, raising her eyes to the crowd of people who had congregated in the street—weddings always attracted interest, especially society weddings—her attention was caught by a solitary man standing on the corner of the street. A coldness crept over her for she was almost certain it was Mr Barrington. She took her eyes off him for a moment and when she was seated inside the coach and looked again, he had gone. The mere thought that it had been Mr Barrington she had seen alarmed her.

Alone with her in his shiny black carriage, Christopher took her hand and raised it to his lips and kissed her fingertips lingeringly, one by one.

'At last I have you to myself—if just for a few minutes.' Seeing her sudden pallor, he looked at her with concern. 'What is it, my love? You look as if someone has just walked over your grave.'

She laughed, striving to keep her unease to herself, determined to let nothing, not even Mark Barrington, spoil this day. 'Nothing—nothing at all. I'm merely overwhelmed with everything and so very happy.'

'You look beautiful,' he uttered quietly, continuing to hold her hand in a firm clasp. His tone held an odd note of pride, and perhaps awe, that made her turn her head to him. With the dappled shade of light playing across her creamy skin and wisps of hair escaping from their pins caressing her cheek, she was the most beautiful woman Christopher had ever laid eyes on. He could not believe his good fortune that she as his wife at last. Whether due to the gently curving bosom beneath the confines of her gown, the satin softness of her skin, or the rosy blush that infused her cheeks, brightening her eyes until they seemed to glow with a brilliance of their own behind the thick, sooty lashes, or the way her lips were softly parted, his attention was firmly ensnared, such enticements being too much for any man to ignore.

Returning to Curzon Street, Lady Sutton served them a splendid meal. Course after course of exquisite, mouth-watering dishes were served, followed by a magnificent bride cake. They drank champagne and toasts were made, and as Lucy raised her glass she was acutely aware of the gold band on her finger that bound her to Christopher for ever. There was only one thing that marred the day and that was Mr Barrington's threatening form which hovered on the perimeter of her mind like the spectre at the feast.

As the afternoon drew to a close giving way to the evening shadows heralding the night, the guests began to leave. To give the newly-weds some time alone, Lady Sutton had taken the Duke up on his invitation to spend the night at his town house with Amelia. Christopher and Lucy were to join them for luncheon the following day.

No sooner were they alone, in moments Christopher and Lucy were on the threshold of her room. The bed, where Lucy would lose her virtue, was hung with lustrous panels in lush green velvet. It was a welcome sight to them both. Without more ado, grinning broadly, Christopher swept his bride of a few hours off her feet and carried her inside, closing the door behind him with his foot. Giving her a long, lazy kiss, making her prey to all those delicious sensations that had never been so sweet, he placed her on her feet and did not let go of her until he had released her lips.

'I've waited a long time for this,' Christopher murmured, caressing her throat, his fingers exploring the softness. 'What are you thinking?' he asked, beginning to remove the pins from her hair himself, having dismissed her maid earlier.

She sighed and looked at him. 'Oh—about our wedding and what a handsome husband I have. I never believed it possible that this could happen.' A cloud crossed her eyes and a note of sadness and regret entered her voice. 'My only regret is that my father is not with us.'

Christopher embraced her comfortingly. 'He will not be far away. I am certain that he is watching you from the mysterious place where we all go to one day.'

'I would like to think so.'

'Me, too,' he said softly, his eyes gleaming into hers, lazy and seductive, feeling a driving surge of desire at the sultriness of her soft mouth and the liquid depths of her eyes.

She stood quite still while he continued to unpin her hair, towering over her, his physical presence rendering her weak. In the soft glow of the candlelight her eyes were huge, like those of a wide-eyed kitten, luminous and infinitely lovely. Removing the last of the hairpins, he spread the gleaming raven mass over her shoulders. She ran her tongue over her lip, unconsciously teasing.

'This,' Christopher said, glorying in the tender passion in her eyes, feeling the heat flame in his belly as he drew aside her curtain of hair and placed a kiss on the warm, sweet-scented nape of her neck, 'is the moment I've been thinking of ever since you entered the church.'

As his lips trailed over her flesh, with a gasp of exquisite pleasure Lucy threw her head back and closed her eyes. 'I cannot believe this is happening to me,' she breathed softly. 'I feel that I am heading for something I cannot possibly know how to handle.'

'Then I think it's about time you learnt,' he replied softly, seductively.

He touched her cheek in soft reassurance—then his gaze travelled down over her body. She followed his stare, glancing down at herself, still clad in her wedding finery. Smoothing her skirts, she looked at him again in rather helpless uncertainty.

Christopher gave her a gentle smile. 'You look wonderful,' he soothed, reading her thoughts, 'but I would like you better without your wedding gown. I want to see you wearing nothing at all.'

Grinning lazily, he turned away, taking off his jacket.

'You would?' The smile still on her lips, she kicked off her shoes and, sitting in a chair, proceeded to remove her ribbon garters and then the stockings without taking her eyes from his as he removed his neckcloth and began to unbutton his shirt. 'I think you are going to have to assist me in removing my finery,' she said, getting up and going to him, turning her back to give him access to the fastenings of her dress.

'It will be my pleasure.' Sweeping her long hair forward over her shoulder, he made short work of the fastenings down the back of her gown. 'I've waited so long for this moment,' he whispered as he slipped the bodice down off her shoulders, kissing the nape of her neck.

Lucy's heart pounded as she stepped out of her gown. He continued to undress her slowly and with reverence, occasionally bending to kiss an exposed inch of flesh as her petticoats fluttered to the floor. When they were both naked, magnificent in their nudity, Lucy's breath caught in her throat, fascinated by the play of light over his lean-muscled body. Happiness, joy and delight were welling inside her, filling her because this handsome, vital man belonged to her, every glorious inch of him. They almost fell on to the bed. Skin to skin, their chests pressed together, their hearts beating in unison, Christopher's lips claimed hers. It was as she'd always dreamed of, this wild, sweet abandonment in his arms.

He aroused her slowly, with a skill that left her trembling. His kiss overwhelmed her while his hands beguiled her, running over her body, caressing and touching. She lay on her back while his lips explored every delectable inch of her, taking his time as he kissed her breasts and his hand ventured between her thighs. Trembling with pleasure, she reached for him, her fingers light and tentative, unsure. Staying her hand, his eyes flickering over her with desire, he covered her body with his own. His lips hovered inches from her own.

'I love you, my darling,' he whispered, 'more than you will ever know.'

Arching her body, she wrapped her arms about him, urging him on, clutching, clinging. She moaned softly as he cradled her to him, throwing her head back against the pillow as he entered her, and after a few moments he began to move, soothing away her fears, bringing her close to the oblivion of bliss. The beauty of it was almost beyond endurance, a shimmering and a shattering that lifted them both into a realm of sheer enchantment. Slowly he became part of her and she felt the joy and wonder of it in her heart. Nothing she felt was suppressed or hidden from him.

As they twisted and rolled across the sheets, rocking together, locked as one for all time, she held him to her. There was exquisite joy in every plane and curve of her face. She was assailed by waves of lust and passion as he thrust her higher and higher to those dizzying heights that made her ache and burn with an ardour she had never felt before.

Then they slept, waking again to more loving, lazy, leisurely, and all the while Christopher watched her flushed face, the way her breath quickened and her dazed eyes widened with startled desire. He had awakened his young bride into a tantalising creature who breathed passion and sensuality.

There were times when words were unnecessary, when the body knew better, and neither of them was capable of holding back. Their lovemaking was stormy. Lucy had never experienced such intensity of feeling, nor such wanton abandonment to passion. They gave each other everything with their bodies, each possessing the other.

They slept again, with nothing but a sheet to cover them.

When Lucy awoke she was content to lay still, content to savour Christopher's hard-muscled body pressed next to hers. How well he had taught her and how well she had come to know his body. She was as familiar with it now as she was her own. She knew the touch, the taste and the feel of him—never had she realised such depths of passion and feeling existed. Neither had she thought a man's body could be so beautiful until she had known his and admired the perfect symmetry of flesh and muscle. How could any woman not want such a man?

With her head against her husband's chest and feeling the steady beat of his heart, satiated and drowsy still with sleep, she nestled closer to him. A glow warmed her as she remembered everything they had done together. She opened her eyes. Now that she had recovered from the shattering passion of the night, the memory of the man she had seen when she had emerged from the church after the ceremony returned like a dog worrying a bone.

'Christopher?'

'Mmm, what is it?' His voice was low and sleep-laden.

'There is something I have to say. I might be wrong—indeed, I hope I am, but you should know.'

Christopher chuckled softly, tightening his arms about her and placing a kiss on the top of her head. 'Whatever it is, can't it wait? I have the urge to make love to you again now you are awake.'

'You can still do that after I've told you what it is that's bothering me.'

'If you are going to tell me you regret marrying me, then it's too late,' he said sleepily. 'This is for keeps, my love. There is no escape.'

'I love you too much to leave you, Christopher. I think I proved that last night.'

'Then what is it that is troubling you that is so important it takes precedence over my making love to you?'

'Yesterday—when we left the church I—I saw someone watching us across the street.'

'They were not alone, Lucy. I swear half of London came to witness our nuptials. What was so very different about the person you saw?'

'I—I think it was Mr Barrington.'

Christopher's relaxed state quietly vanished. 'Are you certain about this?'

'In truth—no, I'm not, but it did look like him. I saw him as I was getting into the coach. When I looked again he had gone.'

Christopher gave a heavy sigh. 'Then if it was Barrington, if he means mischief we must wait for him to make his move.' Wide awake now, he extricated himself from their tangled embrace.

It was Lucy who noticed Amelia's absence. She thought little of it at first, but thought it strange that she had not been downstairs to welcome them along with Aunt Caroline and the Duke when they arrived for lunch. When Amelia failed to appear she went to her room, only to be told by one of the female servants that she had left the house with her maid one hour earlier on a private matter. Curious, she had looked out of the window and saw them get into a coach that was waiting across the road.

Becoming concerned when the servant informed her that Lady Amelia had not been her usual cheerful self when she had returned from the shops earlier, Lucy went in search of Christopher. An inner sense told her something was wrong. Where on earth could Amelia have gone and without informing anyone of her destination?

Christopher was just coming out of the study and looked at her when she came rushing down the stairs.

'Lucy! What's wrong?'

'It's Amelia. She's gone out apparently and told no one where she was going. Where on earth can she be?'

Every muscle in Christopher's body went rigid as he looked at her. 'Gone? Gone where?'

'I wish I knew. One of the maids told me that she hadn't seemed herself since she returned from the shops earlier.'

'Was she alone?'

'No, she was accompanied by her maid.'

'I cannot believe Amelia has done something so irresponsible as going out by herself. I'll check and see if she's taken the carriage.'

'There's no need. They were seen getting into a coach waiting across the street.' Lucy went to him, gripping his arm. 'It isn't like Amelia to do something so inconsiderate and irresponsible as to leave the house so suddenly and without a word.'

Things became chaotic as they tried to find out where Amelia might have gone. It was when the maid who had seen her leave the house told them that her maid had mentioned that a gentleman had approached

Lady Amelia when she had been leaving a shop on the Strand that they became seriously concerned. Not having seen him herself, she could give no description, only that he had appeared to be acquainted with Lady Amelia.'

As he listened, Christopher's face became hard. His eyes were ice-cold and shining with a light that seemed to come from the depths of him. 'Barrington. It has to be him.'

'How can you be certain?'

'I am. You thought you had seen him yourself yesterday—it has to be him. Who else could it be? So—at last he shows his hand,' Christopher said bitterly. 'How dare he make Amelia the instrument of his vengeance? I do not intend letting him destroy her all over again because of all the real and imagined grievances he has for myself.'

'But—how do we know where to look for her? We didn't even know Mr Barrington was in London.'

'I have to try. I'll go and make some enquiries at his old haunts. He might have been there and even taken Amelia there. Thank God she had the presence of mind to take her maid with her.' In the grip of an unnamed terror, Christopher wouldn't let himself even imagine what Barrington might be subjecting Amelia to.

In a fever of apprehension Lucy watched him leave the house, praying he would find his sister and bring her back safely. She went to tell the Duke and Aunt Caroline what had happened. The three of them sat down to wait for Christopher to return. The longer

Lucy waited, the tighter her nerves stretched. She listened to the clock on the mantelpiece chime two hours away.

Christopher finally returned, having scoured all the places he thought Mr Barrington might be, but his efforts had come to nothing.

Lucy was in despair when she looked with pain-filled eyes at Christopher's drawn face as he paced back and forth across the room.

'Where the devil is she? How dare she go her own way—defy me in this outrageous manner? I expressly told her not to go anywhere without notifying me first.'

Lucy knew that what he was feeling was rage at his own inadequacy to know where else to look and pure madness and cold murder flared in his eyes. 'Well, what is clear is that she wasn't forcibly abducted. She went with him of her own volition. They must have arranged to meet. Apparently she took nothing with her, which indicates that she had no intention of leaving the house for long.'

'Barrington is devious, don't forget. He might have other ideas. No doubt he had it all well planned.'

'Perhaps I might make a suggestion.'

Christopher stopped pacing and looked at her with avid interest, willing to listen to anything that might throw some light on the whereabouts of Amelia.

'I've had a thought,' she said, 'although it might come to nothing—but at the Skeffington ball he was in the company of a man called Sir Simon Bucklow. Perhaps he might have seen Mr Barrington.'

Christopher stared at her, absorbing her words. 'Sir Simon Bucklow,' he repeated. 'Of course. Why didn't I think of him? I know where he lives—in Kensington. I'll go there right away.'

'I'm coming with you.'

Christopher turned on her sharply. 'You will do no such thing. I forbid it. You will wait here with my grandfather until I return.'

Lucy stood her ground, facing her husband with defiance in every line of her body, her face taut and determined. 'Don't try to stop me. I insist. I think we both know it isn't Amelia that he's interested in—that he's only doing this to strike at you. In the meantime she might return. With any luck she'll come back of her own volition.'

Seeing she was not to be deterred, and not wishing to lose any more time arguing, Christopher nodded. 'Very well.'

On reaching Sir Simon Bucklow's house in Kensington they were admitted immediately and shown into a large drawing room. Christopher walked in, his jaw hard and set, his face far more ominous than amiable. There were four people in the room, two men and two women. The women, seated on a stylish sofa, were Amelia and her maid and the men, Simon Bucklow and Mark Barrington, were standing a little way from Amelia. Sir Simon, who was most put out at having his friend accosted in his own drawing room, excused himself and quietly left the room. Christopher glanced at Amelia's maid and she did likewise.

The air crackled with tension as the two men eyed each other. Christopher was icy cold, in complete control of himself, but a muscle in his cheek tightened almost imperceptible. Mark Barrington's eyes were sullen, his mouth curled in defiance, the lower lips thrust out. He stared at Christopher's menacing figure, who looked as though he could kill without blinking.

After summing up the situation, Christopher was the first to speak. His voice was calm, frighteningly calm. 'So, Barrington, we meet again. Our last encounter was a memorable one as I recall. You still owe me—or has it slipped your mind.'

'I've been in New Orleans and only recently returned to London.'

'I trust you found New Orleans entertaining. There are enough gambling halls to satisfy even you. Although knowing your luck you probably lost a bundle,' Christopher retorted with contempt.

Barrington shrugged. 'It happens. New Orleans is a gambler's paradise.'

'If you want to squander your money, Barrington, it is no concern of mine. No doubt you have creditors as well as me who are baying for your blood.'

'A few—but it might surprise you to know that I am here to settle my debt to you. New Orleans was lucky for me. I intend to return as soon as I am able.'

'Good riddance, Barrington. Send me what you owe and disappear. My concern is for my sister and what she is doing here.'

'Why, we met earlier today and I was most eager to renew our acquaintance, is that not so, Amelia?'

'Yes,' she said, her answer barely discernible.

'Are you hurt?' Christopher asked.

'No. I'm sorry, Christopher. I saw Mark when I was at the shops. He—he said it would be good for us to meet—to talk. In a moment of impulsiveness I agreed. I—I know what he did to Lucy—how he hurt us both—but I had to see him. Try to understand, I beg of you. We parted suddenly. I had to know why he didn't stay and fight for me—how he could have left me like that.' She turned to Lucy. 'I tried to see him as Christopher portrayed him—a calculating, conscienceless predator—but I wasn't convinced—not until Christopher told me what he had tried to do to you and how many other women I didn't know about. I was gullible and foolish—but I had to talk to him. After what happened to me—I—I couldn't talk about it for a long time. It didn't alter how I felt about him— how much I loved him. This way, seeing him again, will enable me to draw a line under it. I didn't dare tell you, Christopher, because I knew you wouldn't let me see him.'

'You're damn right I wouldn't,' Christopher ground out.

Amelia flinched from his wrath, tears beginning to run down her cheeks.

'Did it not occur to you what his intentions were? Had it not been for Lucy remembering he was acquainted with Simon Bucklow we would never have found you.'

'I'm so sorry for all the trouble I've caused,' she cried. 'I didn't mean to.'

'Christopher, please,' said Lucy, going to sit beside her and putting a comforting arm round the distraught young woman. 'Let us not go into this now. Amelia is clearly distraught.'

'And now you have seen him,' Christopher said, 'what conclusion have you come to?'

'We haven't discussed what happened yet.' She looked at Mark. 'I hope you have not prepared some intricate fabrication for I shall not believe it.'

'I've told you that the man is a dangerous opportunist, Amelia,' Christopher retorted harshly, unable to believe what he was hearing. 'Have you forgotten what he did to you—what he did to Lucy? Had she not fought back this devil would have raped her. The man should be horsewhipped.'

Barrington smiled smugly. His gaze went past Christopher and settled on Lucy. 'I see you have brought your *wife* with you, Rockley.' He smiled. 'She appears to be none the worse for the assault you speak of.'

'It was fortunate for you that she didn't kill you after what you put her through.'

Barrington's eyes narrowed and began to glitter dangerously. His smile was unpleasant as he shrugged himself away from the fireplace. 'I'm not that easy to get rid of. The incident you speak of occurred over a year ago.'

''It hardly matters how much time has passed as long as justice is done.'

'There were no actual witnesses and I shall disavow any knowledge of that. Where the betrothal is concerned, the whole thing was concocted by Sofia, your stepmother,' he pointed out, looking coldly at Lucy, 'who, on the demise of your father, acted in your best interests by arranging your marriage—not an unusual occurrence, I might add.'

'And you were eager to participate,' Christopher bit back.

'Of course, and in the eyes of English society so did Lucy—at least that is what everyone surmised when I introduced her as my fiancée—whom she jilted in favour of you. So you see, I was seen as the injured party.'

'Not any longer. Are you aware that there is a warrant out for your arrest?'

'I am. If you wish to call in the police from Bow Street, then do so and we'll see what they have to say. But I think even you would prefer not to air our dirty linen in public. But,' he said, looking from Amelia to Lucy, 'if you feel honour must be satisfied then go ahead. Of course we could settle this as gentlemen and arrange pistols at dawn and all that, but you are by far the better shot, so killing me could indeed be construed as murder. No doubt the authorities would be reluctant to lock up the heir to a dukedom and it could be talked out of, but the scandal would get out and do your aristocratic name no good.'

'I'm willing to risk it.'

The air inside the room was charged with tension as the two men faced each other, hate trembling in the air between them.

'Please, Christopher—leave it,' Lucy said. 'I don't

want this, I don't want anyone to be hurt.' Christopher's angry eyes bored into hers like daggers. 'I mean it. Now is not the time to argue with your notions of honour.'

He nodded. 'I suppose you are right, damn it. No matter how much I want to put this man behind bars, I can see no point in dredging up a scandal. It would serve no purpose. Your reputation is already tarnished thanks to this man, but I can see no reason to destroy Amelia's.'

'After what you did in Charleston, separating me from Amelia, you deserve to live in wretchedness till your life's end,' Barrington retorted. 'I'm not proud of the way I treated her, but you had no right to separate us.'

Christopher's mouth curled cruelly. 'I had every right. She was underage at the time and both her parents were dead, leaving me her guardian. You didn't put up much of a fight. The way I remember it, when you realised there would be nothing in it for you, you hotfooted it back to New Orleans. You didn't give a damn what she might do.'

'Do? Why, what did she do?'

'Please, Christopher,' Amelia cried. 'He doesn't know—I haven't told him.'

Perplexed, Barrington looked from one to the other. 'Told me? What haven't you told me?'

'Unable to live with the shame of what you had done to her, she tried to take her own life. I found her in time, thank God, but she lost the child.'

The silence that fell on the room was so profound

that if anyone had entered at that moment they would have heard their hearts beating. Barrington's face became filled with honest puzzlement as his mind took its time to register what Christopher was saying.

'What the devil are you saying, Rockley?'

'You mean to tell me,' Christopher said, a sudden chill entering his bones, 'that when you left my sister in Charleston you were unaware that she was carrying your child?'

Horror flashed into Barrington's face. 'She was to bear my child?'

'You didn't know?'

'Of course not. My God,' he said, looking at Amelia. 'Why didn't you tell me?'

'I would have—if you hadn't left me.'

He glared at Christopher. 'Why didn't you tell me when you insisted I leave her alone?'

'Because I didn't know, either. But later I thought you did.'

His shoulders sagging, as if all the life had drained out of him, Barrington lowered his head. 'No.' And he said nothing more. It was a quiet sound that hung between them, without anger or emotion, but it held all the cruel and bitter anguish which he felt.

'I don't think we have anything left to say to each other except that I will give you one week to settle your affairs. If, by that time, you are still in London, I shall have you arrested for the crime you committed against my wife and to hell with the scandal.' Striding across the room, Christopher took the lapels of Barrington's coat and thrust his face close to his. 'If you ever touch either of these women again or even speak to them, I swear by everything I hold sacred that I will personally kill you. Do you understand, Barrington?' Releasing his hold on his lapels, Christopher pushed him away. He turned to Lucy. 'Let's go. Amelia?'

Amelia got to her feet. She looked at the man who had caused her so much misery, the tears having dried. 'Goodbye, Mark.'

Without a word the three of them left the room.

Lucy told Amelia's maid to take her out to the carriage before turning to Christopher.

'I did not expect Mr Barrington to be so affected by what he learned.'

'No—and I feel no satisfaction for what I have just done, no sense of victory for overcoming a man who is my enemy—only a bitter taste of self-loathing, despising myself for having completely annihilated someone who believed he had every justification in the world to hate me.'

There was much relief and many questions when they arrived back home. Amelia was quiet, but not too downcast after seeing Mark Barrington. It was as if seeing him again had laid to rest any fears and questions that had been left unresolved. Before retiring for the night, she was already planning her social life for the following two weeks she was to remain in London with her grandfather.

It was a great relief when Lucy and Christopher closed the door to their room. Lady Sutton had returned to Curzon Street and the house was quiet. Seat-ing himself in a chair beside the hearth, Christopher pulled Lucy down on to his lap.

'I never thought I needed a wife to complete my life. Now I couldn't imagine living without one.'

'Well, that's a relief,' Lucy said, wrapping her arms around his neck and planting a kiss on his lips. 'Although after just twenty-four hours you haven't had much practice at being a husband.'

'I intend to enjoy every minute of it,' he murmured, nuzzling her neck. In his opinion this was a fine way to spend an evening, but sitting in a chair with his wife on his lap when there was a perfectly good bed in the room called for a change. Breaking the kiss, he stood up with her in his arms, a move that surprised her.

'Where are you taking me?'

'To bed,' he said, trailing kisses along her throat as he carried her to the bed.

'Why, do you feel like sleeping?' she enquired softly.

'The feel of you in my arms banishes all sleep from my mind, my love, and tempts me to exercise my husbandly rights. Today was the first day as husband and wife and it hasn't turned out as either of us expected. So this is our time, to be enjoyed.'

'How exciting,' she murmured and placed a warm kiss on his lips.

He gave her a lusty look that made her heart skip a beat.

There followed a period of loving which left Lucy filled with a marvellous languor that glowed inside and warmed her whole body. Christopher's kisses trapped the sensations inside her as love rushed to the surface to meet the outpouring of passion. Afterwards there was teasing and soft laughter, and Christopher looked at his wife, loving her. He was sprawled on the bed in a blissful state of collapse. Lucy looked at him and smiled to herself, overwhelmed with a shimmering happiness that seemed to sing inside her.

Rolling on to her stomach, she rested her arms on his chest and felt she had to question his frowning countenance. 'You're looking terribly fierce, my lord. Has something displeased you?'

'We're leaving.'

'We are? And where are you taking me?'

'Rockwood Park. I wish to be completely alone with my wife. We, my darling girl, are on our honeymoon. Grandfather has decided to remain in London with Amelia so we will have Rockwood Park all to ourselves—for at least two weeks.'

'Alone?' she murmured, preoccupied with the matt of hairs on his chest as she attempted to curl some of them round her finger. 'And how do you suggest we pass the time?'

'There are lots of things we can do. We could go walking or riding, or…should the weather turn against us, we could play cards—which I am very good at—as you already know—or chess, we could play chess. Do you play?'

'Yes. I am quite good at it.'

'So am I—as I am at a number of things, which

brings me back to how to occupy our time. We could make love…'

'Which you are also good at.' He grinned. 'Of which you have had plenty of practice, whereas I…'

'Need to be taught.'

'Since it is the only thing I cannot compete at, then I shall be happy to accept your tuition. I'm a fast learner and how will I learn if I don't practise?' she teased. 'When do we start?'

* * * * *

*If you enjoyed this story, why not check
out these other great reads by Helen Dickson*

Carrying the Gentleman's Secret
A Vow for an Heiress
The Governess's Scandalous Marriage
Reunited at the King's Court
Wedded for His Secret Child
Resisting Her Enemy Lord